FATAL LIES

ANITA WALLER

Boldwood

First published in Great Britain in 2023 by Boldwood Books Ltd.

Copyright © Anita Waller, 2023

Cover Design by Head Design Ltd.

Cover Photography: Shutterstock

A CIP catalogue record for this book is available from the British Library.

Paperback ISBN 978-1-80415-337-6

Large Print ISBN 978-1-80415-338-3

Hardback ISBN 978-1-80415-336-9

Ebook ISBN 978-1-80415-340-6

Kindle ISBN 978-1-80415-339-0

Audio CD ISBN 978-1-80415-331-4

MP3 CD ISBN 978-1-80415-332-1

Digital audio download ISBN 978-1-80415-333-8

Boldwood Books Ltd
23 Bowerdean Street
London SW6 3TN
www.boldwoodbooks.com

To Brad and Beth's daughter, Mia Josie, born 28 April 2023, and Jamie and Sommer's daughter, Amber Jade, born 15 June 2023. With love and thanks for bringing our total of great-grandchildren to four girls and one boy!

'Three things cannot long be hidden: the sun, the moon, and the truth.'

— CONFUCIUS

1

Carol Flynn stared up at the façade of the Forrester Detective Agency and gave a slight nod of her head. Over the previous few weeks, she'd watched men coming and going, carrying wood and anything else they needed to turn what had been a detective agency for several years into an upmarket detective agency for the future.

She had got to know Dave Forrester and Johnny Keane through seeing them around the area, and had wondered what would happen to the business after their untimely deaths. Everyone in the locality had been stunned by it, and flowers had covered the front of the shop as people arrived to pay their respects. Today she was not only here to pay her respects, but she was also here to tell the new partners that they needed her.

The new sign shouting loud and proud that it was the Forrester Detective Agency had been put in place at the end of the previous week, and she looked up at it – it was smart, to the point, and no frills. On the right-hand window was a notice that said 'under new management', and she stepped forward with confidence to go in the front door.

Once inside the compact entrance, three doors faced her. The one to the left said 'Matt Forrester', the one to the right said 'Steve Rowlands' – she liked that, the use of shortened versions of their true names. The one immediately facing her said 'Reception', and there was a man fitting a sliding window into the wall, by the side of the door.

She walked up to the man. 'Is Mr Forrester around?'

He pointed with a chisel, and said, 'He's in his office. Just knock and wait, he'll pop out and get you unless he's on the phone.'

He carried on lining up the glass panel and she moved to the door he had indicated. She took a deep breath and knocked.

It was opened by a child, who looked her up and down and said, 'Hi. You want my dad?'

'Probably,' she said with a smile. 'Is he in?'

'He's in the kitchen making the biggest cup of coffee in the world. Or that's what he said he needed, anyway. Come in.'

The boy held the door open for her, just as the door at the other end of the office opened.

Matt Forrester walked through, carrying a cafetiere and a mug. He saw a lady who he felt he knew but couldn't place where he had seen her before.

'Sorry,' he apologised. He placed the drink on his desk and held out his hand. 'Matt Forrester. Can I help you? Oh, and my assistant here is Harry, my son. Half-term break,' he said, in explanation.

She took his hand in her much tinier hand, and shook it. 'I'm hoping that you can.'

'Please,' Matt said, feeling a little flustered, 'take a seat. Can I get another cup and offer you a coffee?'

'No, I'm good thanks. I had one just before I came across.'

'Across?'

'I live over there. The house with blue-painted walls. My husband was a Wednesday fan.'

He waited, taking in her appearance. He would guess around forty years old, but he would freely admit to being useless at guessing women's ages. She was slim, had on a navy-blue suit that had clearly cost more than she would have paid at Primark, and a smile that wasn't forced.

'My name is Carol Flynn. I was an acquaintance of your dad and Johnny, dropped the occasional box of scones in for them, that sort of thing.'

Matt's eyes lit up. 'You're the scone lady!'

'I am indeed. I miss both men very much. My husband did running repairs to your dad's wheelchair when they were necessary, and they always waved when I passed by the window.'

He waited. This wasn't why she had ventured inside, something else was on her mind.

'Do you have a problem I can help with?'

'Kind of.' Again she smiled. 'My husband was twenty years older than me and in poor health. He caught Covid six months ago and was gone in less than a week. His body wasn't strong enough to fight it. I wound up his affairs fairly quickly considering there was a lifetime to go through and although I don't need to work, I want to work.'

She handed a plastic sleeve containing a printed piece of A4 paper across to him.

'I think you need a receptionist. I have only seen you and Mr Rowlands actually working here. I'm not asking for favours. I have always done reception and secretarial duties, both in recent years, and earlier in my working life when I worked for a solicitor. This is my CV,' she tapped the plastic sleeve, 'and all I ask is you read it. Working here would mean no costs for getting to work, that's for sure.'

Again the smile came.

'And is mind reading one of your skills?' Matt picked up his cup and sipped at the coffee he'd been pouring.

'Don't think so, but I can work on it,' she confirmed, her tone serious.

He spun his laptop around so she could see the screen. 'I was putting together an advert for a receptionist, and was about to send it to an agency.'

She glanced at it. 'Don't use that agency, they treat their staff badly. I can tell you at least three that are much better. And you've spelt negotiate incorrectly. It doesn't have two Gs.' She stood. 'I won't trouble you any further. All I ask is that you read my CV before you contact an agency – a different agency to that one. Thank you for your time, Mr Forrester, it's been a pleasure to finally meet you and speak with you. Your dad didn't half love you and your sister. He was so proud of you both.'

* * *

'She's nice,' Harry said, peering through the blinds he was holding to one side.

'Come away from the window, monkey. I liked her as well. I'll discuss it with Steve when he gets back, but I think it's possible we may have found our receptionist without even having to look.'

'Will she bring us scones?'

Matt laughed. 'I saw your eyes light up when she said that. I don't think she will if she starts working for us. So you liked her?'

Harry nodded. 'She was polite, wasn't she? Like Mum is. And Karen. And Aunty Herms.'

'I'd better give her the job on the strength of that little lot, then, hadn't I?' He ruffled Harry's hair. 'So, Harry boy, I've got you for a full week. I'll try to keep parts of it free for us to go places, but if you've got anything special you want to do, just shout up.'

'Will I ever be able to live with you and Karen all the time?' he asked.

Matt froze. 'Why?'

'I don't like him. Dickhead. Sorry, Brian.'

'He's okay with you, though? And don't call him Dickhead. He's a superintendent, and the title is worth some respect.' He didn't complete the sentence with *even if he isn't*.

'He's nothing with me and he's nothing to me.'

'Not sure what you mean, Harry.'

'What I say. He doesn't talk to me, and now Mum's having a little girl I'm well out of it. He sometimes drops me off at school, but only if it fits in with what he's doing. It was him who persuaded Mum to let me come here for the week, but it was only to get me out of his hair.'

'Or could it be because your mum is struggling to sleep at the moment, and is exhausted? In answer to your question, I don't see her ever agreeing to your coming to me full time, but you're getting older, Harry, and one day you can make your own decision on that. Can we leave it like that for the moment? And now I'm not in the police, I'm only ever a phone call away, day or night. Now don't let me catch you calling Superintendent Brian Davis a dickhead again! Especially in front of your mum.'

Harry grinned. 'I don't, but nobody can stop me thinking it.'

The sound of the office door opening and closing, followed by the sound of a second opening and closing, told them Steve was back, and Harry went in to bring him through to his dad's office.

He told Steve about his interesting fifteen minutes or so, and handed Steve the CV.

Steve read through it, then read it again. 'Have you looked at this?'

'No, she's only been gone five minutes, and Harry insisted on talking to me. Is she good?'

'You've let her go without making her sign a contract?' Steve's voice was incredulous. 'Seriously? This woman is our Mary Poppins. She's exactly what we need, just going by this document. What's she like?'

'She's lovely Uncle Steve. She makes scones.' Harry grinned again, enjoying watching the interaction between the two men.

Steve turned his eyes back to Matt. 'She makes scones as well? And according to this she only lives thirty seconds away.'

'Thirty seconds across a main road and two sets of tram tracks.'

Steve laughed. 'I should imagine the last twenty-odd years have taught her how to cross that road without getting squashed under a tram. I suggest you read through this, see what I'm seeing with her skills and experience, then risk your life on the tram tracks and go get her signed up. See if she can start tomorrow, we need help sorting out what goes where now all the building work is done, and Herms hasn't got time to help us.'

'Look, for what it's worth, I really liked her, and if it had been my decision alone I would have offered her the job there and then. She even caught a spelling error in the job ad I drafted. Keep your eye on Harry, and I'll nip over and see her. I'll make us sound like two hopeless idiots who don't know what they're doing, then maybe it will persuade her to start tomorrow morning. I need to offer her a salary. What sort of figure are we looking at?'

'If she's as good as this CV would lead me to believe, you

need to start at 30k and see what she says. That'd be for full time, though – it depends what hours she'll be working. You want me to come with you?'

Matt shook his head. 'No, I'll ring if we need to have an agreement on anything.'

He spent a couple of minutes reading through the CV, with Steve pointing his fingers at various sections of it to make sure he saw them, and he stood. 'I'll be back shortly. We could be being a bit optimistic at 30k. And I hope to God I don't call her Mary now you've said she'll be our Mary Poppins.'

He walked outside, waited on the kerb until a tram had fully rattled past, then ran across towards the blue-painted house.

She opened the door as he walked up the path. 'You've read it then?' she asked.

He nodded. 'We need you. I'm here to negotiate your salary, no matter how many Gs are in the word.'

2

MONDAY, 24 OCTOBER

Carol Flynn smiled as she stood at her window watching her new employer running back across the tram tracks. She knew she would enjoy getting to know him, and definitely enjoy working for him.

The discussion about her salary had been quite funny. She had said don't pay me for a month and then we'll talk, and he had said he daren't go back to the office without a contract being signed. She asked if he had brought the contract, and his sheepish expression had said it all. The agreement ended up being that she would type up the document as her first job the following day, she would work for free until the beginning of December and then they would discuss her salary again.

He had vaguely waved his arm in the air when admitting they'd not actually employed anybody before at the agency – he had been a DI in the police until the murder of his father pushed him into leaving and taking on Dave Forrester's existing business, and while Steve, his partner in the agency, had employed people, he also employed a part-time accounts lady to see to his wages and everything connected with that, for his landscape gardening company that was currently taking a bit of a back seat.

'Leave it to me,' she said. 'I'll be there for nine tomorrow, but I'll adjust the hours accordingly when I see how I need to manage the job. Is that okay with you?'

'Carol, I've seen your CV, I've seen who you've worked for, particularly the last employer, and whatever you say is fine by me. I'll make sure I'm there early, but today I'm going to get you a set of keys cut. I'll show you where all the security cameras are, explain the alarm code setting which is being installed as we speak, that sort of thing. Steve and I are both very much hands on with the business; if we have to go out, we tell each other, but more than that, we use a handwritten diary that stays on my desk. Just a bit of security for the two of us that Hermia insisted we get. We got into a bit of bother when we investigated the deaths of Dad and Johnny, and as Steve is her partner, we have to do as she says. Or else.'

'That's what sisters are for.'

And he had gathered up the bits and bobs he had brought across and headed back to the office.

She turned away from the window after watching him run across the tram tracks and then the road, deciding her first job would be to tell him there was a traffic-controlled crossing not twenty-five yards from her front door, and maybe he should think about using it.

* * *

Harry and Steve were waiting for Matt in Steve's office, their faces expectant.

'She said yes?' Steve asked.

'Mary Poppins will bring her own umbrella.' Matt grinned. 'I reckon we're lucky to have dropped on her at this point in our business development...'

'She dropped on us,' Steve pointed out. 'We didn't choose her, she chose us, and she's definitely getting more like Mary Poppins every time we speak. She chose her employer, didn't she?'

'Mr Banks, Mr George Banks,' Harry said helpfully.

'Thank you, Harry,' Steve said, 'but you don't get paid for being our resident expert on Mary Poppins. Unless we actually need an expert on Mary Poppins, that is.'

They all turned at the sound of tapping on the large front window, and Harry, being nearest to it, pushed aside one of the vertical blinds.

'Karen,' he yelled, and went to press the newly installed door release to let her in.

DS Karen Nelson was as big a favourite with Harry as she was with his dad. Huge steps had been taken in Matt and Karen's fledgling relationship over the previous six months, and now, with the sale of Karen's home she had shared with her ex-husband, they had created a more solid footing and moved in together at Matt's home.

Matt kissed her cheek in greeting. 'How did you know to knock on Steve's window?'

'I'm a detective.'

'Okay, that's a good enough answer.' He grinned at her. 'You called in for a cuppa?'

She shook her head. 'No, much simpler than that. I'm taking five minutes out. I actually wanted a chat, but it's about a case so I'll wait till after a certain young man has gone to bed.'

Steve stood. 'I'll take Harry with me. We've got a big job on at Bradway, and I want to check it's all going as well as they keep reporting it is. Besides, it doesn't hurt them to see the big boss turn up occasionally. Grab your coat, Harry – and a football. This house is next door to a public field so we can grab half an hour's kick-about.'

'Don't damage Uncle Steve,' Matt warned his son, and led Karen through to his own office. He carried on into the kitchen and switched on the kettle, despite his earlier offer having been refused.

She smiled at him. 'You know me so well, Matt.'

'I know that sometimes you say no, when you really mean yes, please,' he said, winking at her.

'Cheeky.'

'You okay?'

She shook her head. 'Not really. Because we've got one or two off with Covid, I had to go to a burglary site. I wouldn't normally do that, I'd send uniform, but as I said, we're short staffed. I brought Ray Ledger, but he's gone back to write up the reports, so I thought I'd come here, wash my hand,' she waved her wrist about, 'and tell you my concerns about this case. And also to say how chuffed I am that Ray Ledger, Jaime Hanover and Ian Jameson are properly on my team as DCs, promoted from PCs. And all on merit after their work on your dad's murder and the Anthony Dawson murder.'

Matt headed to the kitchen as he heard the kettle switch off, and then turned back. 'They all deserved the promotion to Major Crimes. Wash your hand?'

She held her right hand out towards him.

'That's blood.'

'It's my own.'

'Thank heavens for that. What have you done?'

'There was a lot of glass and I fell over an iron.'

'An iron?'

'A plastic child's iron. I saw it at the last minute but I stepped on it, and it broke, I catapulted forward and saved myself by putting my hand on the windowsill. The glass from the broken window was everywhere. And now my blood is too. I've confessed to forensics, showed them the part that is all me, and they laughed. Amateur, they called me. But I actually think I might need a dressing on it, and I happen to know you've got a super-duper first aid box here. You do, don't you?'

He grinned at her. 'It might have a plaster in it. Let me get the tea made, and we'll clean the cut. Don't bleed on the carpet.'

'You're all heart, Matt Forrester.'

* * *

With the cut cleansed until a germ wouldn't dare trespass anywhere near it, and a large pink plaster protecting it, Karen sat back with a sigh. 'That's much better. It was actually quite painful, but if I'd confessed to that I'd have been known as wimpy Karen for the rest of my police life.'

'And what about the iron?'

'I've promised the little girl I'll get her a new one. The bloody burglars had tipped her toybox over and scattered stuff everywhere, but the mother knew better than to move anything until we arrived. Hence my size fives landed on a plastic iron.'

She took a sip of her tea. 'So, the house is about ten properties from here, along this little service road. The mum and her two kids went to her brother's house for a meal last night, but both kids fell asleep so all three of them ended up staying. When they arrived home this morning, the front window had been smashed, the front door left open, and inside was... well, I suppose you'd say wrecked. She rang us to say she thought they might still be inside because she could see her television still on the wall, and the front door was open, so we were with her within about six minutes. There was glass everywhere – they'd been in every room and trailed it around the place; it was a dangerous environment for the two little ones. Her brother's been and collected them, got them safely out of the way, and the lady herself is quite calm and composed.'

'Really?'

'That's for our benefit. I know she's seen some CCTV from next door's camera, and I think she's recognised somebody. It was a couple of thugs, teenage thugs. Just learning their trade, I reckon. Didn't have a car unless it was parked round the corner, though they didn't look old enough to be driving. It happened about nine last night. They took a television, about fifteen years old, but left the brand-new one on the wall in the lounge. Left a laptop upstairs in the main bedroom, that sort of thing. They took her jewellery box, but she says that's no great loss, it was just costume jewellery that the little one played with.'

'And you think she'll go after them herself?'

Karen nodded. 'I do. I've tried to warn her off doing that, explained they might only be teenagers but their families will back them in every way and it could be a dangerous game she's playing, no matter what they've done. I'm going to have a closer look at them when I get the CCTV transferred to our system and hopefully enhanced. I kind of thought I knew one of them, but I can't give a name yet.'

'You want me to take a look?'

'I'll download it to a stick and bring it home with me tonight, then nobody will realise I'm showing it to you. Two heads are probably going to be much better than one. The victim is called Elise Langton, lives at number 83.' Karen replaced her cup on the desk. 'I'm calling round at Smyths before I go back into the station. I need to buy a plastic iron.'

Matt stood and moved round the desk to take her into his

arms. 'Take care, drive carefully, et cetera et cetera. Oh, and remind me to fill you in on our new receptionist tonight. You'll be impressed.'

'I am impressed already. You hadn't even contacted an agency when we left this morning.'

He laughed. 'Fate intervened, big style.' He kissed her, and she left him with a small wave and a huge smile.

He watched as she drove away, then picked up his phone.

'You still at Bradway?'

'Yep, you need us? The job's fine, but we've not even kicked a ball yet.'

'Tell Harry you have to come back for work, but I want us to go for a walk when you do get back. Harry can come with us.'

'Problem?'

'Stolen goods type of problem. I'll explain when you get here.'

* * *

Harry grumbled most of the way back, and Steve had to promise him a game of football for the following day, with the proviso that it wasn't raining.

'What's Dad want anyway?'

'You're not going to believe this, but it seems we're going for a walk.'

'Dad? Walking?' Harry sounded shocked. 'I thought he went everywhere in the car.'

'Well, it just goes to show you don't know your dad as well as you think you do. Although now you mention it, I thought he went everywhere in the car as well.'

They laughed, fist-bumped at their agreement on Matt's

walking attitudes, and Steve put on his indicators to pull onto the forecourt of their office.

'Safely delivered,' he said. 'We'd best get inside and find out what he wants us to do on this walk. Could be an interesting evening, this one.'

'Reckon he'll buy me a bag of chips?'

'He will if we steer him towards Base Green shops. You know he can't resist the smell if we walk past the chippy down there.'

'Okay, let's see what his plans for us are, then.' Harry opened the passenger door, ready to negotiate the planned walking route.

3

MONDAY, 24 OCTOBER

Elise Langton was quietly angry. She hadn't shown it in front of Jack Mitchell, her brother, because she knew he would insist on her returning with them instead of staying in her home, and she had things to organise. She needed all the locks changing because the little bastards had taken a set of keys from the kitchen, and she needed to get the window boarded up, with arrangements made to have the glass replaced.

And she needed to get on Facebook and start naming names. Her time as a social worker had left her with a memory of kids who would develop into criminals in future years, and she thought she had recognised one of them on the CCTV video. She wanted to let the brain-dead morons know that she knew who they were, and they'd picked on the wrong person.

Forensics had found nothing. Apparently shows like *Vera* and *CSI* had taught the criminal fraternity all about wearing gloves, covering hair with a hat and wearing black clothes. These two obviously hadn't learnt enough about CCTV, though.

She escorted the forensic people to the door and thanked

them for their trouble, and they said she could begin to put her home back together.

She began with three-year-old Skye's toys, scrubbing out the toybox with bleach just in case they'd touched it, then shaking and washing each toy, making sure there was no glass caught up anywhere in them. When all the toys, except the broken iron, were back in the box, she carried it into the kitchen. Apart from the bunch of keys which had been in a bowl on the work surface, the thieves didn't appear to have taken or done anything else in there, so she stacked things as she cleaned them on the kitchen table.

Six-year-old Daniel had been furious that they'd taken his PS4, but a little bewildered that they hadn't taken the cables that went with it. And she realised he had been even more angry that they'd taken his *Minecraft* disc that had been in the machine – he'd spent months reaching a high level on it. Elise had blocked the machine within minutes of discovering it had gone, and she hoped that had worked.

Most of his toys and games had been in his bedroom, and it appeared that the burglars hadn't bothered with the rooms that were clearly for kids. But her own bedroom had been trashed beyond all recognition. Tonight she would be sleeping on the sofa in the lounge, tomorrow was soon enough to begin the big clean-up in that room. They'd taken her old television and the jewellery box she had owned since she was a child, but there was nothing of any significant value inside it. Skye loved to play with it, dangling odd earrings from her ears, wearing multiple strands of beads and chains around her neck, but Elise knew the value was zero. Her wedding and engagement rings that had been removed from her finger and taped inside her Bible, as soon as she had ordered Rick out of her life, were safe. She had had some vague thought in her head that burglars wouldn't consider a Bible worth stealing. Thankfully, she had been right on that one.

With the lounge looking quite bare and the kitchen table full to overflowing, Elise began to sweep up the glass. She didn't want to wreck her vacuum cleaner by scrunching over it, so patiently swept and tipped it shovelful by shovelful into a cardboard box. It was only when she couldn't see any remaining glass that she got out the vacuum cleaner and hoovered the entire house except for her bedroom. That was for another day, but at least she could get her children home the next day and know they would be safe from cutting themselves.

The window took half an hour for her neighbour to board up, and after he refused to take anything for doing it, she handed him a six-pack of lager.

'Happy to help out,' Malcolm said. 'And I'd got the stuff I needed in the shed anyway. I'll measure up properly for the glass tomorrow, and you'll be back to normal within a couple of days. You contacted a locksmith?'

Elise nodded. 'Coming tomorrow. Early.'

'Have you told Rick?'

She shook her head. 'Not yet. You know what he's like, he'll cause uproar trying to find out who's done it, and I can't handle that at the moment. Let's give the police a chance to make the arrests, before Rick gets to them.'

Malcolm laughed. 'Then let's hope he doesn't hear any Chinese whispers about this, because he'll be round here causing merry hell. And if he gets sight of my CCTV, he'll know who they are, won't he?'

Elise sighed. 'He might. Please don't let him know your camera was working and caught them.'

He stared at her. 'You know who they are, don't you?'

'I think so.'

'Then take care how you deal with it, Elise. You've two kiddies to think about. Just tell the police their names, and let them do their job.'

* * *

Matt, Steve and Harry made sure they were protected against the cold of the night air, before setting off down Seagrave Avenue, looking in front gardens using torches, the whole time checking Harry was with one or the other. They concentrated on houses that were in darkness, and while they were shining torches at one such home, a man came out of the front door of the adjoining house.

'You lost something?'

Matt approached him, holding up his ID. 'Matt Forrester. From the Forrester Detective Agency at the top of the hill. We're looking into a burglary that happened last night, and we think they may have hidden some items to collect later. Just taking an hour or so to have a look in the locality, just in case.'

The man checked the ID, then nodded.

'Charlie Anson. You looked down the side of this house yet?'

Matt shook his head. 'My partner's heading down the side now...'

'There's a television with a black bag over it. Stashed behind a wheelie bin.'

As the men finished speaking, they heard Harry call out, 'Dad! We need you.'

Matt and Charlie moved to where Harry and Steve were, and all four of them looked at the television.

'Not the brightest of burglars, are they?' Charlie said.

'I'll lay odds on them being bright enough to keep gloves on,' Matt said. 'I'll ring DS Nelson and tell her what we've found.

She'll send somebody round to pick it up. Let's have a look round and see if they've dumped anything else, like the PS4 or the jewellery box.'

'The owners of this house are in Spain at the moment,' Charlie said. 'They'll be sorry they've missed all of this. I've been keeping an eye on things for them, that's why I knew the television had been put there after their departure.'

'On the plus side,' Matt said, 'this wouldn't have been dumped here if they'd thought the house wasn't empty. It must have been in complete darkness for them to stash it here. They probably know the homeowners aren't home and obviously think there's no rush to pick it up, so they're going to be pretty pissed off when they do turn up and it's gone.'

When Matt called her, Karen answered her phone immediately, and listened as he explained what was going on. 'Tell me what you want to do.'

'Can you hang on there until I get the forensics people out to pick up the television? I'll tell them to be quick. They might just get a fingerprint off it, but there's no point getting surveillance, we don't have the manpower to do that. And Matt – thank you.'

He smiled as she disconnected. 'She's sending somebody from forensics to pick it up,' he explained. 'I suggest you two go and buy a bag of chips and head off home, and I'll wait here until it's been collected. That okay?'

Steve and Harry laughed, gave him the thumbs ups, and began to walk up the road, heading back to the office to collect Steve's car.

The elderly neighbour looked at Matt. 'You're Dave Forrester's lad?'

'I am. You knew my dad?'

'Everybody round here knew your dad. It's a privilege to meet you.'

'Thank you. I miss him, and he's why we've done this walka-round tonight. It's what he would have done, albeit in a wheel-chair. He could see into the minds of criminals, almost second guess them, and I try to emulate that. I'm just not as successful as he was, but we'll get there.'

'I'll wait with you until your mates arrive to take this away.' He indicated the television set. 'I'll go and get the missus to make us a cuppa tea; it's a bit chilly out tonight.'

Within five minutes, Charlie was back with two cups of tea and a packet of ginger biscuits in his coat pocket. 'The missus says I can have two, and you can have as many as you want.'

'She's a star,' Matt said, rubbing his hands together to warm them before wrapping them around the cup. 'But I'll not tell her if you have more than two.'

Charlie looked down. 'She'll know, she'll know.'

The two men sat on the front garden wall, and sipped at their drinks, dunking ginger biscuits.

'Is there a reason she limits your biscuit consumption, then?'

'Aye, my bloody doctor told her I'd got diabetes and she needed to change my diet.'

'And have you? Got diabetes, I mean.'

'Aye, I have, and she checks everything before I have it.' He fished in the packet for a biscuit.

'That's the fourth one you've had.'

'Yes, but the last two don't count.'

'Why not?' Matt was enjoying the company of this man.

'I'll tell her you had them. You were starving because you've had nowt to eat since lunchtime.'

'Which happens to be true. If we hadn't found this televi-sion, I was on the promise of a bag of chips from the chippie.'

'Well, there you are then. You needed a couple of extra ginger biscuits to keep you going.' Charlie sipped at his cup of tea, and smiled. 'There's always a way round things, lad. You just have to look for 'em, where women are concerned – they're a lot smarter than we are.'

'Think I don't know that? That DS I rang earlier? She's my life partner. Proper smart cookie. I've also got a sister. More brains in her big toe than I have in my entire body.'

'Hermia? Or something like that?'

'That's right. You know her?'

'Met her once. Your dad introduced me to her. Beautiful lady.'

'Certainly is. She lives with Steve, the feller who's gone off with my son to get a bag of chips before they go home and pretend they've had nothing to eat.'

'So you've two smart women keeping an eye on you? Don't know how you cope. I've enough with one.' He reached for another biscuit.

'Am I eating that one as well?' Matt asked.

'Afraid so. You really are hungry, aren't you?'

'Obviously.' He picked up the packet of biscuits, now much depleted, and twisted the top of it until it resealed the pack.

Charlie watched him, then smiled. 'Think I'll get suppertime biscuits tonight then?'

'Doubt it. As you said, your wife's a lot smarter than you, and she will know exactly how many you had. Plus, your CCTV camera is pointing at this stretch of road.'

Matt suddenly realised what he'd said.

'CCTV, for fuck's sake. You have CCTV. Does it work?'

'Think so. Our son put it in about a year ago, but we've never had to check on it. It's linked to the wife's phone.'

'Just don't touch it. I'll get somebody out first thing in the morning, and they'll download the previous thirty-six hours or so.'

'No problem, lad. I'm always up early. So she could have been watching me scoffing all these biscuits?'

'Yep.'

'Bugger. That's no chocolate for me for a month then.'

The small forensics van pulled up to the kerb, and Matt and Charlie stood. The two men shook hands, and Charlie collected up the cups and what remained of the biscuits.

'Been good chatting to you, Matt. Hope you catch the little bastards.'

4

TUESDAY, 25 OCTOBER

Karen verified the two lads caught on the Ansons' CCTV were the same two lads seen at Elise Langton's neighbour's property, and asked that files be checked to try to come up with names. The television had fingerprints all over it, but it had been confirmed they belonged to Elise and her children, so Karen picked up the iron in its pretty gift bag and headed down to her car.

Ten minutes later, she was outside the Langton home, waving at the little girl's face peering at her through the bay window.

Elise opened the door, and ushered her in. 'You have news?'

'Kind of. But first of all I have a new iron for Miss Skye, to say sorry for standing on yours, sweetheart.'

Skye smiled shyly, and took the gift bag proffered by the nice lady. She squealed in delight when she saw the sparkly new iron; it was much nicer than the one the lady had trodden on. She ran to the kitchen to get her ironing board, then returned to collect some tea towels that she thought desperately needed ironing.

Elise laughed. 'That'll keep her busy until my brother comes to collect her. He's taking both kids for the day, so I can sort out the bedroom. Skye irons absolutely everything. Bet that changes as she gets older. So, you have news?'

'It's not a lot, but it's a start. I just want to explain something about burglaries. There really are only two kinds. One is planned meticulously where the thief knows exactly what is inside the property, where it is, and the likelihood of people being in the house. The other sort is the opportunistic thief. They usually work in twos, go out for a supposed walk, and look for houses that are in darkness.'

Elise nodded. 'I always leave a light on and my curtains closed if we're going to be out for the night, but I didn't know that was going to happen. We were only going over to Jack and Pippa's for a meal, but both kids fell asleep, so Pippa suggested we stayed. This house was in darkness, and the curtains were open, letting them see nobody was inside.'

Karen nodded. 'They were definitely the opportunistic type. That's why it was all so rushed. They took the TV from upstairs, but they didn't have transport so couldn't manage the even bigger one that's on your wall. They left the PS4 cables still plugged in at the wall, and they missed the laptop altogether. They probably imagined they'd got a fair haul in the jewellery box, but even with that they'll get nothing for it. Then last night we had a bit of a breakthrough in that the people who own the Forrester Detective Agency went for a walk around the nearby area to see if these particular little scrotes had behaved as all little scrotes behave with stolen goods that are too big to carry. They hide them to collect later. And they found your television hidden behind a wheelie bin. We collected it last night. They were caught once again on CCTV and it is the same pair, so we've tested for fingerprints but there's only yours and some little ones, so that doesn't help. We'll get it back to you as soon as we can.'

'You know who they are?'

'I...' Karen hesitated. 'I feel as if I do. I'm going back to the office now, and I'm going to look through some photographs. See if anything jogs my memory a bit further. I intended doing it last night, but we had to deal with getting that telly back to the station and logged into forensics. But you know them, don't you?'

Elise shrugged. 'Maybe. I'm not 100 per cent sure, but maybe. I'll let you know as soon as I find out for definite.'

'Elise...' There was a warning note in Karen's voice. 'Do not take matters into your own hands. You've two kids to think about, and they could easily get hurt, as could you. Whoever these lads are, they're probably from one or two of the criminal families and they're learning their trade. But it's their families who are the problem. They'll think nothing of a sharp knife in your neck, or a baseball bat smashing your kneecaps to smithereens. Leave the rough stuff to us, and if you do feel you can tell me who you think they are, I promise I'll follow it up. It won't be left in my in-tray.'

* * *

Carol Flynn proved to be just as good at crossing tram tracks as she was a receptionist. She had watched for the arrival of a car carrying somebody who looked as though they belonged in the agency, then moved at speed across the road to begin what she hoped would be the last job she would ever need or want. And the need was social rather than financial. She was a woman who needed to be needed!

Matt and Steve arrived together and as she stood behind them, they both turned.

'Good morning!' Matt's smile was huge. 'I'm glad you've arrived. At four this morning I had a fear that it had all been a dream and I still had to find a receptionist.'

'I'm real, and I'm here,' she said, leading the way into the office, ushered in by both men. 'And don't be on your best behaviour on my account. I'm here to be part of the team.'

'Good. Shall we start with a cuppa made in our new coffee machine?'

'Can do,' she agreed. 'I haven't had a chance to orientate myself yet, but I'm assuming I can access the kitchen from my office?'

'You can. We all can, because now the kitchen kind of runs along the back of the building, and our offices are built in front of it. Yours is slightly smaller than ours to facilitate this little vestibule where people can enter, then ring the bell for you to deal with their problem. We initially tried to sort it out without major changes from the way Dad had it, but then we decided to just go for it and reconfigure the whole of the downstairs. There are now two access points to the upstairs flat. The first is via that little door on the outside of the shop. Dad had a lift to transport him and his wheelchair up there, but we don't need it, so we've removed it, and the second entry is the door in the kitchen which takes you to a flight of stairs. Upstairs is sort of a large filing system really. We've used Johnny's old bedroom for storing all his files, and there's a separate filing cabinet for ours. In theory it could still be used as a flat with external access. When we removed the lift – with a degree of sadness – it gave us considerably more space.'

'Okay, I'll begin by getting us all a drink. Is Harry not with us today?'

'No, he's decided to spend the day with Aunty Hermia. She booked a day off work for what she hopes will be her discharge from hospital, all mended and put back together, then they're going to the cinema, probably McDonald's, and other nefarious places. I keep saying she's a bad influence on him, but he thinks she's the best person in the whole world.'

'She is,' Steve said.

Carol laughed. 'I'll get used to the relationships. You live with Hermia, Steve?'

'I do. Chased her for years, and finally caught her. Not before somebody chucked her over a balcony unfortunately, but I've caught her now.'

'And you'll meet my better half later this morning, because she's calling in. She's dealing with a burglary along this service road.'

'Elise's house? I heard she'd been burgled. They're all okay, though?'

'They are, but I know Karen is concerned Elise might take matters into her own hands. She's DS Karen Nelson, by the way. I've asked Herms to call in at some point today to meet you. I want you to be able to recognise the bona fide guests instantly, and turn the AK47 on anybody you don't know. Because if we don't know the person at the door, they don't get in.'

'This sounds like fun,' she said, 'I've never had a job before where I could shoot people.' Carol turned towards her reception door, and asked for the code.

'At the moment it's 12345, but change it to one you want, then let us know as well. We are conscious that although we caught the bastard who killed my dad and Johnny, he was part of something much bigger, and our security here as a result is a work in progress. After you've found your feet, I'll take you round the entire property, show you all the cameras, which are the dummy ones and which are the real ones, then you'll know just how safe a working environment this is. But trust me when I tell you it will eventually be like Fort Knox.'

She keyed in 12345 and entered her office for the first time. Steve and Matt followed and stood in the doorway, watching her reaction.

'It smells deliciously of wood. Somebody should bottle this fragrance for a room freshener spray; I'd buy it by the bucket-load. And it all feels so new.' She moved behind her desk and sat. 'Nice chair,' she said, approval written across her face. 'Much better than mine at home. I think I'm going to like it here.'

'That's good. Right, first things first. Reset this entry code to one you can remember, then come into my office,' Matt said. 'I'll make us all a coffee to welcome you, but that door at the back of your office leads directly into the kitchen. Just take a break whenever, and an hour for lunch. Does that suit you?'

'It does,' she said.

She stood, ushered the two men away from her door and looked at the door entry pad. She gave a brief nod, and reset the number.

Matt disappeared into the kitchen and Steve and Carol sat on the client side of his desk. He returned quickly with coffees for all three of them, and raised his in salute to Carol. 'Welcome, I hope you're going to be okay with us. We're a bit of a step down for you, I know, so we will understand if you find you want more than we can give. And I think we need to change your title, because you'll be so much more than a receptionist. Does Personal Assistant sit okay with you?'

'It does. And as for being a step down, that might have been relevant at some point in my life, but it isn't now. I know I worked for the so-called great and good of our country, but they're not. I hated having to constantly lie for them, be nice to people I knew weren't nice, that sort of thing. Here I feel an honesty, not just you two, but the whole ambience of the place. And, of course, I knew Dave and Johnny. Dave once told me that if ever they decided to expand, he would come knocking at my door to offer me a job. But when my husband died, I decided it was time to leave a working life, and take up knitting.'

'Knitting?'

She laughed. 'I can't do it. I thought I'd learn from YouTube. I bought some wool and some needles, and they're safely tucked away in a drawer now. And then I spotted all the comings and goings here, and knew this was Dave and Johnny controlling you from heaven, expanding the business. Have you?'

'Expanded? We have. We've retained all of Dad's old clients, and picked up new ones. And it seems we've also acquired a pretty smart lady who even worked out how to reset the entry box. What's the number, by the way?'

'It's 37192.'

'How on earth am I supposed to remember that?'

'I've known it since I was five,' she said with a laugh. 'It was my Mum's co-op number. To me, it's the easiest five-number code in the world, but I doubt others will remember it.'

Steve looked at Matt. 'We'd best write it down, pal.'

5

TUESDAY, 25 OCTOBER

Hermia and Harry buckled on their seat belts and Hermia turned towards him. They gave a mutual high-five, and both of them laughed.

'The NHS has thrown me out, Harry, they've banished me forever with instructions never to darken their doors again.'

'Then make sure you don't,' Harry responded. 'I thought I was going to lose you like I lost Granddad. And then Uncle Johnny died as well, so I thought I was slowly losing everybody except Dickhead.'

'Don't call him Dickhead.' Hermia made the automatic response to her nephew's words that they had all got used to making.

Harry turned to her as she started the engine. 'But he is.' Harry's face held no glimmer of a smile, and Hermia knew they had a serious issue. With the new baby due very shortly, Harry was going to feel even more left out, and she vowed to herself that she would have a discussion with Matt about what they could do to help Harry.

'Okay, McDonald's before or after the cinema?'

'Before, I think. We going to Centertainment?'

'You decide. The other option is Meadowhall cinema.'

'Centertainment, please.'

Hermia pulled out of the car park and headed towards Barnsley Road, feeling a huge sense of relief that her visits were finished. Her bones had mended, the bruises had disappeared, and all was right in her world. Just not in Harry's world.

* * *

DS Karen Nelson left Elise's home feeling disgruntled. She'd hoped that Elise would come to her senses overnight, but clearly she hadn't and was withholding the name or names of the lads who had wrecked her home. Karen was convinced Elise knew for definite who they were, but she wouldn't admit to it.

She got in her car and drove the fifty yards to the office of the Forrester Detective Agency, parking up next to Matt's car. She rang the intercom bell, and held up her warrant card towards the camera, knowing the new receptionist had started that morning.

The door clicked, and she pushed it open.

The sliding window opened, and Carol smiled at her. 'Hi, you're DS Nelson?'

'Karen. I'm only DS Nelson if I bring my boss with me.' She smiled.

'Matt doesn't have anybody in with him at the moment, but if it's Steve you're wanting, he's gone out.'

'No, it's Matt. Good to meet you, Carol, and I'm sure we'll get to know each other much better in the future. Congratulations on getting the job, by the way.'

'Thank you.' Carol grinned. 'I bullied them.'

'That was smart of you. I've found they usually respond to a bit of bullying. Has Matt got anybody due in?' She patted her bag. 'I've got some photos I want him to take a look at, but it can wait if he's any appointments.'

'No, he's free until half past three, so with a bit of luck he'll take you for lunch as well.'

'You mean he'll nip across the road to the shop and bring me a sausage sandwich?'

Carol shrugged. 'They're nice sausage sandwiches, though. Play your cards right and he might even stand you some tomato ketchup as well.'

Karen held up a thumb, and turned away towards Matt's office. He opened the door as she lifted her hand to knock, and stepped back to let her walk in.

* * *

The book of mug shots was open on Matt's desk and he was simultaneously, and with difficulty, watching his iPad screen as it played the CCTV of the two lads, and checking the actual photographs of known rogues.

Karen was silent, not wishing to disturb his concentration. He had watched the CCTV first, pausing it at a couple of spots where he needed a prolonged look, and then had combined the book with the CCTV. Every inch a DI. He was taking it slowly, keen not to miss anything, but at the end he sighed.

'It's strange, but the taller one of the two I feel I know. Yet I can't match him up to anything in the mug shot pictures, and the CCTV isn't making me think that's so and so.'

'It's the taller one I've been concentrating on. I don't know the other one, but this is really bugging me now. They're both obviously only kids, but...'

'They've not really arrived on the police's radar yet. It's

perhaps as well they're just learning their trade, they could have taken so much more from that home if they'd really known what they were doing.' He pushed the mug shots to one side. 'You have to get back or can you stay for lunch?'

'What constitutes lunch?'

'Sausage sandwich?'

She tried to control her laughter but failed miserably. 'Much as that sounds really tempting, I have to decline. I'm going back to the station, need to wind this one up. I can't give it much more of my time, so I'll complete the report and move on. I've delivered the iron and that was my main reason for visiting Elise this morning. It may be that she finds other stuff missing, because she's tackling her own trashed bedroom this morning, so I imagine she'll be feeling murderous by the time she's finished it.'

The house felt eerily silent. Once the children had left with Uncle Jack, the quiet had been immediate. Elise had until their promised six o'clock return to sort out the damned bedroom.

She found the largest mug in her cupboard and made a coffee, then carried it upstairs along with a bucketful of cleaning materials. She couldn't bear having the knowledge that the gits had been in her bedroom, and every part of it would have to be cleaned so that every speck of them, every thought of them, was removed.

She put the bucket in the bathroom, then carried the coffee into the bedroom, placing it carefully on the windowsill. Then she cried. For the best part of ten minutes she was distraught, then she closed her own personal relief valve, and shook her head. This wasn't getting her anywhere.

She began by stripping everything off her bed, then she staggered back downstairs with the wash load and set the washer going. She carried the vacuum cleaner back upstairs with her and hoovered the mattress before turning it over and hoovering the underside.

She looked around. Having done all of that, the room looked no better. She gulped at the coffee; there was a need for caffeine. And the curtains would have to be taken down and washed – they had definitely touched them because they had been closed, and she knew she hadn't closed them before heading out to Jack's. She dragged her bedroom chair over to the window and climbed up on it to reach them.

Her thoughts were in turmoil. She knew exactly who had done this to her, and she sure as hell was going to let his fucking family know what he had done as her first action. Her main decision was whether to take it into her own hands, or tell DS Nelson. She sensed it wouldn't be ignored by Karen; she had seemed to genuinely care, but would a slap on the hand be enough to make amends for the heartache and angst brought into her life? Because Elise knew that the courts would be far too lenient – and she knew enough people to have the lads dealt with more effectively.

She dumped the curtains on the landing and took the spray window cleaner out of the bucket. Cleaning the windows was something she had always enjoyed, and she took her time, making sure every part of the frame and glass was spotlessly clean. Her bedroom overlooked the road below, and as she looked down several people walked by and all waved at her. She attempted to smile at them, but didn't allow the smile to reach her eyes. The struggle was real – tell Karen Nelson the name, or get in touch with Rick and let him know what had happened. And she had one day to make the decision because Rick would

be standing on her doorstep at ten the following day to collect
the kids for a couple of half-term days with him.

She doubted that Skye would say anything beyond telling
Daddy that she had a new iron, but Daniel, in his new role as
the six-year-old man of the house, would definitely spill the
beans.

She didn't want Rick back in her life but she knew once he
learned what had happened he would begin to interfere. But he
had made his choice by sleeping with someone from work.
Although she did acknowledge to herself that it wasn't so much
Rick making this choice, but one she'd given him when she
discovered his dirty little secret. She'd given him no option. Get
out and get out now.

But he seemed to have difficulty letting go. Yes, he'd moved
out but it was mainly because he couldn't get into the house. She
had organised changing the locks the second he'd walked out of
their home, and when he returned after visiting the cow from
work, he couldn't get through the door.

He would be collecting the kids, and he would collect them
from the doorstep, but she couldn't disguise the wood replacing
the glass in the bay window of the lounge.

And Daniel would say Mummy had cried, and he would
explain in detail about his PlayStation having disappeared, and
that there had been glass all over the floor. And that Mummy
had used naughty words.

She could, of course, refuse to tell Rick anything. She could
also tie a gag around Daniel's mouth, but neither of those
options would work in the long run.

She sat down on the newly cleaned mattress, and her head
dropped forward. She remained unmoving for a couple of
minutes, wondering how on earth everything had managed to
go pear-shaped in just a couple of days. She could see glass glis-

tening in the pile of the carpet, and she knew exactly where they had stood. Although no glass had been broken in the bedroom, it had been trailed upstairs in the soles of their trainers.

Anger exploded once more inside her, and she lifted her head, searching for where she had dumped her phone as she had begun the clear-up. She spotted it on the bedside table, and reached for it.

She hesitated, lost in thought for a moment, then opened up Facebook. Time seemed suspended while she thought about the words. Then she began to type, tagging the person she was addressing.

Luke Peters, tell your brat that he's dead meat. He picked the wrong one to rob, and I'm giving his name to police tomorrow.

She waited a couple of minutes to see if there was any response; there wasn't so Elise stood, plugged in the vacuum cleaner and began to clean up the glass that had triggered her rage.

She meant it. She would give Peters time to sort out his lad, and if he didn't confirm it had been dealt with and that she would get everything back, there would be a phone call to Karen Nelson.

6

WEDNESDAY, 26 OCTOBER

Daniel Langton, at six years of age, was a child used to obeying his mother's rules about getting up. This didn't apply yet to his little sister, and he felt her tiny fist pummel him on his face as she tried to wake him.

He opened one eye. 'Back off, Skye. I'm asleep.'

'Mummy sleep.'

'Go back to bed. It's not a school day.' He closed his eyes, but she thumped him again, this time on the nose. He sat up. 'Stop it, Skye! That hurt!'

She tugged at his arm. 'Mummy sleep. On floor. I want to iron this,' and she held up the crocheted blanket she took to bed every night.

Slowly his brain began to wake up. 'Where's Mum?'

'On floor.'

'In her bedroom?'

Skye shook her head. She tugged at his arm. 'You get my ironing board. Mummy won't wake up.'

He sighed. 'You're a pest, Skye. Okay, I'll go and get it for you. Then will you leave me alone?'

She nodded without speaking, and tugged once again at his arm.

He unwrapped the twisted bedclothes from around his legs and sat on the edge of the bed.

'I need a wee first,' he said, and he saw her mouth begin to open and object to this massive waste of time. 'Don't say anything,' he warned. 'Be back in a minute.'

Because he knew it would annoy his sister, he took his time washing his hands, but as he came out of the bathroom, Skye was waiting at the top of the stairs.

'Now can we go to my ironing board?' she asked, clutching the blanket to her.

He went downstairs in front of his sister, again following rules ingrained in him. The door at the bottom of the stairs led into the lounge, and it was partly open. Mum must be up, he figured.

He pushed it open fully, and Skye followed him as he entered the lounge.

The smell hit his senses before he realised his mother was on the floor, her head lying in a pool of sticky dark red blood.

'Skye, we need Mum's phone.'

She nodded, and walked towards the kitchen door. 'And my ironing board?'

Daniel felt unable to move. 'I'll get that in a minute. We need a phone.'

Skye found it on the kitchen work surface and handed it to her brother who was now searching the lounge – without going anywhere near his mother, of course. He couldn't.

He pressed his mother's favourites list and clicked on the name 'Rick', as he did at least twice a week when he had a chat with his dad.

It was answered quickly, and he felt relief wash through him. His dad would know what to do.

'Elise? You okay?'

'Dad, it's me. Can you come round?'

There was a momentary hesitation as Rick recognised the abnormality of an early-morning call from Daniel. 'Not at the moment, son. I'm on Derek Dooley Way, heading to work. I'm picking you up at ten. Something wrong?'

'There's a lot of blood,' Daniel whispered. 'And Skye needs to do her ironing.'

Rick heard the panic. 'A lot of blood?'

'From Mum. She's not moving, and she's on the floor.'

'Ten minutes, Danny. Ten minutes. Don't touch Mum, don't do anything. Can you and Skye go do some ironing in the kitchen?'

Rick couldn't believe he was making such inane comments. He checked his mirrors, cut across three lanes of traffic and took an exit that almost allowed him to do a U-turn to head back the way he had just driven. He forced the U-turn amidst blares of horns and angry hand signals from other drivers. But they hadn't just been told about lots of blood, had they?

He drove erratically, his foot hard down, almost hoping he would have a police-stop, but he pulled up outside Elise's home nine minutes later. The front door was unlocked, and he pushed it open, making an immediate right turn into the lounge. He stared in horror at the scene in front of him.

* * *

Karen kissed Matt, then picked up her briefcase. 'I shouldn't be late home,' she said. 'Shall we go mad and eat out tonight? Book a table somewhere nice?'

Matt smiled. 'Whatever you say, my love. Your wish is my command, or should that be your command is my instruction? Anywhere in particular?'

Her phone rang and she held up a finger. 'It's the station,' she said.

She held it to her ear.

'DS Nelson,' she said. She listened for a moment. 'It is my case, but about to be handed over.' Again there was pause. 'I'll be there in about five minutes. Get Ray Ledger, Jaime Hanover and Ian Jameson to meet me there. You say the husband's already at the scene?'

She listened to the response, then disconnected before turning to Matt.

'You got the gist?'

He nodded. 'Just go. I'll not book a table, go and do your job. It's your burglary case, isn't it? Is she dead?'

'Yes, it's Elise Langton, and yes, it seems there's now a fatality. The kids found her and rang Dad. That's as much as I've been told. I'll keep in touch. This is shit, Matt, utter shit. And it's a priority that we identify those two lads now, because my instinct is screaming this is all connected.'

Karen pulled up outside the house numbered 83 and saw a squad car pull up behind her. The three officers she had requested must have really blue-lighted to get here so quickly, she mused, then waited as they all piled out of the car.

'Ray says it's the lady from your burglary case,' Jaime said.

'It is. Let's not assume a connection just yet. Come on, let's suit up. Forensics are on their way, so let's not contaminate the scene by hot footing it in there. Her husband and kids are inside.'

They covered up quickly, and followed Karen to the front door which had been left open for their arrival, and as they entered the lounge Rick Langton stood from his seated position in an armchair.

'Hi, I'm Rick Langton, and this is my wife.' He waved his arm in the general direction of the body. 'About to become ex-wife, but she is still my wife.'

'Where are the children?' Karen asked.

'I've told them to play upstairs. Skye is apparently ironing everything in sight. I didn't want them seeing this...'

'Have you touched your wife?' Karen asked.

He shook his head. 'No, with all that blood I knew she was gone. I kept the kids away, and I've rung Jack, her brother. He's coming to get them any time now. He was in bed asleep when I rang him; he's a teacher, so they're more than happy to be going with him. Elise wouldn't hurt anybody. Who the fuck would do this to her?' Rick was babbling; he knew his sentences were disjointed, and he took a deep breath.

'Well, hopefully we'll have answers for you before too long.'

Karen turned at the sound of voices outside, and heard Ian explaining to someone that it was a crime scene and he couldn't enter.

She moved to the door.

'You're Uncle Jack?' she asked, and he nodded.

'I am, I've come to collect the children. What the hell's happened? I only spoke to her last night...'

'What time did you speak to your sister, Mr...?'

'It's Mitchell, Jack Mitchell. It would have been about half past nine, I was in bed for ten. She was telling me she'd cleaned the bedroom to within an inch of its life. She said there was someone at the door...' His voice trailed away as he realised what he had said. 'And we said goodnight, and love you.' He shrugged. 'Our standard way of closing down.'

'Mr Mitchell, I need you to get the children to safety, then one of my officers will be down to take a statement from you.' She turned to Ian. 'DC Jameson, get Mr Mitchell's address, and leave it a good hour before you go down. The children are a priority at the moment. They're upstairs in their rooms, so I understand.'

She stepped aside to allow Jack access to the stairs, then moved back into the lounge as the forensics team arrived. It suddenly became an efficient, fully functioning crime scene. Karen watched as Elise was officially pronounced dead, then turned her head as she heard Skye loudly proclaiming that she would iron all of Uncle Jack's shirts for him if he would let her take her ironing board as well as her iron. Jack waited at the foot of the stairs while Daniel returned to Skye's bedroom to get the ironing board, and two minutes later his car disappeared, bearing Elise's children.

She took Rick out to her car, and spoke briefly with him, telling him she would organise for a more formal statement later, and he explained that Daniel knew how to call his dad, so had used his mother's phone. He handed his phone to Karen so she could see the time he had been notified.

'That's fine, Mr Langton. Can you tell me where you were last night between nine and eleven o'clock?'

'I can. I took my partner to the George at Hathersage for a meal. We arrived about eight, left about half ten, back home before eleven. Then we went to bed. It was apparently an anniversary of the first time we made love. I had to pretend I remembered.'

Karen felt a slight frisson at the bitterness in his tone. This was not a happy relationship this man was apparently in.

'I was supposed to pick up the kids at ten this morning to have them for a couple of days,' he continued. 'I wasn't supposed to be working but I was on my way in, was going to work just for an hour because I needed to reroute a few deliveries following one of our lorries being broke down. I've left them to sort it out for themselves now I have things to organise here for Daniel and Skye.'

Karen made a note in her book. 'Thank you, Mr Langton. And your partner's name?'

'Jenna Glaves.' He handed her his card, after scribbling his address on the back. 'The kids will probably be with me from later on today; we're all set up for having them. Jack has to move his kids around, due to only having three bedrooms, to accommodate mine.'

'You and Jack are still friendly?'

He sighed. 'We are. I buggered everything up by screwing around with Jenna, but I've only myself to blame.'

'And you were divorcing?'

'Elise insisted on it. Said she wanted a clean break. I don't think she had anybody else because the kids have never said anything.'

'You ask them?'

'No, I don't, because I don't want to know that she loves somebody else when I still love her and can't tell her, but Daniel would have told me if there was somebody popping in to see her anyway. He's like that. He's quite a mature little lad, likes to have serious conversations, and is very protective of Skye. And his mother.'

He dropped his head as if reflecting on the words he had just said.

'Can I go now?' he continued. 'I need to see Jenna, she's panicking she's going to be next, I think. She's asked three times when I'm coming home, and she's come out of work, "to be my support," she says.'

His tone was sarcastic, and Karen once more inwardly winced. He really didn't love this woman he'd given up his wife and family for. What an idiot.

'Yes, you need to be away from here and let us do our jobs now. Someone will visit to take your statement, and we'll get in touch with the George to check out your alibi, but if you have to leave Sheffield, please inform us before you go.'

He nodded. 'Just find the bastard that did this, DS Nelson. We've been together since we were at school, and it's going to be a funny old world without her in it.'

He got out of Karen's car and she watched him stop for a moment and look at the house windows, still with their curtains closed, before moving further down the road to where his car was parked somewhat haphazardly, reflecting the speed and distress with which he had arrived.

7

WEDNESDAY, 26 OCTOBER

Hermia perched her bum on the edge of the bath and stared at the little stick she held in her hand. How the hell had that happened?

Then she giggled, in a nervous explosion of her emotions. She knew exactly how it had happened – probably in their king-size bed, but maybe on the sofa downstairs, or even a memorable episode halfway up the stairs.

And now she had to find some way of breaking the definitely unexpected news to Steve. She had no idea how he would initially feel, but she hoped she knew him well enough to judge that after the initial shock it would be a positive reaction.

It certainly would cause mega upheaval in her own life, she reflected, still holding the stick. Maternity leave for one thing. That was a complication to concern her; thoughts of being in the middle of a requested council report and it having to be shelved for an indeterminate length of time filled her with unease.

And would Steve be as thrilled as she was? They had never really discussed children – had never discussed their lives beyond the present situation. She had moved in with Steve while she took time to look for her own new place to buy after selling her flat, but she hadn't even been to look at anything. They had become almost like an old married couple, happy in each other's company, and, she thought wryly, with amazing sex.

Sex that had consequences…

She left the bathroom, and popped the stick into her bedside drawer. She would tell him tonight, she decided, while they were having their evening meal. Then she would be able to see his face, gauge his true feelings on the matter of becoming a daddy.

She sat on the bed, a huge smile on her face. Now with her suspicions confirmed, she had everything to smile about. She hoped.

* * *

Matt and Harry arrived at the office; the lights being on told them that Carol was already at work, and Harry's face lit up.

'Will she have baked us some scones?'

Matt laughed. 'Doubt it. We don't employ her to bake scones for us. She's our PA, and from what I've seen, she's damn good at it. So, you have a choice for this morning.' He held the door open for his son to enter. 'I have a client coming in at ten, and I think Karen will possibly be in as well at some point, so you can either go into Uncle Steve's office with your iPad until he arrives, or upstairs into Grandad's flat where the PlayStation is set up.'

Harry frowned, thinking through his options. 'I'll go on the PlayStation,' he said. 'But if there's scones…'

'I'll bring you one up. There's Cokes in the fridge, so help yourself. I'll take you over to Graves Park this afternoon, we'll go see the animals then have a bit of a kick-about. That okay?'

Harry gave him a high-five, and headed straight upstairs.

There was a soft knock on the door and Carol popped her head around.

'Morning, Matt. Do you know what's going on down at Elise's house?'

'Nothing much, but brace yourself. I'm afraid she's been murdered. Karen was called in earlier, and from what she's managed to tell me, the kids found her. Head injury it seems, but other than that I don't know anything. Karen'll pop in later, I'm sure, but if she doesn't I'll catch up on it all tonight.'

'Oh, no!' Carol looked distraught. 'Those poor children.'

'I imagine they're out of the way now. It still feels strange that I don't dash down to the crime scene as DI Forrester, but I can't, so I'll have to wait for news of what's happened. Karen looked shocked to the core when she left this morning.'

'You think it's connected to the break-in?'

'It's the logical conclusion, I suppose.' He pursed his lips, deep in thought. 'But that was only kids. Karen thought that Elise knew them, but she wouldn't tell her their names. Whoever those lads are, they've not come under the scrutiny of South Yorkshire police. Yet.'

Carol nodded her head slowly. 'So very sad. Did I see Harry?'

'You did. He's gone upstairs to play on the PlayStation until he gets fed up with that, then he might just turn to his book. Book four of *Harry Potter* is proving a big hit at the moment. He tried reading it in bed last night, but it's a bit big for reading when you're lying down.'

'There's an answer,' Carol said. 'Make sure he has the box set so he has the physical book, then buy it on Kindle so he can actually read it.'

'Why didn't I think of that? I knew it was a smart move, employing you.'

She laughed as she closed the door behind her.

'Happy to be of help,' she called out, before remembering what she'd gone to see Matt about, and it hadn't been *Harry Potter*, so she returned.

He looked up as his door opened once more. 'I've just been chatting to somebody who looks just like you.'

'I guess it must have been me. Two things. The first is I don't know where Steve is. According to my diary he's here, but he clearly isn't. And the second is I think an intercom system linking the three rooms would be beneficial. It's not good that I have to leave my office to come to yours or Steve's to tell you that you have a client. You stressed the safety and security of working here, but no intercom negates it.'

'I have no idea why we didn't think of that.' He took out his wallet and flipped through some cards. 'Here, give this chap a ring, explain to him exactly what you want, and tell him we need it yesterday. I think maybe we should have it connected to the room upstairs as well, where we file everything. And as for Steve, he picked up a job at seven this morning – his crew turned up at a property to do some fencing work, and found the garden destroyed. The owner's called the police, and he's gone over there to find out what the homeowner wants to do. We can't add it to the diary until I have an address for where he is; he shot off at a hundred miles an hour to make sure his team knew the boss was in control. I imagine he has two heads on at the moment, landscape gardener and private investigator. His surveillance is in the diary for this afternoon, isn't it?'

'It is. I'm assuming that's what "Fulwood surv 2 p.m." means.'

'Yes, it's a client at Fulwood, a lady. Steve has the file in his safe until the case is ended, then it will go through to you to add it to a tidied-up filing system that I'm hoping you'll put in place.' He shuffled through some mail that had been placed on his desk. 'This lady thinks her husband is straying, with someone she believes to be a friend of hers. Steve has taken it on, he's become quite adept at just sitting and taking photographs. Since we started officially back in May, this is his fourth adultery issue. Every case has been proved, and the other three are in the throes of divorce. Faced with his photographs, they just threw up their hands and said okay.'

Carol laughed. 'I'm sure there's a motto in there somewhere, just not sure what it is. I'll go and organise this intercom, and when you're having a coffee, give me a shout. I've brought us some scones.'

It was Matt's turn to laugh. 'Harry is already half in love with you, this will seal the deal, I reckon.'

Steve arrived to find a scone covered by cling film on his desk. He sat down with a sigh, leaned back in his chair and let his tiredness settle on him for a minute. He needed a coffee to liven him up, but still he sat there.

It had been a distressing morning. It appeared as if someone had taken a scythe and had walked all around the rear garden haphazardly swinging it and chopping all the late summer and autumn flowers down to ground level. The owners slept in a bedroom at the front of the house, and whoever had done it had targeted the back garden. They had poured weed killer all over the lawn and sprayed paint all over the expensive garden furniture.

Anna and Paul Bancroft had been almost incandescent with rage, but the thing that had upset Anna more than anything had been the rips and tears in the walls of the trampoline, meaning their grandchildren would no longer be able to use it.

He had sat for an hour with the couple while his team tidied up the broken stems and crushed flowers, measured for the fencing and generally helped everything look a bit more normal. They were dismantling the trampoline as he prepared to leave.

Nothing had shown on the couple's CCTV, as the camera pointed to the road outside their home, covering their driveway where they kept their car parked. The police hadn't stayed long; the two uniformed constables gave them a crime number and left with words of half-meant platitudes, saying they would be back if they had anything to report.

Anna had immediately locked the cat flap on the back door to prevent their two cats going out into the back garden and coming into contact with the weedkiller, and Steve promised that the garden would look much better within a week. He recommended instead of a five-foot fence they had a seven- or even an eight-foot one, which would help prevent anybody climbing over it again.

As Steve was leaving, Paul Bancroft was making arrangements for CCTV to be fitted facing their back garden. His team were to stay until everything that could be done had been completed, and he had felt sick as he climbed back into his car. He knew how he would feel if the same happened at his home. His garden was a joy, and he spent a lot of time keeping it that way.

It had remained within his mind all the way back to the office, and he wanted Matt to go back out to the property with him. The Bancrofts had asked him to do some digging around, but not in the garden.

'Find out for us who did this, can you?' Paul Bancroft had asked quietly. 'Don't tell Anna, keep it between us, but I would like answers and I don't think it's a priority with the police.'

And Steve had nodded, asking Paul to go out to the car with him to sign a contract.

'It's to cover both of us,' he had explained, and Paul hadn't argued, simply signed it and headed back indoors to his still upset wife.

Steve, now sitting at his desk and eyeing up the scone, took the contract from his briefcase, and placed it on the table. He opened a new file on his computer, and scanned in the contract signature, then removed the cling film from the scone.

Truly delicious was his silent comment, and he walked through to the kitchen where he made himself a coffee to wash it down with. He popped his head around the door leading into Carol's office and thanked her.

'Truly delicious,' he repeated to her. 'I love scones. Has Harry had one?'

'No,' she said. 'He's had three.'

'Three? Does that mean there's more?'

She removed the lid from the plastic container and held the box out to him. 'Help yourself. It's lovely to have somebody to bake for. I stopped doing it after losing Dave and Johnny, then my husband.'

Steve grinned. 'Well, I'm glad you've resurrected the skill for us,' and he helped himself to the largest in the box.

8

WEDNESDAY, 26 OCTOBER

Karen sat at her desk feeling sick. DC Kevin Potter had used his skills to check out Elise's activities on social media, and had very quickly come across the Facebook post with Luke Peters tagged in it. She knew Elise had shown her naivety; some people you could threaten, some people you couldn't. Luke Peters was in the latter category.

Clearly Elise had believed one of the lads was Peters's son.

Karen glanced at her watch. She had despatched Ray Ledger and Jamie to bring Luke Peters into the station, and a second car with two uniformed constables had accompanied them to bring in the boy. They'd only been gone five minutes and she was already tapping her foot, waiting for confirmation that they had been locked in back seats of cars.

She picked up her personal phone and rang Matt. He listened patiently while she explained in guarded words what had happened, hoping that nobody else could hear her. Only six months ago Matt would have been the one leading the investigation; now it had been made very clear to her that he wasn't to be involved with anything that she was tasked with solving.

'I never came across the Peters lad. Aaron, did you say he was called? No wonder we didn't recognise the CCTV image. I suppose it was only a matter of time before he came onto the radar, though, with a dad like his.'

'I'll be glad when he gets here. Although I already know he'll have a bloody good alibi for where he was last night. His sort plan stuff like this to the last second. Luke Peters is a thug, always has been. Can't wait to hear what he comes up with. I'd better go, don't want anybody accidentally hearing any of this conversation. See you tonight, and I'll fill you in on the rest.'

* * *

Matt smiled to himself as he recognised Karen's disappointment at not being able to call in to the office.

He looked up as his door opened, then listened quietly as Steve talked him through the events of the morning.

'It means completely re-laying the grassed area, and we won't really know about the plants until the spring – they may have caught some of the spray that was all over the grass or even have been sprayed directly. They've all been chopped down; it looks like a barren wasteland. Everything is destroyed, even the very expensive garden furniture.'

'And they've signed a contract? Paid a deposit?'

'Not paid a deposit yet. He was sitting in the car with me when we were discussing it, didn't have his card on him. I asked him to ring me and pay over the phone.'

Matt dipped his head in acknowledgement. 'Have they upset anybody?'

'I asked him that, says no. They keep themselves to them-selves, have a daughter, son-in-law and two young grandchildren who have now lost their trampoline. Their main interest is the garden. Although I think I might know someone who can restore it to how it was – I'll check on that later before I offer them that hope, but I'll tell them not to dump it.'

'Are they in this afternoon?'

'They are. You want to go and see for yourself what's happened?'

'I can look with a policeman's eyes. We can take Harry, maybe go and have a kick-about after we've been there. Or have you got something else on this afternoon?'

'No, that's fine. I'd hoped you wanted to be involved. And I'm always up for a game of football. Can't be home late, though, Hermia's cooking tonight because I said I had nothing much on today, so I daren't suddenly find something. You know what she's like.'

Matt laughed. 'I do. She'd just take it as normal, and put everything off until tomorrow. But I reckon you'll be home on time. Go and check with your contact about refurbing the garden furniture, then we can use that as our excuse for going back to see them.'

'Karen been in?'

Matt shook his head. 'No, they had a lead so she went back to the station. You ever heard of anybody called Luke Peters?'

Steve hesitated. 'Married to Vanessa Peters? If that's him, I can't say that I know him, but Vanessa is one of my clients. We're booked in for February with her to take down an old shed and build her a large new summerhouse. Very strong lady, knows what she wants.'

'That's him. He's being brought in for questioning about the Langton murder a few doors away. Apparently Elise, the deceased, put a threatening post on Facebook tagging him in it, and now she's dead. Karen is back at the station waiting for him to be brought in for interview.'

'Well, they're certainly not without a bob or two. Massive house, massive grounds. Vanessa's very proud of both. I asked if she wanted the plans running by her husband and she almost bit my head off, so I guess I know who wears the trousers in that relationship.'

'Interesting insight,' Matt said. He'd come across Luke Peters in the past, and had found him to be aggressive. There was a lot of anger in him, but his wife had obviously worked out how to deal with it. Take control. 'Have a chat with Karen, this might be of interest to her. She could maybe use Vanessa as a lever when she's interviewing him.'

He stood. 'I'll just go and make some notes, then I'm free whenever you're ready.'

* * *

They reached the Bancroft home an hour later, and Paul confessed to admitting to his wife he had asked the Forrester Agency to help them find who had done the damage.

Paul led the two men and Harry through to the back garden, and Matt felt an unusual waft of anger engulf him. He could virtually see the grass dying blade by blade as he looked at it. The furniture, covered in red and green paint, was stacked in one corner.

'You mentioned you may be able to help with the furniture?' Paul said.

'I definitely can. I've explained what's happened to my colleague, and he says he can do something with it. He will liaise with you every step of the way. And he wants you to give him a ring when you've spoken to me.' Steve handed over a business card he had taken from his wallet.

Suddenly aware that Anna Bancroft had tears in her eyes, he said gently, 'Don't cry. Between us we can put everything back to the way it was. It would have been starting to look pretty bare around now anyway, so by the time spring arrives, everything will be flourishing again. If it isn't it means the weedkiller spread to it, but it can easily be replaced. My lads will have the new fence up by the end of next Wednesday, and they'll take your old fence away and smarten everything up. Once that is erected, and effectively stopping anybody from encroaching on your property, we'll get started on sorting out the lawn. We have a machine that cuts turf, so we'll remove the entire top surface, put down fresh soil and then lay new turf. In two weeks' time you'll wonder why you let it get to you,' he finished with a smile. 'I know you'll be contacted about the furniture before he starts any work on it, just to make you aware of costs and how long it will take, but I know he's very fair. It's obviously an expensive set and I'm sure replacing it will be much more money than you'll be charged for repairs.'

Finally a smile touched Anna's face. 'We insured it against theft and damage because it was so expensive,' she said, 'so we're okay with that. We just didn't expect to have to insure our grass.'

'Is it okay if we ask you a few questions?' Matt asked.

'Of course it is, but I'm sure Harry would like a glass of orange juice or something, and maybe a piece of cake?'

'Yes, please,' Harry said, thinking maybe this detective work had a positive side to it, the offerings of the day being scones and cake.

Anna headed for the kitchen, and Paul leaned forward.

'Thank you,' he whispered. 'I can see Anna feels much happier now that something is being done, and believe me, that makes life so much better for me. I'll just go and give her a hand, because although we've all asked for tea, there's no guarantee that's what we'll get,' and he stood to help his wife.

'I fully understand,' Matt laughed. 'Keep the ladies happy, and everything takes on a better appearance.'

Anna returned with Harry's drink and a piece of chocolate cake, then Paul followed a few minutes later with tea for everyone else. While they were eating the cake and drinking the tea, Matt turned the conversation towards things he and Steve needed to know.

'Do you know of anybody you've upset recently?'

They both said no, and Paul continued. 'Since I retired, we rarely see anybody except our family. We love having the grand-children, so they're pretty frequent visitors, but we rarely have anything to do with anybody else. We go shopping, occasionally out for a meal, and we go to the local garden centres. We've never felt the need to have a large circle of friends, and keep pretty much to ourselves.'

'So you haven't had an issue with somebody who made you feel uneasy or threatened recently?'

'No,' Anna said. 'We don't actually see much of others around here.'

'And your CCTV points to your drive, covering your car?'

'It does, and it doesn't show anybody going through to the garden via that route. However, the back garden fence is only just over four feet high and easily accessible from several other back gardens. It's why we asked Steve to come and quote for a new one, six feet high, but that's now been bumped up to eight. And I might get a Kalashnikov as a garden ornament, for a bit extra security.'

'You want a quote?' Steve joked, and Anna said a simple, 'Yes, please.'

'Do you leave a light on in the back garden?'

Anna shook her head. 'No, but we're having one fitted by the chap who's coming to put us a camera in to cover the back of our property. It will be one triggered by movement so I expect it'll be on and off all night as we have two cats, but it will be worth it. I think we also need a more secure gate for getting into the back from the front. Maybe you can look at that for us, Steve? That's what we want, isn't it, Paul?' she asked, turning her head to check with her husband.

Paul nodded his agreement, his smile strained.

'Of course. I'll measure it as we leave, and get on the internet tonight to see what we can come up with. I'll give you a ring tomorrow to discuss it. And you're right. There's absolutely no point securing all these things if you leave one weak point, because that's what they'll use.'

'There's really nobody you can think of who might have a problem with you?'

Both of the Bancrofts shook their heads.

Steve and Matt stood.

'We'll be in touch tomorrow,' Steve said. 'Don't buy that Kalashnikov without my approval, and try to relax. I know it will be hard, but they've done the damage now, they're not going to come back.'

They stepped out of the front door, followed by Paul.

'I don't know about relax.' Paul laughed. 'I have an insurance claim to fill in. I've just done one for the car, so they're going to really love us – a second claim in two weeks.'

'You had an accident?'

'Sort of. No big deal, but the other party insisted on going through insurance. I reversed out of our drive, done it for twenty years with no issues, but this day he had parked on the road and not on his drive. I caught his with the back of mine. He wasn't happy, so I went along with the claim.'

Matt looked at Steve. 'Can we go back inside, Paul? We'll not keep you much longer. Steve will measure up for your new gate while we're chatting.'

9

WEDNESDAY, 26 OCTOBER / THURSDAY, 27
OCTOBER

Hermia felt nervous, a new feeling for her. Telling somebody she was pregnant was a totally new experience, and this wonderful person already seated at the dining table was definitely the main person she had to tell. After this, it would probably be fun, but she had no idea how Steve would react.

She carried in the dishes and placed them on the table, then lifted the lid of the casserole.

'Tada!' she announced with a theatrical flourish of the tea towel she had used to remove the lid. 'Corned beef hash.'

'Oh, my God. Oh, my God.' Steve half stood and stared into the dish. 'Honestly? You've finally tackled it?'

'I have. You wore me down with talking about your mother's version, so I thought I'd give it a go. Especially after you rang and said what a rubbish day it was turning out to be. So help yourself, I've made loads, and if there's any left we can freeze it.'

He chuckled, picking up the ladle. 'If there's any left...'

She watched as he filled his dish before helping himself to a couple of chunks of baguette.

He dipped his bread and took a bite. His eyes closed and he

sighed. 'Delicious.' He looked across the table. 'You not having any?'

'I am, but I want to talk to you first. While your mouth is full of hash.'

His hand paused on its way to his mouth. This didn't sound good.

'Then talk to me...'

She took a deep breath. 'We're pregnant.'

There were a few seconds of silence, then Steve pushed back his chair, shouted, 'Back in a minute,' and left the room at a run.

Hermia didn't know whether to laugh or cry. She sat in a kind of stupor, wondering how her announcement could have gone so dramatically wrong. She heard his footsteps jumping back down the stairs and he returned to the room to stand by her side.

He dropped to one knee, opened the box clasped inside his fist, and took his own deep breath.

'Hermia Forrester, will you marry me?'

She leaned forward and gently kissed him. 'Of course I will, but did you hear what I said?'

'I did, but I didn't want you thinking I was doing this because you're pregnant. I've had this ring for about a month, and was going to ask on your birthday in a couple of weeks, but I need you to know this is us, not us and a child.' He took the ring out of the box, and slid it onto her finger. The solitaire diamond exploded into sparkling dazzles of light as it reflected the glow from the candles. 'I love you so much, Herms, and knowing we're going to have a baby just puts the icing on the corned beef hash.'

'Well, it's still early days, I reckon I'll be due sometime in June, so maybe we keep it to ourselves for a little bit longer. Can you?'

He shook his head. 'No. You know that rule will only last until tomorrow, and then I'll have to tell Matt. And he'll tell Karen. And Harry's not stupid...'

'You're okay about it then?'

'I'm... much more than okay. I can't even think of words to describe how I feel.'

She kissed him again. 'Then eat your hash, and I'll try some now. I've been on tenterhooks all day wondering how you'd take the news, but I think I can manage some food. Maybe after that we can nip over to Matt's and tell them?'

'Saves me getting into trouble for letting the cat out of the bag.' He grinned at her. 'Can I get up now? This is hurting my knees.'

* * *

The champagne flowed, with Harry saying he would be like Aunty Hermia and stick to lemonade. Matt and Karen were delighted at the news.

Karen had immediately closed down her laptop and tried to forget about work for the rest of the evening. It was only when she was lying in bed, by Matt's side, that she allowed her mind to drift back to the morning, the awful sight of Elise in the middle of the floor, the bewildered children... She cursed the power of social media. She knew deep inside that the post from Elise targeting Peters was the most likely reason she was dead.

She was equally frustrated by their inability to bring in Luke Peters and Aaron Peters. It seemed Luke was in Fuerteventura, and Aaron was simply not at home. Vanessa Peters had shrugged, denying all knowledge of her son's whereabouts, but confirming that Luke was in Fuerteventura with some friends on a golfing holiday, and had been there for five days. Two officers were on duty outside the Peters home, but she had no hopes the errant lad would return there, not after his mother had sent a text warning him of the presence of police. Karen had no doubt that had happened.

She listened to Matt's gentle breathing, deduced he was fast asleep, and slid her legs out of the bed.

Once downstairs, she made herself a hot drink to counteract the effects of the champagne, and opened her laptop.

She found nothing on Aaron Peters, not even from logging into the police system, so entered the name Luke Peters.

Most of the hits came from work files – Luke was an individual who appeared in their records for a variety of crimes, going back to when he was a fifteen-year-old and was caught shoplifting cigarettes. He did a short sharp prison sentence when he was twenty-one, but that seemed to make him smarter as he became much cannier at avoiding prosecutions after that.

And he had grown in the criminal world. He married Vanessa, who had been Vanessa Beardow prior to her name change... Suddenly Karen felt sick. Beardow. As in the late Andy Beardow, another stalwart of Sheffield's crime scene in years gone by, and the reason Matt's father was murdered.

She added Vanessa's name to the document she had created, and moved on. She urgently needed a photograph of Aaron to establish if he was on the somewhat blurry CCTV of the two lads who had committed the burglary. She checked her watch, deciding 2 a.m. was a bit late to be contacting colleagues. She scheduled a message to go to Ray Ledger at six, asking him to be at Vanessa Peters's home early in the morning to get a photograph of her son. She had no doubt that the son wouldn't be there.

She sipped thoughtfully at the dregs of her drink, letting her mind roam towards the news of a new baby in their circle, and hoping with all her heart that everything would go well for Hermia and Steve. It brought back memories of the two babies she had lost, both at sixteen weeks, and she briefly wondered how her life would have evolved if those babies had gone to term. Would she have stayed with Finn? She suspected she would have; she wouldn't have been at Moss Way police station to fall in love with the handsome DI Forrester.

She closed her laptop, carried her cup to the sink unit and headed upstairs. Her handsome ex-DI was still fast asleep, unaware of her absence.

In the house just across the driveway, Steve was having a similar sleepless night. A baby. That would make him a daddy.

The only child he had ever really known was Harry, and he couldn't say with any surety that he had had to deal with him as a baby; he'd just been Uncle Steve who played football with him.

That was one good thing – he knew how to teach football! His son would be the next Pele of this world, fast, skilful, Sheffield Wednesday supporter – he'd have all the benefits he could give to him. Unless he was a girl, of course. Steve stared at the glass of cold milk he was nursing. A girl? He couldn't teach her ballet...

He finished the milk and went upstairs to try once more to sleep. His mind had been all over the place, but hopefully two paracetamol and the glass of milk would help him nod off. He needed to be up early.

Hermia was sitting up, a pillow tucked behind her to support her back. 'Can't sleep?'

'No,' he said, trying to keep his tone serious. 'It appears I'm pregnant, and it's stopping me sleeping.'

'Well, actually, it appears you're stopping the real pregnant one in this partnership from sleeping. And she thinks you should have brought her a hot chocolate to bed to help her to drift off, but apparently that hasn't happened.'

He took the blatant hint, retraced his steps, and five minutes later entered the bedroom carrying a mug of chocolate. Hermia was fast asleep.

* * *

DC Ray Ledger was awake when his phone pinged at six. He had felt abnormally angry at their failure to bring in the two suspects required for questioning, and he knew the lad, Aaron, was around somewhere, keeping out of the way. He had suffered a restless night as a result of trying to work out where he could be, and he was relieved to see the message was from the boss.

He read the instructions and got out of bed. There was no need for a response beyond a thumbs up, and he headed downstairs to make a drink and some toast before going out to his car.

He parked behind the two constables who had been left on duty, out of sight of the house, and had a quick word with them before heading up the drive. They moved their car closer to the target property, blocking off the exit from the house with their vehicle, then prepared to watch and listen with windows down.

They had remained alert all night and had seen no activity – nobody in, nobody out, much to their disgust. There would have been some kudos for taking in Aaron Peters.

The two officers knew Ray wasn't expecting trouble at all, and he had told them to keep their eyes peeled, but not to approach the house. They had responded with tapping their radios, and telling him to shout if he needed them.

They saw him knock on the impressively large knocker twice before the door opened, watching as he held up his ID. The door closed, as if a chain was being removed. It reopened and Ray stepped one foot inside then halted.

The officers in the car heard what Ray heard, the slam of a door closing elsewhere on the property.

Within seconds, they were out of the car, and saw Ray Ledger turn and run to his left. A figure shot around the corner of the house and abruptly stopped.

Faced with the sight of three police officers all sprinting towards him, Aaron Peters turned and ran, but with a shoe on one foot and the matching shoe clutched in his hand, he didn't stand a chance.

They heard a loud 'Fuckin' 'ell', and saw him drop to the floor, holding his foot. There was a considerable amount of blood by the time they reached him, and it was clear where his immediate future now lay.

'Aaron Peters?' Ray's tone was conversational, without tension. The lad wasn't going anywhere under his own power. 'Don't worry, we'll get you medical attention when we get you back to the station. Try not to drip blood in the back of the car, though, these officers like to keep it spotless.'

10

THURSDAY, 27 OCTOBER

Ray watched as the car carrying Aaron Peters disappeared from sight, then he rang Karen.

'He's waiting for you at the station, boss,' he said.

There was a moment of silence and he guessed Karen hadn't fully surfaced. 'What? Who is?'

'Aaron Peters. I did better than getting a photo, I got *him*. I'll have to confess to it being accidental. I was almost in the front door. Then there was a noise, like a door being slammed shut, so I stopped. He must have been inside. You might want to ask him how he bypassed our two lads in the patrol car. They saw nothing all night, the lights went out around half past ten and until I arrived they saw nobody else. There must be a rear access to the property, I think. I reckon he guessed why there was someone there at that ungodly hour, so listened for me getting inside, and then he legged it. The funniest part was he didn't manage to put both shoes on, one was in his hand. The two surveillance officers joined in the chase, and we soon got him because he was on the floor, his foot in a bit of a state. They've taken him in, and are going to get the duty doctor to take a look at it.'

'Ray Ledger, you're a bloody star. Remind me to buy you a coffee.'

'Don't worry, I will.'

* * *

Karen stared at the miserable figure of Aaron Peters, but felt not a shred of sympathy. For all she knew, this was the murderer of Elise Langton; if that proved to be the case, she hoped his foot would turn gangrenous and drop off. She kept the thought to herself.

She watched as he picked up the bottle of water, and twirled it around in his hand, staring at the label. He removed the top and took a small sip, then replaced it on the table. His expression didn't change; this was one unhappy boy, but they couldn't proceed without an appropriate adult. As he was sixteen, they had to tread carefully.

His left leg was resting on a chair, the doctor having cleaned and dressed the toe that had taken the brunt of the damage, but it seemed it wasn't life-threatening, merely painful.

She stayed five minutes in the observation room, then went towards the reception, where she asked to be informed as soon as an appropriate adult, the person deemed to represent a suspect under the age of seventeen, arrived to be with Aaron.

She felt a presence behind her, and turned to see an attractive woman dressed in a jogging suit, her hair scrunched up into a messy top knot.

'Is he here?' the woman demanded.

'Who?' Karen asked, guessing who she was talking about.

'My son. Aaron Peters.'

'And you are?'

'Vanessa Peters, his mother.'

Karen looked her up and down. 'Ah, yes. Wife of Luke Peters. Currently playing golf, I understand.'

'On his way back as we speak,' Vanessa replied. 'Where's my boy? You do know he's only sixteen, don't you? He should be in school.'

'We do. He'll be questioned and possibly released after we have an appropriate adult for him. Maybe you should contact his school and let them know what's happening.'

'*Possibly* released?' Vanessa's words came out as a squeak. 'What the fuck are you talking about? He's done nothing...'

'Then if that is the case, he will be released. And as soon as I'm sure of that, you can take him home. In the meantime, please feel free to have a seat in here.' She waved her arm to indicate the waiting room. 'I'll keep you informed.'

* * *

After notification of the arrival of the appropriate adult, Davina Charlton, a lady well known to Karen for being part of the Social Care team, Karen decided to wait a further fifteen minutes before going to the interview room, just for the hell of it. Vanessa had truly annoyed her.

She had read quickly through the Elise Langton post-mortem results, where time of death had been confirmed as between eight and ten on the evening of Tuesday, 25 October 2022. The cause was blunt force trauma to the head. The deceased was in excellent health otherwise, with no underlying illnesses.

Karen made a note in her diary to call Rick Langton and see how the children were, then picked up her file folder before heading downstairs. She collected Ray Ledger on the way and they took a moment to stand in the observation area before entering the interview room; Davina was going through a note-book, and Aaron was staring morosely at his hands, both his feet now firmly on the floor. There was no interaction between the two people.

Finally Karen and Ray moved. She opened the door, and Ray switched on the recorder. 'DS Karen Nelson and DC Raymond Ledger entering the room. Also present are Davina Charlton, appropriate adult, and Aaron Peters.'

She sat and placed the file on the table, then covered it with her arm. Ray leaned back in his chair, his eyes never leaving the young boy's face.

She saw Aaron's eyes move as they took in the presence of a file, and she smiled.

'Aaron. Have you had chance to speak with Davina?'

He shrugged. 'Yeah. Told her I ain't done nowt. What you want me for?'

She sensed he was pushing the Yorkshire accent to make himself sound tougher, more threatening.

'Okay, Aaron. You can talk normally now. I've just spoken with your mother and I know your family don't speak like that.'

Again he shrugged.

'So, can we go to the night of Sunday, 23 October. That's last Sunday. I need you to tell me where you were between eight and ten that evening.'

Aaron began to interlock the fingers on his hands. His head dropped and he said nothing for a few seconds. The he looked at Karen.

'Last Sunday?'

'That's what I said.'

'I went to my mate's house. His mum and dad will tell you.'

'Who's your mate?'

Again there was hesitation. He clearly realised he was getting into 'opening his mouth without thinking' territory. He could almost hear his father telling him to keep his gob shut.

He lowered his head and mumbled a name.

Karen heard him speak but he could have been saying Elton John for all she could discern.

'I'm sorry, what did you say?'

Aaron repeated what he had tried to disguise. 'George Jackson.'

'Address?'

'Why do you need his address?' There was a degree of belligerence in his voice, and Karen smiled.

'I need to go see him before we can even think about letting you go home. And if he doesn't confirm what you're telling me, your mum is going to be very uncomfortable spending the night in that waiting room. You, of course, will have a bed. In a cell.'

'I don't know his address. I know the house.'

She removed a piece of blank copy paper from her file, pushed it across the table and handed him a biro. 'A map,' she said. 'What area is it?'

'Gleadless,' he mumbled.

'Well, what a surprise. Start with White Lane, and draw where it is from that point. I know you know where White Lane is.'

There was anger in the way he stabbed the pen into the paper, but she said nothing.

She immediately recognised Seagrave Crescent, and knew a minimal internet search would reveal the Jackson home, but she let him struggle with working out which house had supposedly been his refuge on that Sunday night.

'So, Aaron, help me out a bit here,' she said in a chatty tone of voice. She pointed to his hand-drawn map. 'When you and George walked out of his house on Sunday night, did you walk to the top of Seagrave then turn left along the main road? Along White Lane? And did you happen to see a house in complete darkness on the parallel service road that runs ten metres away?'

'Didn't see no house with no lights on.'

'So you didn't spend the entire evening in George's house, you two did go out? That's what you've just said, isn't it, Aaron? Let me go through what I think you did. You walked along here,' she pointed on the map, 'along White Lane until you reached its junction with Carson Mount, then you turned left and almost immediately left again, so that you were on that small service road. And then you went to the fifth house along, the one in darkness, and you had a bit of a look around to make sure nobody was about. Then you broke the window to gain access. Want to know how I know this, Aaron?'

'Get stuffed, copper.'

'I know it because you were caught on the CCTV from two houses nearby. Two little children lived in the house you burgled, and you stole the little boy's PlayStation. Bit of a bastard on the quiet, aren't you, Aaron?'

'Fuck off, pig.'

Ray leaned forward, resting his hands on the table. 'We can terminate this interview right now, Aaron,' he said mildly, 'and restart it tomorrow. Is that what you want? Because your attitude towards my boss suggests that's exactly what you want.' He allowed his voice to increase in volume, and Aaron seemed to shrink.

'Sorry,' he mumbled.

'No, you're not, but we'll continue. For now.' Karen stared at him. 'Cut out the bad language in this room, and we'll soon get to the bottom of this part.'

'This part?' Aaron's head swivelled towards Davina, and she shrugged.

'We haven't pulled you in at such an early hour to simply talk about a burglary, although that little boy crying because he no longer has a PlayStation and the even littler girl crying because one of you trod on her toy iron will be forever imprinted on my memory. One day their daddy will hunt you down, I'm sure.' She mentally winced at the mention of the iron.

His head now seemed to be on a permanent swivel; he didn't know where to look, what to say, what to do next.

'Can she talk to me like this?' he asked Davina.

'She is,' Davina answered.

'So,' Karen continued seamlessly, 'let's move on to Tuesday night. Where were you at half past nine? And that's p.m. And I need some precision on this, Aaron.'

Aaron sensed the change in the atmosphere, and he wondered what the fuck had gone off on Tuesday night that he was getting dragged into. He took a drink from his bottle of water and stared at the woman who seemed to be pretty mad at him. He hoped to God she wouldn't search his bedroom because they'd find that bloody PlayStation tucked under his bed...

'Tuesday? That's my boxing night. Eight till ten, at the Clinton Woods gym on Waterthorpe. They'll verify it, because me and George stayed a bit longer and helped to put the equipment away before we caught the tram home. We caught the tram around half past ten, but it might have been a bit later.'

Karen wrote *check with CW* in her notebook, then turned as the door opened. A uniformed officer handed her a piece of paper and she read it quickly.

'Okay, Aaron, we've finished searching your home, and it appears you have a spare PlayStation hiding under your bed. And that's without its cables, because as you probably realise now, you left them plugged into the sockets at the property you burgled on White Lane. It's currently being forensically examined, and I think we all know it's going to show the fingerprints of the family you stole it from, as well as yours, and possibly George's.'

'You can't just—'

'But we can, Aaron. You handed us your keys and your phone when you were brought here, and we quickly got a warrant to search the property. I expect your mother will be pleased we didn't use the enforcer to gain admission, but I think you're going to have some explaining to do when she does see you again. DC Ledger, please inform Aaron's mother that she might as well go home, as we'll be keeping her son overnight while we investigate further.'

11

FRIDAY, 28 OCTOBER

Susan Hunter approached the doorway of the Forrester Detective Agency, and pressed the admittance intercom.

She heard a woman's voice say, 'Good morning, can I help you?' and she hesitated before responding.

'Good morning, my name is Susan Hunter, and I was a friend of the late Dave Forrester. Is it possible for me to have a quick word with Matt, please? If he's not available, I'm happy to make an appointment.'

'Just let me check his availability,' Carol said.

The woman spoke to Matt quickly, after which he left his own office to go to the front door to allow his visitor admittance.

'I'm sorry, I don't recognise your name...'

She smiled. 'I know.'

He waited for her to speak, to say who she was and how she knew him.

'I loved your dad.'

Matt tried to hide the shock from showing on his face. 'So did I.'

Again she smiled and then began to explain. 'I've known

Dave for many years, and after the shooting we became close in a different kind of way. Very close. Johnny, of course, knew about our relationship, but we kept it very quiet because Dave was afraid there would be repercussions because he didn't die. He didn't want them going after me and using me as a way of getting to him. But then five years ago fate intervened anyway.'

Matt waited. And wondered why he had never known anything of this. He was pretty sure his father had never mentioned a Susan Hunter, neither as a client nor as a lover.

'I had to leave everything. I was a housing officer with the council, loved my job, and it was how Dave and I met in the first place. Some random stabbing in one of the council's properties. We both attended as part of our jobs. We clicked straight away, and after he was shot and hospitalised our relationship changed. I realised I didn't just like him, I loved him, so I told him.' Matt watched as her face crumpled. 'But it wasn't meant to be. We were happy for the first years, with Johnny knowing our secret but recognising the importance of hiding it from everybody, even you and Hermia. Five years ago, my own life changed, and I emigrated to Australia.'

It was Matt's turn to feel shocked. Of all the things she could have said, this was the last thing he would have expected.

'Australia?'

She gave a slight nod. 'My daughter and son-in-law emigrated ten years ago, and had twin girls two years later. Around the time the twins were born, my son-in-law's parents moved out to join them, so all seemed to be going well for them. Then Nicola, my daughter, rang me to tell me Tom had left her, had moved back to England, leaving her in Melbourne with the babies. I went out to join her to give help with the children as much as anything, then returned home. Then she found a lump in her breast. I packed everything up here and moved to

Australia to look after her and the children. Dave and I kept in touch via email.'

Susan removed a tissue from her bag and dabbed at her eyes.

'I'm sorry, I truly loved him. I thought I'd cried all my tears... Four months ago, Nicola passed away and I decided to return to England. The twins had never known anything but Australia, so it seemed the sensible decision to leave them with their other grandparents. I never felt settled there, missed my life in England, but it's not that far away that I can't get there in a couple of days tops.'

'How did you find out about Dad?'

'I have a close friend in Sheffield who knew how we felt about each other, and of course it was all over the news here. I couldn't come back because it was getting very close to the end with Nicola. It was like being torn in two. I didn't sell up when I went to Australia, I rented my home out with the understanding that when I came back they would have to move out, and it all went very smoothly. And now I'm back.'

'It's good to meet you. Dad never said a word, and Johnny died within a week of Dad. We had very little conversation in that week. You don't mind if I tell Hermia?'

'Not at all. Your father made me the happiest I've ever been, and I miss him so much. But there is a reason I'm here. I would like to visit his grave, if he has one. Also Johnny's grave.'

'They're both in Hutcliffe Wood cemetery. Pretty easy to find if you go in the Abbey Lane entrance. I'll sketch out some directions.' He pulled a piece of copy paper towards him and explained as he drew. 'I'm happy to take you if it will help, but somehow I feel you'd rather be on your own.'

'I think I would rather be on my own. I can stay as long as I want, cry as much as I want, and generally be a weak female.

Thank you for listening to me, Matt, and it's lovely to finally meet the man your dad was so proud of. He loved you both so much.'

* * *

Matt stood in the doorway and watched her walk towards her car. The grief of his father's loss suddenly began to overwhelm him. This stranger had awoken everything all over again, and he was glad Harry had been with Hermia and not with him. He knew Harry wasn't accepting of the fact that he wouldn't see his granddad ever again, and if he had overheard any of that conversation, he would have been immersed in grief all over again.

And then he smiled, recalling what he had just learnt. This was certainly a turn-up for the books. His dad! Having another woman in his life! It was such a shame he hadn't lived to see her return from Australia after five years of being on separate continents.

He brought to mind his dad's journal which had led them ultimately to solving a couple of their first cases, and yet he couldn't recall any mention of Susan Hunter. He must have felt it was really necessary to keep her out of the limelight, well away from any connection to Andy Beardow, the man who had taken away his mobility, then finally, through his brother, his life.

And how had they communicated? Susan said they had emailed. The tech-savvy Dave Forrester must have set up a separate email address that he used purely for Susan, maybe one where he could delete every interaction between them. To keep her safe.

Matt hoped she had made his dad happy.

Since taking on the responsibility of the Forrester Agency, Matt had worked a little harder at becoming more proactive on the technical side; he had always been well aware of his failings in the subject but as a DI he hadn't had to use any sort of expertise. He had DCs, all younger than him and actually interested in IT, so had tended to not worry about anything beyond basic email sending, and saving whatever reports he wrote.

His dad, on the other hand, had been a pretty smart cookie when it came to everything computer linked. Would he have set up some sort of automatic delete for all emails between him and Susan? Was that even possible? Herms would know...

And would it be possible to recover automatically deleted emails?

* * *

It was only as he retook his seat at his desk that he began to query why he would want to read the email correspondence between Dave and Susan. Was he just reverting to his DI days and suspecting everybody he came into contact with of underhand activities?

He heard the gentle double tap on his door, and waited for Carol to pop her head around.

'Everything okay?' she asked.

'It's fine. Come in and sit down a minute, will you?'

He slowly began to sort out his thoughts. He told her who Susan Hunter was, how it seemed that Dave Forrester had kept her well under anybody's radar, even his own son and daughter. He told her everything he could remember of what Susan had told him, and at the end he sat back.

Carol waited a moment before speaking, as if digesting what he had said. 'So what made the finger ends tingle, Matt? Didn't you believe her?'

'I don't know,' he confessed. 'I think it's more that I'm struggling to believe we have found no mention of her name, and believe me, with everything that happened after Dad's death, we searched everywhere for anything. But if it is all some sort of a con, what on earth can she get out of it? All she wanted was to visit his grave. I think I'm leaning towards her being genuine; I suppose I just needed to talk it through. It's the policeman in me that won't lie down and play dead.'

'I'm glad you have,' Carol said with a smile. 'And I may be able to help. I know you'll probably have glazed-over eyes when I finish telling you what I'm doing, but the filing system here is more of an unfiling system.'

He grinned at her. 'You think I'm not aware of our shortcomings?'

'Matt, there are shortcomings, and there are shorter shortcomings. You and Steve are in the latter category.' She smiled and then began to explain. 'I'm doing a bit each day. If it's a quiet day I get more done. But what I'm doing, and I've taken it right back to Dave's first ever case, is adding every single name to a file. Each name has a file number where it originated from so what we will end up with is a sort of mini-HOLMES, a Forrester version of the police Home Office Large Major Enquiry System, where we can cross-reference everything. For example, if something shows up, even if they're only a bystander in a case that happened in 2014 say, but the name crops up in a current case, it will show up immediately and take you straight to any connections that have happened in the intervening period. Now when I say a mini-HOLMES that's what I mean. It's a way of keeping track of everything this business deals with. So if Susan Hunter isn't a part of any case but she did arrive on a random visit, it will be logged on our HOLMES as such.'

Matt shook his head. 'I assume you can tell I'm gobsmacked. We can't keep calling it mini-HOLMES, we need our own name for it. Bloody hell, Carol, Steve's going to be as gobsmacked as I am!'

'I call it WATSON. It stands for We Are Tracking Some Outstanding Numpties. But I must just confess that's my name for it. I'm sure you and Steve can come up with something that will make sense.'

'That's brilliant! WATSON it is. And off the record, I do still have access of a sort to the real HOLMES, as you've probably realised, but WATSON will no doubt be the one we turn to first. So you can already check if Susan Hunter is anywhere in our system? It seems she was with Dad for a long time before she had to leave for Australia five years ago.'

'I checked as soon as she entered your office, but no, she's not on it yet. I've only worked through the first eighteen months of Dave and Johnny's files so far. If her name does crop up, you'll be the first to know.'

12

SATURDAY, 29 OCTOBER

Matt lay with his arms behind his head, pondering on the past week.

It had been a busy one, and the jewel in the crown had been the arrival of Carol Flynn. She had already earned double her non-existent salary, and he thought her setting up of WATSON was pure genius. He had no doubt it would be completely accurate and totally pertinent to their business, not the whole world.

Beside him, he felt Karen move slightly, and she rested her head on his arm. He turned and kissed her forehead.

'Coffee?' he whispered, not totally sure whether she was awake or not.

'Thought you'd never ask,' she murmured, her eyes still closed.

He grinned and eased himself away from her. 'You got to go into work, or shall we go out for breakfast?'

One eye opened. 'No work today unless I'm called in. I could be persuaded for the breakfast bit. What time is it?'

'Just after seven. Don't go back to sleep in protest. I'll go and make us a drink.'

* * *

He had to shake her out of the half sleep she had fallen back into, and Karen pulled herself up into a sitting position. She took the cup out of his hand, and nursed it for a moment while she put her brain into the right gear.

'All my villains have gone home. I feel a bit bereft.'

'I used to feel like that. I bet you could have thumped somebody when young Peters had his alibi at the boxing gym confirmed.'

'I knew it would be. He's a trainee burglar, and I must be honest, I don't see him advancing to murder just yet. We've charged him and his thuggish mate with the burglary, but it's only a slap on the wrist for them because it's a first offence. I don't think he'll learn anything from it, but his mother's got him home now, so maybe she can instil some sense into him. I doubt it, though. And although we picked his father up from the airport and questioned him, that was never going to go anywhere. He was in the bloody Canaries, for heaven's sake, so I had to let him go as well. He'll be at home right now training his son how not to get caught again.'

'That's good parenting,' Matt said. 'Look after your kids and make sure they don't end up in jail. He always smirked did Luke Peters, as though he was a top dog of some sort. He probably thinks he is, but one day you'll put him away for a long stretch and maybe he won't smirk any more.'

* * *

Matt pushed his now empty plate to one side, then picked up his and Karen's cups to go and top up their coffees. Harry simply shook his head at the silent question of whether he wanted another Coke.

'Has Dad said we're going to the match?'

'Not to me. You hoping to use Aunty Herms's ticket?'

He nodded. 'Dad says next year they're having season tickets where the three of us can all sit together. There isn't a spare place where they sit now, which is why I can only go if one of them doesn't.'

Karen grinned at the youngster who was becoming a big part of her life. 'Life's really hard being a young kid, isn't it? It's awful not having your own season ticket...'

'Are you having me on, Karen?'

'Course not. As if I would. You want me to message Aunty Herms, see what she's doing? But be prepared, you know what your dad and Herms are like about going to the match when they can.'

She looked up as Matt returned with the fresh drinks. 'Just had a text from Herms,' he said. 'She wants to know if you want her ticket for the match.'

Karen and Harry high-fived.

'Result,' Harry said. 'She's the best aunty ever.'

It was a quiet afternoon. With Harry and Matt settled on the Hillsborough kop, Karen sorted out the laundry then opened her laptop. It had been her intention to have an afternoon on the sofa with a good psychological thriller, but her mind kept focusing on Aaron Peters and his mate George. She had watched them leave the police station after being charged with the burglary offence, and had seen the fist bumps and the bout of laughter between the two of them.

What did they think they had got away with? Murder? They'd certainly made nothing from goods taken from the Langton home – everything had been recovered, even the value- less jewellery box that little Skye played with, so what had they actually benefitted from, causing the hilarity between them?

She sat quietly, staring blankly at the opposite wall for some time; she allowed her mind to roam. It roamed long enough to convince her she needed another coffee or she would fall asleep, and she stood. She picked up her phone that was on the kitchen work surface and looked at it for a minute, telling herself it was Saturday afternoon, her team were entitled to a day without work, and she clicked on DC Phil Newton.

He answered somewhat breathlessly. 'Boss?'

'Phil? You sound out of breath.'

'I'm playing frisbee with the dogs and the kids. Tell me it's urgent and I'll come into work.'

She laughed. 'No, sorry, it isn't. I just wanted to ask you something, to clear it up once and for all in my mind. I asked you to give Clinton Woods gym a ring, and check the alibis of our trainee burglars for last Tuesday evening, didn't I?'

'You did, boss, and I did.'

'Who did you speak to?'

'It's all in my filed report, but it was Clinton.'

'Oh.' For a second Karen felt deflated. 'What exactly did he say?'

'He sounded like me, a bit out of breath. I told him who I was, so he went away for a minute to speak to his client, who turned out to be an eight-year-old little girl he had been spar- ring with. The man is a legend.'

'Certainly is. My ex used to train there. So what did you ask him?'

'I gave him both names and asked if they'd been there on the

Tuesday evening, and what time they'd left. He said they were regulars, went every Tuesday and sometimes Fridays, but always Tuesdays because they had a bit of a routine going, staying behind to help him clear away all the equipment. He did offer further disclosure, something I didn't ask because he said they usually caught a tram back up to Gleadless about half past ten. He said sometimes he dropped them off at George's house, but they usually declined, saying they wanted to get off at Crystal Peaks, have a McDonald's before recatching the tram and going home. He didn't take them home on Tuesday because his daughter attended the gym with him, and she was tired. I pushed him a bit, asking if they ever left early, and he said no, they were good lads, always helped with a bit of training of the younger kids.'

Karen paused for a moment. 'I'm going to clutch at a straw, just to clear it fully. Find out what time the gym opens on Monday, and nip down to actually see Clinton. Just say you have to verify his records for your report. It's actually for my peace of mind, because I want to really make sure they were there on Tuesday, and if they were he would have a record of their fees payment, wouldn't he?'

'He certainly would. I'm sorry, boss, I should have done this personally instead of ringing the gym.'

'I said to ring,' she reminded him gently. 'You obeyed to the letter. And it's nothing major, it's just confirmation, really, of what the lads said. Clutching of straws, Phil, clutching of straws. If they were there till half past ten on Tuesday there's no way they had anything to do with Elise Langton's murder, so we can officially switch our activities to another avenue. Although God knows what avenue that will be. The ex-husband has a solid alibi, her brother was on the phone with her when somebody came to the door at the relevant time, and that's confirmed on her phone, and whoever it was at that front door didn't show up on any CCTV in the neighbouring houses; he or she was considerably smarter than the lads when they burgled the house.'

'Maybe we need to look more deeply into her life?'

'That's my plan for Monday morning, but to be honest I can't stop reliving it. It's why I had to speak to you now, while it was all fresh in my mind. They shouldn't leave me on my own in the house. I start to think.'

'Matt at the match?'

'He is. He's taken Harry. Hermia let him use her season ticket. I can see next year we'll all have to have season tickets, because Harry has already been making suggestions about me going with them.'

'Well, so that you're prepared for when they arrive home singing "Hi Ho Sheffield Wednesday" in an hour or so, it's just flashed onto my phone that the result is Wednesday four, Burton Albion two, so they'll both be bouncing and they'll want to tell you every kick of the match.'

She laughed. 'See you Monday, Phil. Take care, and let me know when you've seen the register at the gym so we can forget about the two yobs.'

13

SUNDAY, 30 OCTOBER

Matt pulled up at the cemetery gates, and Karen jumped out to go to the flower seller. She bought two bunches of chrysanthemums on his instructions, and carried them back to the car.

'You sure two is enough?'

Matt nodded. 'I'm expecting there to be fresh flowers there already, because I think Susan Hunter was planning on visiting two days ago. I just felt I had to come tell them both that we won yesterday.'

'So it's nothing to do with you missing them?' She smiled as she spoke.

'Shut up, woman.'

'Okay. You're not missing them, it's all about football. I understand.'

'He said yesterday how much he missed Granddad,' Harry piped up from the back seat. 'And I'm missing him as well. I'm glad you found out who hurt him, Karen.'

'And I'm even more glad you weren't at your dad's house that night,' Karen said, with a degree of feeling. 'I would have had to be a lot more careful if they'd got you tied up as well.'

'But they're all in prison now?'

Karen hesitated then looked out of the car window as they began to progress up the main cemetery drive. 'Yes. Yes, of course they are.'

She sensed Matt's head swivel towards her, and knew he was registering her words to be dissected later. She also knew she couldn't answer him; it was only seeing the name Beardow in connection with yet another crime that was making her uneasy. All the Beardows and any other guilty parties from the killing of Dave Forrester and Johnny Keane were safely tucked away in their cells.

They stopped a few feet away from where the two head-stones were, and all three got out of the car. They walked across and Matt bent down to touch his father's grave.

'Love you, Dad,' he said softly, and then slid the flower container out of its holder. The flowers in it were dead.

'I guess Susan whatever her name is hasn't been to visit yet.' Karen glanced towards Johnny's headstone. 'Johnny's flowers need dumping as well.'

'I'll bring these,' Harry said, and picked up the second container.

Father and son walked to the large wire mesh cage and deposited the dead blooms, then turned towards the water tap where they cleaned out the containers and refilled them with water, each managing to successfully soak both their feet as they did so.

With the new flowers installed on the headstones, Matt and Harry began to tell Dave and Johnny all about the previous day's match. Karen walked back to the car and sat inside it while she waited for the two to return. She felt an overwhelming shudder of love for both of them, and knew Harry was dreading being taken back to his mother's home after leaving the cemetery. He'd loved the week spent at Ridgeway, but he also knew there was a birth imminent – Becky Davis, ex-wife of Matt, mother of Harry and current wife of Superintendent Brian Davis, was huge – so would have been counting down the final few days to the birth. He didn't mind having a sister, he'd said, he just didn't want the sister to have a father. Therein lay the problem.

She watched as they walked back to join her, and saw Harry give a half turn and blow a kiss to both graves.

'Okay?' she asked as Matt got into the driver's seat.

He nodded. 'It's still bloody unreal. How can he be there on a Saturday morning and not there by Saturday afternoon. Okay, he was paralysed, but he wasn't ill. If he'd died of natural causes, I could have handled that a lot better than I'm handling this.'

He started the car, and she squeezed his hand as he put it into drive. 'Just keep talking about him, we can keep him alive. That seems to be Harry's way of managing.' She turned around and smiled at the young boy. 'I'm right, aren't I?' she asked, and Harry grinned at her.

'My dad says you're usually right.'

* * *

Dropping Harry off had been hard for both of them, and they had left him standing by his mother's side at the front door, his face a picture of abject misery. Matt hadn't gone inside the house – he preferred to keep well away from Brian Davis – but he did tell Becky the news that Harry was to have a new cousin, although not for quite a long time. He guessed Harry wouldn't be able to keep the news to himself, so thought it better to prewarn Becky.

They arrived back at Ridgeway ten minutes later, and Matt

leaned back in his seat, rubbing his eyes. 'I thought it would get easier, visiting Dad, but it's not happening yet.'

'Will it ever? He was such a massive personality, and that leaves memories, footprints in your life. Sorry, I don't think it's supposed to get easier. Tell you what, though, wherever he is right now, I bet he's proud of you. You've stepped up to the plate with the business, you've modernised the premises, found your new Mary Poppins, and increased the cases he already had. Plus you've brought Steve in, which was a brilliant idea. It's back-up for you if you need it, just as Johnny was for your dad.'

'And the funny thing is,' Matt said, 'I don't regret walking away from my job. Maybe if Brian Davis hadn't appeared on the scene, I wouldn't have done it, but I do think it was fate he had to take over at that point. And I actually love what I'm doing now, which feels a lot more like helping people than ever it did as a copper. Strange, isn't it?'

'No, I get what you mean. And just because I'm feeling a little uneasy about this Susan Hunter, I'm going to do a quick check on her on Monday. That okay?'

He held up his hands and laughed. 'I'm saying nothing! I didn't get the impression she was up to no good; perhaps it wasn't her intention to go visit the graves immediately, maybe she needs to build up to it. I struggled, the first time I went. She did seem genuine, and I felt happy that she'd cared for Dad, and that circumstances had been the cause of the separation between them, not a falling out. You think I'm wrong?'

'Not at all. I didn't meet her, so I can't form any views on her, but I can rule out anything a bit suspicious because of what I can use at work.'

'Well, I can tell you she's not in WATSON.'

'That really makes me smile. And I know you said Carol had

only added the first eighteen months of your dad's cases, but I bet she's done a lot more now. The woman is a miracle worker.'

'And she makes scones. She's a much-valued employee already, and we've only known her four or five days.'

'You'll have to pay her.'

'I know, and we're more than happy to do it, but she keeps saying not yet, we can pay her when she's proved her worth. She did that on the first day.' He shook his head. 'WATSON. I have this strange feeling it's going to be such a valuable asset.'

* * *

Carol spent most of the morning at the antiques centre, after calling to fill up her car with petrol and also her purse with real cash. The vendors at the antique centre were usually open to offers, and she hated then having to say *can I pay by card, please* after they had agreed a substantial discount.

It was always a busy place, and after an hour she made her way to the café, where she ordered a pot of tea and a blueberry scone. She placed her pile of goodies she intended purchasing on the end of the table, away from the teapot and cup and saucer. Most of her choices were made of paper, and she didn't want them ruined with splashes of tea before she got them home to judge whether she needed to tea or coffee stain them.

The thought made her smile, and she stroked the book of music scores she'd found rummaging through a trunk full of books. The date inside read 1890 and the papers had aged, giving all the edges a brownish hue. Perfect.

She watched as a woman walked up to the counter and asked for a blueberry scone, then felt a little guilty as the waitress told her they'd just sold the last one but they had cheese or coconut. She settled on a cheese one, then turned around to look for a free table. All were occupied.

Carol stifled a gasp as she realised who it was. Susan Hunter.

She knew Susan hadn't actually seen her, so there was no danger she would be recognised, but nevertheless she felt a little uncomfortable. She felt even more at odds when the woman moved towards her, and asked if the place at her table was free.

'Yes, that's fine,' Carol said, and moved her pile of things nearer to her, allowing a little more room for when Susan's scone and drink arrived.

'Thank you,' Susan said. 'Busy, isn't it? I came last week and it wasn't like this.'

Carol smiled. 'It rained last week. Today it's quite nice, so people decide to go out for the day. That's why I'm here.'

'And you already have quite a collection.' Susan gave a slight nod towards the eclectic selection of goods.

'I make stuff,' Carol said. 'I don't quite know how to explain what I do, but it feeds the creative side of my soul. I make journals – junk journals they're called, but that's because they're made with beautiful old papers and pictures, and this place is ideal for getting that sort of stuff.'

'I've just bought a roll-top bureau. I saw it last week, and wasn't sure if it would fit where I wanted it to fit, so decided not to buy it. It's quite expensive, but even so I measured up when I got home and it would fit perfectly. I've spent all week deciding whether to splash out on it or not, and today I came to buy it. I've managed to get fifty pounds off, so I'm well happy. And that lovely young man on the desk is going to deliver it tonight on his way home, because he lives only a couple of roads away from me, in Norton.'

Carol felt a shiver run through her. Norton was far too close to Gleadless. Far too close. She had no idea why this tiny piece of information affected her. Susan Hunter hadn't left an address or even a contact number with Matt, and he had no reason to ask her for one as she wasn't a client.

The absence of any mention of a Susan Hunter in any of the old files was causing Carol's brain to go into overdrive.

She felt truly grateful that the woman had only had the briefest of glimpses of her that day when she visited Matt, if she even saw her at all. Matt had gone to the door himself to let her in, he had enjoyed a fairly lengthy chat with her and had escorted her out after their conversation, so this was pure coincidence that she and Susan would meet up in the tea shop at the antique centre, and actually begin to talk while sitting at the same table.

She hoped coincidence was the right word.

14

MONDAY, 31 OCTOBER

Karen had her full team in the briefing room by half past seven and she brought them up to date on the release of Aaron and George, confirming they would be charged with the burglary, but it seemed they were in the clear for the murder.

'Phil, you're going to the gym this morning?'

Some bright spark in the background muttered that he needed to, and Karen smiled. There was always one joker in any pack, even so early in the morning.

'I am, boss. It opens at ten for training, so I thought I'd go down for about half past nine and speak to whoever is there. I only need to see the register, so I don't need Clinton himself. I'll ring to let you know as soon as I'm back in the car.'

'Thanks, Phil, and do we have any new reports in?'

Jaime stood. 'The George at Hathersage has confirmed officially by email that Rick Langton and his girlfriend were there for a meal until around ten-thirty, so that rules them out of being at Gleadless at the time of the murder. It would have been getting on for eleven by the time they arrived home. And the PM report is through, no different to what we were told initially. Blunt force trauma and she would have died quickly.'

Karen gave a slight nod, trying not to let her frustration show. The old maxim of looking at the close family first in cases of murder didn't seem to be working with this one, because everyone in Elise's close family seemed to have strong alibis. And to top it all off, even her bloody husband wanted to be back with her, admitting he still loved her. Funny how you could form an instant impression of somebody, without really knowing why. And her instant impression of Rick Langton hadn't been a good one.

There were a couple more minor queries which were speedily dealt with before everyone began to move either towards their desks for the background research needed at this stalemate period, or to slip on coats to leave for outside visits.

Karen headed back to her own office and moved to the window. It looked down onto the car park and she spotted Phil as he was climbing into a squad car. She smiled. Seeing that parked outside the gym might make one or two gym enthusiasts think twice about entering the premises, but his bulky frame slid more efficiently into that car than into his wife's Mini, which he was currently forced to use while his own Civic was in for repair.

She made herself a drink and opened up her laptop.

Staring blankly at the screen didn't offer any bright ideas, and with a sigh she read the official autopsy report on Elise Langton. She'd only met the feisty young woman a couple of times, but had been impressed by her no-nonsense attitude, the obvious fighting spirit despite the devastation to her home the burglary had caused, and for her to end up in the mortuary was almost unthinkable.

Karen felt sure it was all connected to the Facebook post, and yet their two trainee burglars seemed to be in the clear for heading to Gleadless that night. But somebody had been there and had given no thought to the fact that it would be little children who would find their mother dead the next morning, with no other adult immediately present to help. And Skye, with her iron and ironing board, not realising how her life was about to change...

Karen shook her head and sipped at her drink. She'd pick up some sweets and nip over to Rick Langton's home, ostensibly to check on how the kids were doing, but mainly to see that the new arrangements for the rest of their lives would work in their favour, and not Rick Langton's and Jenna Glaves's.

She zipped up her bulky jacket, wondering briefly when the transition from blazer-type coat to winter-weight coat had happened, but it definitely had. There was a frosty feel to the air every morning now, and she knew it would be April before there was a return to the ease of slipping on a lightweight jacket for appearance's sake, not for warmth.

She walked across to the local Asda and picked up some sweets for the children, along with a couple of books for them, and returned to her own car. She was half tempted to take the one remaining squad car, but then decided against it. A dislike of Rick Langton didn't mean she had to be heavy on him, and he wasn't a suspect; they had confirmation he'd been at the George.

* * *

Rick was just walking down the garden path as she pulled up. He waited for her to join him, before going inside.

'I've just taken Daniel to school. Stayed a bit to chat to his teacher, made sure she knew what was happening. I know he's a resilient little kid, but he's been too quiet, so I've asked them to be aware.'

With that, he shot up in Karen's estimation. He wasn't quite as selfish as first impressions may have suggested. She gave a small nod in acknowledgement, and followed him inside.

Skye was sitting at the kitchen table eating a bowl of corn-flakes, and she waved when she realised who the visitor was.

'Lady,' she said.

'Karen,' her visitor responded. 'Okay if I sit here?'

Skye nodded, tipping another spoonful of her breakfast into her mouth. 'Where's Mummy?' she mumbled, forcing cornflakes to drip down her chin.

'Hey, young lady,' her dad said, hunkering down beside her chair. 'We've explained Mummy isn't going to be able to come back, haven't we?'

Skye nodded. 'I thought she was with this lady.'

'Karen,' Karen repeated. 'And, no, she isn't, Skye. I was just there to look after her, but she's with a doctor now and can't come back to you any more. You're living with your daddy now, just as Daniel is.'

'And Jenna?'

Jenna placed a sippy cup of orange juice in front of Skye. 'Of course, sweetheart. There's your juice. And when you're dressed we'll go to the shops, and then to the park. That okay?'

Skye smiled a little uncertainly, then nodded. 'Okay. Can I wear my pink wellies?'

'You can. But you have to eat all your cornflakes first.'

Karen handed the bag containing the Asda goodies to Rick. 'For the children,' she said. 'Can we talk?'

He nodded. 'Let's go through to the lounge. You okay with her, Jenna?'

* * *

They sat facing each other in the two armchairs.

'Is everything going okay with the children?' Karen asked.

'Kind of. Daniel seems to understand, but Skye doesn't. And meanwhile I have to find the happy middle ground of keeping Elise's memory alive, but not the person. I don't know how to do it.'

'You'll be fine. Skye's clearly happy with you, and she'll always have Elise's brother to fight her corner as well. In a year's time, whatever is happening in her life now will seem the norm. Children are remarkably resilient. The advantage here is that they have a caring father to step into the breach. Not all kids have that. You're off work?'

'I am. They know the situation, and I've good employers. I've booked a month off, and they said if I need more, it's not a problem. I'm half working from home to be honest, keep getting phone calls. But we can cope with that. It's how we kept going through lockdown, and we can do it again.'

The door opened and Jenna brought in two mugs of tea. 'We're going out in ten minutes. You don't need me, do you?'

Karen smiled. 'Thank you for the drink. No, I just came to check the kids were doing okay, really. And you two. It's a big responsibility, suddenly having two kids here permanently, when I know it was shared custody before. If you need help or advice, there are professionals who can step in to give it, and who will be contacting you, but I'm sure you'll be fine.'

Jenna left them to talk, returning to the kitchen to get Skye into her wellies before their trip to the shops and the park.

Rick watched her leave, then shrugged. 'I just feel a bit guilty,' he said. 'They're my kids, not Jenna's. Yet it seems she's stepped in and is doing so much for them. She never grumbles, just gets on with it, but I can't help but feel...'

Karen noticed his hesitation, and smiled. 'Hey, don't beat yourself up about it. Even if Jenna decides she doesn't want this new life, you'll manage perfectly well. You have back-up with Elise's brother's family, and there are always after-school clubs and breakfast clubs and other such helpful things. People adapt to fit circumstances, Rick, but at the moment you're coping. And what those children need right now is to know they're loved. I'm sure they do, because I'm sure you tell them constantly. Just be a dad, Rick, because you are, and let Jenna cope with having motherhood thrust upon her.'

He picked up his cup. 'Do you have anything to tell me?'

'Only that the two lads we brought in have been charged with the burglary, but they have a pretty solid alibi for the night of the murder.'

'And Luke Peters?'

'He was in the Canaries. He's back home now, came home when he found out we'd taken in his lad, but they all seem to be in the clear.'

'Personally, I agree they are, but Luke Peters has long arms. Pushy bloke. What he wants he expects to get.'

'You've met him?'

'Indirectly. I don't want to talk about it, because I've the kids to think about now, but nothing would surprise me about him. He has a way of taking revenge if you don't do what he wants you to do.'

'Tell me.'

Gone was the friendly Karen, to be replaced by an authoritative DS Nelson.

'Not much to tell, because I don't know much. About three

years ago one of our drivers was approached by him, via somebody else of course, to bring in stuff from the continent, from Amsterdam. I'll leave you to guess what it was, but it wasn't tulips. The driver came to me to report it, and I laughed it off. He said no, obviously, and two days later they set his lorry on fire overnight. They contacted him the next day and said his house was next, so he left. Last I heard, he was living in Norfolk. I lost a truck from the fleet, and one of our best, most reliable drivers. But you'll never prove they did it, of course. So don't think that he didn't have something to do with my Elise dying just because he was in the Canaries.'

Karen listened carefully, making a note to check out this driver on their records, but doubting he would be there.

She finished her drink and stood. 'Thank you for listening to me, Rick. If you need to talk about anything, you have my number. I'll keep you informed, because we will find out who did this, I promise you. Don't forget there's a carrier bag in the kitchen with some sweets for the kids, and a couple of books. Hope it's not too many E numbers, I'd hate to think it sent them hyper.' She grinned at him.

'Thanks, Karen. You're all heart. I'll be ringing you at midnight when they're still wide awake...'

'Well, it'll make a change to the duty sergeant ringing to me to tell me they've evidence a crime has been committed, and can I just get out of bed, nip out and sort it. I can tell you to bog off, but it's not done to say that to the bloke in charge of the night shift.'

Rick escorted her to the door, and she touched his arm.

'Take care, Rick. You're doing okay. I'll keep in touch.'

15

MONDAY, 31 OCTOBER

Karen drove to Gleadless and parked outside the Forrester office. She heard the door buzz as she approached, and guessed Carol had recognised her car.

'Is Matt free?' she asked.

'He is. And I've just taken him a couple of scones, so if you're quick he might share. If not, I've got some more.'

'I'm fine, thanks. All the way here I've been dipping into a bag of sweets I've bought for Halloween treats. Feel a bit sick now.' She held up the carrier bag. 'I thought I'd drop these in with Matt, because he might be home when we get the little darlings knocking at our door. Do you get many?'

'Normally I do. Rain's promised for later, though, so it might put them off.'

'I hope not,' Karen said. 'I'd hate to have to work my way through all these bags of Haribos.' She turned to go into Matt's office.

He was on the phone, so she waited until he finished the call before sitting down. The two scones were still on the plate, and he indicated she should help herself while he was still talking, but she shook her head.

Matt disconnected, and looked at her. 'This is unexpected.'

'I've bought a bag of sweets.'

'Wow. That's good of you.'

'No, they're not for you. They're in case we get any wizards and witches and ghosts and suchlike before I get home from work. I don't want an egg smashed down the front door just because you're not equipped with treats. However, a couple of the bags may be accidentally open, like the shrimps and the bananas, which is why I don't want one of your scones.'

'Did you buy some Swizzels lollies?'

'I did. For the kids. You tip everything into this big orange bowl that I've also bought, and let them help themselves to whichever they want. And those lollies had better be in that bowl, Forrester.' The threat was evident in her voice.

'You're a cruel taskmaster, Karen Nelson. You're expecting to be late home?'

'Who knows. Everything seems to be at a standstill. We're at the double-checking of everything stage, because it seems as if somebody isn't being totally honest, but heaven only knows who that person is. Everything good here?'

'It is. I was on the phone with the chap with the vandalised garden. It was more a courtesy call really, and it seems Steve's lads are there today using the machine that will get the turf up that's been killed, and fitting the new secure gate into the back garden. He was singing their praises. I just feel a bit puzzled by it all. He doesn't want the police involved, he didn't mention the contretemps with the neighbour when he reversed into their car, nothing showed on the back garden CCTV although it was a bit ineffective. It's almost as if he suspects who did it, and doesn't know how to deal with it. Even if it's an insurance scam, and I don't think it is, it wouldn't benefit him, because he's already got one claim with the company because of the bump with the car, so claiming again would put up his premium. It's as if it's escalating out of his control. I'm going out to see him tomorrow morning.'

'Surely for an insurance claim for vandalism he'll need a police report number?'

'He would, which is why I'm finding it a bit puzzling. There's something wrong. I'm letting it play out, and I'll have a chat with Steve when he gets back. See what his take is on it. In the meantime, I've been having another look at Dad's journal to see if we missed anything.'

'Susan Hunter? You're looking for a reference to her, aren't you?'

Matt smiled. 'You know me so well. Everything is suddenly a mystery. Carol is working her way through all the files, all the cases, right back to the day Dad opened the business, but nothing has shown up yet. That leads me to think she was never a client, that it truly was personal. The journal is a mix of personal snippets and client business, more of a chat-a-day type memoir, with things he wanted to stand out written in capitals, or, as in the case of Anthony Dawson, in red. But nothing – nothing in any colour, capitals or lower case – that even vaguely resembles the name Susan Hunter.'

'You didn't feel suspicious while she was here, did you?'

'Not at all. It's only as I've thought about it, and also saw that she hadn't been to the grave, that I started to think. But I'm pretty sure she gained nothing by being here, except the location of his grave. Suddenly everybody seems to be playing silly buggers, and I'm not getting it.'

'I have to go.' Karen stood and fished inside the carrier bag.

'Here, have a lollipop, and relax.' She handed him a Swizzels lolly. 'See you tonight, and hopefully reasonably early.'

Her phone rang as she walked across to her car, and she glanced at the screen before answering it.

'Phil?'

'Hi, boss. I'm outside the gym now. I've taken pictures of the gym register for that Tuesday night, but there's no Aaron Peters or George Jackson on it. I checked back for six weeks, and they're listed every week, but not last week. So they have no alibi for the night of the murder. I hung around until the owner arrived, and he couldn't apologise enough for giving us false information. He said George and Aaron are there every Tuesday, very reliable, and he simply wasn't thinking straight when he said they were there. He now confirms that if they weren't signed in as they paid their fees, then they weren't there. Everybody else who attended last Tuesday was logged in by him personally. You'll see it's all the same handwriting. He seemed quite shocked that they hadn't been there, he said they never miss a Tuesday session because it's the quietest day and they seem to get more from it.'

Karen hesitated, trying to decide how to handle this. What would Matt have done?

'Okay, Phil. Well done. So here's what we're going to do. This crafty pair think they've got one over on us, so we'll let them think that for the rest of the day. At six in the morning I want them brought in. Let's wake the little bastards up nice and early, they can sweat it out in the station until we get there. You want to interview with me?'

'Yes, boss.'

'Okay. Be at work for nine, we'll have a coffee, and then see what they have to say. They'll be screaming police brutality by then, I don't doubt. I'll get a responsible adult there for them for half nine, and we'll see what happens after that.'

Steve followed the car into the layby, and pulled up some distance away. His camera was on the passenger seat, and he quickly snapped a picture of the Skoda with the passenger climbing out and heading towards her own car. He kept the camera in his hand ready to complete the sequence of a dozen or so photographs already taken that day, and waited.

It had been a long morning. At seven o'clock he had been parked near the family home of Tina and Wesley Thornton, waiting for events to unfold. Their client was Tina. Her problem was her husband, who she now was determined should be her ex-husband. She simply needed the proof.

Using the tram to go to work meant that daily she passed the Forrester offices, and one week earlier she had got off the tram at Gleadless Town End, and walked to her afternoon appointment with Steve, where she had given him a list of times her husband had lied about where he was, or invented excuses for having to go out. She asked for help with gaining proof.

Hence Steve's dawn start following a hurried text the previous day from Tina saying her husband had told her he had an early appointment at work the following day.

Steve had been waiting a mere five minutes when he saw Wesley's car edge down their drive and turn left. He dropped in behind it, and felt relief when a couple of cars managed to get between them. Driving along Bochum Parkway, he saw the Skoda's indicators flash to warn of a left turn, and he followed it onto a large layby, regularly used by a huge van selling fruit and vegetables. The vehicle was there, but it was still a little early for its owner. The Skoda drove past the van, and pulled up behind a yellow Mini. Steve parked so he had a view of what was happening with the Skoda, and waited.

A woman slid out of the Mini, pulling her skirt down as she did so. Her legs, long ones, were still very much on show as she walked around the back of her car, and opened the passenger door of the Skoda. Steve took three or four pictures, then the Skoda left, driving back onto Bochum Parkway. He waited a few seconds before setting off to follow them.

They drove as far as the Travelodge. He got a beautiful picture of the two of them, arms linked around each other's waists, as they entered the doors of the motel.

He sat for a couple of hours before managing to capture another photograph of them, this time exiting the doors, then followed them back to the layby where the woman got back into her own car. Wesley waited until the Mini had left before setting off in the Skoda.

Steve sent a quick text to Tina advising her to ring her husband's office number and check if he was there, telling her he had just seen him set off from Gleadless. Just over a minute later, he received a reply. Her husband hadn't arrived at work. He was due in any time.

Steve was only a minute away from his office, and he headed there to make copies of the photographs before adding them to a presentation folder. He also screenshotted the text message she had just sent confirming the time.

He was just making the folder presentable when Matt knocked and walked in, carrying a lollipop. He handed it to Steve, who smiled.

'My God, you're a star. This is just what I need. You got these for tonight? I'll send Herms round dressed as a witch if you have.'

'Yep. Karen got them, but I've got strict instructions they're for the kids, and I'm not to eat them. So I'm going to blame you. What's that?' He nodded towards the file folder.

'Photos of what I've been doing all morning. Job done, I reckon. Caught him escorting a very attractive pair of legs into the Travelodge, and escorting her back out a couple of hours later. He told his wife he had to be in work early, so I tipped her off, she rang him at work, and he hadn't got there, obviously. We have all the proof she needs, so I reckon its bye-bye Mr Thornton. She's calling in at two to collect this, settle her bill, and then I suspect she'll go home to pack his suitcase. Or just chuck it all out of the window.'

Matt picked up the folder and glanced through the pictures. 'This is a good camera. Better than my phone, anyway.'

'It cost a fair bit, but I reckon it's worth it. Everything's so clear, especially the number plates. I suppose if we had the right police connections, we could find out who owns the Mini, and really earn our money.'

'We could if we had the right police connections. And if I stop eating these lollies, she might listen favourably to us. But she might not. We'll go down that route if the client wants the name. She might not be bothered; it's very obvious what's going on from the photographs, and they're all in timed order. Good job well done, Steve.'

16

MONDAY, 31 OCTOBER

Steve removed the wrapping from the lollipop. 'Did you want something, or did you pop in just to bring me a lolly?'

Matt shrugged. 'I don't know. I wanted to talk about your gardening clients that are now sort of our clients.'

Steve locked the client file in his filing cabinet along with the business copy of it, and turned to Matt. 'I don't know what to say.'

'No, I don't either.'

They both sat, then looked at each other.

'You start,' Steve said.

'But what with?' Matt countered. 'I don't know what to say except I'm a bit uneasy. I saw the damage, which has clearly upset the wife, I saw the CCTV camera that has shown nothing, and I'm now seeing frantic security being installed to turn it all into a fortress. It feels as if we're missing something, and I hoped you'd have picked up on it, or maybe somebody on your team has.'

'Nobody has said anything, but I don't think they would.

They'd just get on with the job. They just want to put the damaged areas back to how they were. But you're right, something is off. Maybe we need to go out and talk to them, see if we can find what it is. Maybe we can get the husband to open up a bit more. His wife seems to be a bit quiet, but he might have thoughts on it now time's moved on a bit. Tomorrow morning okay with you? I'll give them a ring and tell them we're popping out to check everything is now okay with what we've done. They don't need to know we don't really believe what they're saying, do they?'

* * *

Both Matt and Karen were home by five, and Karen put in a pizza so they didn't have to worry if they had a disturbed evening. They took it in turns going to the door, although Matt managed to sneak a sweet back with him every time it was his turn to face up to the witches and wizards. He sent all their visitors to the house next door, telling them they would get double sweets there, while trying to keep his face straight. Harry had said he wasn't bothered about doing it this year, and Matt felt a little sorry that his son should think he was too old to join in the fun.

He was trying to unstick one of the chewy bars from his teeth as he sank down onto the sofa by the side of Karen.

'Been a busy night. You think it eases off around seven, you said?'

'Usually it does. I'm always glad when it's over, even though I love seeing all the outfits they wear. I just think it's paedophile heaven, Halloween. It scares me.'

Matt's phone pinged to indicate a message, and he closed his eyes. 'Do I have to answer that?'

Karen leaned forward and picked the phone up. 'Here, it may be important.'

He glanced at the screen. Davis. For a second, he reverted to being DI Matt Forrester, and shook his head.

'It's Dickhead,' he muttered, and opened up the text.

On our way. Becky in labour. Be there in fifteen minutes or so.

He sat upright. 'Shit. Harry's on his way. Looks like the baby is about to arrive.'

'His room's ready for him. No need to panic, we've known this was getting close for some time. He'll not be a happy young man, but we can look after him. I can drop him off at school if that helps.'

'No, I'm okay to take him. You've got the teenage thugs to interview, haven't you?'

'I have, but I can work around that.'

'No, I'll take him in, have a quick word with his class teacher while I'm there. Just let her know what's going on.'

She stood. 'I'm going to put a hot water bottle in his bed, he likes that. He might feel he needs a bit of comfort.'

Matt smiled as she left to go to the kitchen. She was so good with his son, treated him as if he was her own child. She was pretty good with him as well, Matt reflected a moment later, as he took the wrapper off his fifth Swizzels lolly of the day.

* * *

Superintendent Brian Davis was frazzled. He banged on Matt's door, and when Matt opened it thrust a suitcase towards him.

'Got to go, things are progressing fast.' And he ran back to the car.

Matt and Harry watched as the car turned around, and Harry gave a small wave to the hunched-over form of his mother.

'She hurts,' he said.

Father and son continued to look at the taillights as they disappeared down the road.

'Tends to happen, lad, tends to happen.'

'Well, I wouldn't want to be a woman,' he said with a degree of feeling, and looked up at his dad. 'I've not been fed.'

'Well, I'm sure we can feed you. Come on, let's go see what we've got.'

* * *

The orange bowl containing what was left of the Halloween sweets was put away in a cupboard, and Karen accompanied a satiated Harry upstairs. She turned down his bed a little, keen to keep the warmth generated by the hot water bottle inside the covers, and waited while be brushed his teeth.

He got into bed, and slid down. 'Oooh,' he said, 'this is awesome. I love a hot water bottle.'

'I know. I thought it might make the world a little bit better for you. And by tomorrow, your new baby sister should be here. Whatever you're thinking right now, you'll grow to love her, and to enjoy having her in your life. Look at your dad and Aunty Herms – where would one be without the other? It's special, being brother and sister.'

He thought about that for a moment. 'Think she'll grow up to be like Aunty Herms?'

Karen smiled. 'I'm sure she will with your help. And then, of course, we have Aunty Herms and Uncle Steve's new baby to look forward to.'

He nodded, and in that moment she saw a flash of wisdom cross his face. 'Then let's hope they have a boy,' he said, and snuggled down lower into the bed. 'Night, Karen, love you.'

'Night, sweetheart, love you too.'

* * *

Florence Alice Davis was born two minutes before midnight, and the text with the good news arrived on Matt's phone at just after one in the morning. He didn't hear the ping.

He saw the message as he switched off his wake-up alarm, so after showing the message to Karen, he went to Harry's room to tell him.

Harry was already awake and sitting up in bed reading. Harry looked up as his door opened, and frowned. 'She's had it?'

'Yes, you have a baby sister called Florence. Weighed just over eight pounds, and everybody is fine.'

'Oh, good.' He dropped his eyes back to his book.

'Time to get up now.'

'I'm going to school?'

'You are.'

'But why?'

'It's kind of required by law.'

'But I've just had a sister.'

'Makes no difference to a judge. He'll send me to prison.'

'Really?'

'Yep.'

'Well, take a dressing gown in with you in case it gets cold at night.'

Matt picked up a teddy bear and threw it. It hit Harry in the face, and they both burst out laughing. 'Good shot, Dad! You might need skills like that inside.'

'Out of bed immediately, young man, or you won't have time for breakfast.'

Harry threw back the bedclothes and closed his book. 'Am I coming back here tonight?'

'I think so. I'll make sure one of us can pick you up from school. Not sure when Mum and Florence will be allowed home, so we'll play it safe and bring you back here. I'll know more when I see you after school.'

He left Harry to get ready, and went down to toast the requested bagel with cream cheese.

'That looks nice,' Karen said, peering around his shoulder. 'I was going to grab a slice of toast, but...'

'But you thought, why shouldn't I have that, and Matt can do two more for him and Harry?'

'Exactly.'

He handed her Harry's breakfast and popped in two more bagels. She smiled and thanked him, then took his coffee.

'I was going to wait till I went past Costa, but I need this now if I'm eating a bagel.'

'Good job I made a pot and not just a cup then. Has Ray brought in the two lads?'

'He has. Vanessa Peters kicked off about it, but Aaron was quite calm. Apparently he said he knows he's done nothing wrong, and he'll be back home for dinnertime. George's mother stormed around, but even he said there was nothing to worry about, they'd been charged with the burglary and they'd done nothing else. Wait while we show them the proof that they have no alibi for Tuesday night. That'll be a slap in their cocky faces.' She paused for a moment. 'Florence?'

'Florence.'

'Pretty name. I like the older ones. My nan was called Florence. Was Harry okay?'

'Not really interested. He's coming here again after school, but I don't know what will happen later.'

She put down her cup and picked up her work bag. 'Okay, I'm off. Let me know if you need me for anything, I may be able to pick him up if you're tied up.'

Matt smiled. 'You're a star. I think he kinda likes you.'

'Well, I love the bones of the pair of you, so don't forget that, Matt Forrester.' She waved a hand over her shoulder as she left to go to her car.

'Does she mean me and you?' Harry asked, as he walked through into the kitchen.

'Seems so,' Matt said, grinning.

'Then I'll come and live with you instead of with them.'

'And what would I do with you during the long summer break when I'm at work and Karen's at work? And your mum might have something to say about it. I need you there to take care of her, especially now you have baby Florence to think about as well.'

Matt handed him his bagel, and Harry smiled.

'And here's another reason. I get more cheese on the bagels here than I do at Mum's house.'

Matt shook his head. His son always had an answer. 'Get it eaten, drink your milk, and let's get off to school. I'll go in with you, let them know it'll be either me or Karen picking you up, and tell them the baby is here.'

'Will Karen pick me up in a squad car if she comes for me? That would be cool.'

'Doubt it. They're not taxis, you know. No, she'll be in her own car. It could be either of us, so just keep your eyes peeled when you tear out of that door at home time.'

17

TUESDAY, 1 NOVEMBER

Phil Newton placed a large latte in front of Karen. 'Thought you might need this before we tackle them,' he said.

'Are they behaving?'

'Currently demanding toast and coffee because they didn't have breakfast at home.'

'Have we given them some?'

'Being done now.'

'Well, heaven forbid they should waste away through lack of nourishment.'

'They're definitely stroppy. They think because they've been charged with the burglary offence, that's it. They'll go to court, get a slap on the wrist for a first offence, and they can go on their way. Their responsible adults have arrived, so I've told them to grab a coffee because we're not quite ready. That okay?'

'Perfect.' Karen picked up her latte and sipped at it. 'I stole Matt's coffee this morning, but he always makes it too strong. This one will take away the taste.'

'There's an answer to that,' Phil responded. 'Don't steal his coffee.'

'You sound like Matt. He always says that.'

'You two seem to be settled. You happy?'

'Very. And when Harry's with us, it feels even better. He's a lovely lad.' Karen was tempted to give him the news of the birth of Dickhead's baby, but decided against it. One email from Superintendent Davis would soon give out the details.

'Good. You want to look at the screenshots of the gym register before we go down?'

She nodded. 'You printed them so we can wave them around?'

'I have. I'll go get them from my desk.'

She watched him walk across the room, noticing he was still favouring the right leg. He had been in a car accident at work a couple of years earlier, and he always said it was getting better, but it clearly wasn't.

He handed the file folder to her, and she looked at the listings of attendees for the night of the murder. It had been reasonably busy, but there was no evidence that the two smart arses in the interview rooms had been anywhere near. So where had they been?

She tried to imagine what their answers would be, but couldn't come up with anything. They hadn't had time to prepare, believing they were in the clear. She could, of course, work one against the other, lead one into thinking their friend was singing like a canary, but she would wait and see how it panned out before taking that route. One thing was for sure – if they didn't come up with a reasonable explanation as to why they had lied at their first interview, they wouldn't be going home to Mummy this time!

Even though it was looking as though there was a connection with the death of Elise Langton, she still couldn't see this pair of nincompoops as murderers. But she needed the truth.

Where had they been the previous Tuesday night at around half past nine?

Half an hour later, they entered the first interview room, with Phil logging them in with the recording equipment. Karen had allocated Jaime and Ray to interview George in interview room two, with clear instructions to interrupt her if anything of any significance came up that could impact on their interview with Aaron Peters.

She sat down and placed the file on the desk in front of her, watching as Aaron's eyes swivelled towards it. She always found it amusing that people could find the sight of a file so intimidating, yet most of the time there was precious little in it.

'Okay, Aaron, let's get down to business. You have some things to explain, and I have to tell you that the same thing is being said to your mate next door.'

'George? You've collared him as well?' Aaron looked bewildered.

'You don't need to worry about him. Concentrate on keeping out of the courts yourself. So, we have stuff we need answers about. You lied to us, Aaron.'

'I fucking didn't.'

'Well, unfortunately for you, we followed up on your alibi for last Tuesday night with a personal visit by DC Newton here to the gym at Waterthorpe. Do you pay to use their facilities, Aaron?'

She watched as his face lost all its colour. 'Yes,' was his mumbled response.

'How much?'

'Five quid.'

'And how often do you go?'

'Every Tuesday for definite, sometimes on a Friday as well.'

She could tell he knew what was coming. 'And how much did you pay last Tuesday?'

'I've told you, we pay five quid each.'

'Who to?'

'Sometimes it's Clinton, sometimes it's Barney. Depends who's there first.'

'And they make a note of everybody who pays.'

'Yes.' His tone was becoming surlier by the second.

'Who did you give your money to last Tuesday?'

He shrugged. 'Can't remember.'

'Could that be because you didn't go?'

'Always go on a Tuesday.'

'Not last Tuesday you didn't.' She removed the printout from the file and pushed it across the table. 'Show me where your name is on this list.'

He didn't even bother looking at it.

'What's the matter, Aaron? Isn't it there?'

'No comment.'

She sighed. She'd wondered how long it would take for him to remember he had the option of saying *no comment*.

'You don't actually need to comment. We have the proof you didn't attend the gym last Tuesday. So where were you?'

'No comment.'

'Okay, let me tell you what I think you were doing. You and your best mate, George. I think you saw the post left on Facebook by Elise Langton, tagging your father. Telling him to check what his son was doing on the burglary front. And I think you decided to scare her by paying her a visit. That visit went disastrously wrong and ended with her murder. And murder carries a life sentence, no matter your age.'

Aaron tried to stand, but Phil rose from his seat and leaned over the table. 'Sit,' he said, and Aaron did.

'Don't fucking put that on me,' he snarled. 'I had nowt to do with it. Okay, we were going to put the frighteners on her, but not hurt her. Threaten her, like.'

'You took a weapon?'

'A bat. Just to wave it at her. To tell her to stop with the mouth. To just shut up. I'd had a right phone call from my dad, having a proper go at me.'

'So now you're confirming the alibi you gave about attending the gym is false?'

He nodded. 'But we didn't even knock on her door. We couldn't because when we got off the tram and walked across the road, there was somebody there already. We waited in the trees next to the road, and saw her come to the door. The woman went in with her, so we called it off, guessed it was a mate of hers.'

'A woman? You're saying a woman was at her door? What time would this have been?'

He thought for a moment. 'About half past nine, give or take ten minutes.'

'Did you recognise her?'

As Karen asked the question, her thoughts were *we should be so lucky*.

'Only saw her from a distance. We stood the top side of the trees and saw her crossing the little service road. She must have gone there through the trees as well, because she was only a few steps in front of us. She had on a hoodie, a black one, pulled up over her head and probably over her face. Same as us, really.'

'So you'd gone prepared to hurt Elise? You didn't want to be recognised on the neighbour's CCTV again?'

He shrugged. 'By approaching her house head on through the trees, you don't get picked up on CCTV.'

'You're sure it was a woman?'

'She'd got boobs. Can't hide them in a black hoodie. And a high voice.'

'You heard her speak?'

'I think she said *where the fuck is Mick* but I'm not sure. It sounded like that anyway.'

Karen waited, and eventually Phil prompted Aaron to continue.

'So? You waited for the woman to leave then went in to have a word with Mrs Langton?'

'Nah,' Aaron responded. 'We went down to George's house, played a game then I went home. Decided to go back the following night and hoped she wouldn't put owt else on Facebook 'cos it winds my dad up. Then we forgot about it all anyway when you charged us with the burglary.'

'And you didn't recognise this woman?' Karen asked quietly. Her mind was racing. A woman had been the last person to see Elise alive?

'I didn't. Don't know if George knew her. He was just mad that we'd missed the gym to go and have a word with the slag who was causing us trouble, and then we couldn't even get her on her own.'

'You're such lovely lads,' Karen said as she closed the file and stood. 'You'll be taken back to a cell until I decide what we're going to do with you. I need to verify this, and it could all take some time. Especially if your mate hasn't told the same story as you.'

'I can't go home?' He looked puzzled.

'Not an earthly. As a person of interest in this case, you'll stay until I can no longer legally keep you here. Or until I'm satisfied you're telling the truth.'

The two officers left the room, and five minutes later Aaron was escorted to a holding cell. Karen headed to the second interview room, and added her name to the recording as she took a seat.

* * *

'And you definitely had no idea who the woman was?' Jaime was obviously at the wrapping-up stage.

'No, I've already told you that.' George was sounding belligerent.

'Okay, George, thank you for your cooperation. I'm going to have you taken to a holding cell until we've checked out your story. We'll let your parents know what's happening, but obviously we can't tell them when to expect you home. We don't know how long this verification is going to take.'

The three officers left the room together, making their way to the canteen where they met up with Phil. Coffees and bacon sandwiches were ordered, and they compared notes.

They were basically identical. When faced with the threat of a murder charge, the boys had both suddenly found the truth button. They had admitted to being there to 'have a word' with Elise about her use of Facebook, but had seen a woman at the door who ultimately had thwarted their plans.

'Ideas about the identity of the woman?' Karen asked.

There was a moment of silence as their brains went into overdrive, but nobody came up with a logical thought. Or even an illogical one.

'George didn't say anything about what the woman said?' Phil asked.

'No, we only have Aaron saying he thought she asked about somebody called Mick. Could Elise have been seeing somebody? Somebody else's husband, maybe?' Karen bit into her sandwich.

'Or it could be Rick and not Mick,' Ray said, looking around at the others. 'Was it somebody looking for Elise's husband? We know he was at the George Hotel with Jenna Glaves, but this woman might not have known that, and wanted to speak with him?' It came out as a question.

The other three looked at him. Karen smiled. 'The battering your head took a few months ago hasn't affected your brain cells, has it? We heard Aaron say Mick because that's what his brain told him the woman said, but it certainly could just as easily have been Rick. And if that's the case, who was the woman trying to find Rick Langton? What's he been up to now? He's made such a thing of saying he wanted to get back with Elise and how he regretted the affair with Jenna, but just suppose he's playing around with someone else. We need to bring him in for a more official chat, I think, and take it from there.'

'So you believe what these lads have told us today, boss?' Jaime asked, chewing a piece of bacon as she spoke. She coughed.

'I do, for a couple of reasons. One is that they had no idea we had found out they hadn't been to the gym so didn't have time to come up with a storyline, and two, I didn't get the feeling they had anything to do with the murder anyway. I just couldn't see it. They're not trained in murder yet.'

18

TUESDAY, 1 NOVEMBER

Steve and Matt travelled to the Bancroft home in Matt's Land Rover. They had decided not to announce their visit to the owners, but to treat it as a site visit to inspect that everything was going well with the renovation.

Matt drove in his usual fashion – carefully – and Steve rested his head back, his eyes closed. He felt tired. It had been a late night because they had stayed up planning their wedding. Hermia had initially said let's wait until after the birth, but he had said why?

She couldn't come up with a sensible answer, and their thoughts and plans had progressed to a March date – that's if they could get everything booked in time. They had laughed at the idea of a wedding dress with an elasticated waist which would accommodate the growing bump, and that had been the point when Steve realised that maybe Hermia didn't want her wedding day to be marred by pregnancy. Hermia had roared with laughter when he did a complete change, and suggested they might be better waiting a couple of years, when their child was walking and could take part in the day, and she would be sylphlike as usual.

And the talk had continued until around two o'clock in the morning, when they had finally fallen asleep. They had completed the circle, and decided on March, elasticated dress and all. Hermia said a huge bouquet would hide the bump on the photographs.

Steve opened his eyes as he sensed the car stop, and heard the handbrake. His company truck was in front of them, and the new side gate leading to the back garden was open. Anna Bancroft was standing by the gate, and they walked down the slight incline to meet her.

'Mrs Bancroft? Everything okay?'

She looked at both of them, as if wondering who they were. 'Are you coming to help?'

'I'm just checking everything is progressing smoothly,' Steve said, waving a hand as Paul Bancroft appeared from the back garden.

'Anna!' Paul called, moving quickly towards her. 'Let's get you inside, sweetheart, it's quite chilly and you haven't put on a coat.' He looked at Steve and Matt. 'Be back in a minute. You want a coffee?'

They thanked him and watched as he took Anna by the elbow and steered her towards the back door. Steve frowned and looked at Matt.

'She didn't know who we were.'

'No, she didn't. And I know she's only met me once, but she's met you more times than that.'

'Let's get in that back garden and see what's happening.'

It was a transformation. The new fence was completed and stained to a light oak, albeit a lot higher than the original planned fencing panels; the damaged lawn had been removed, fresh soil laid, followed by new turf, currently being completed by two of Steve's team. Steve and Matt skirted the edge of the newly laid turf.

His two men turned towards him.

'Hiya, boss,' one said. 'Almost finished here, unless Paul wants anything else clearing. We've fitted him new locks on his shed, at his request, but I've made a note of it on the works sheet. That okay?'

'It's fine, I'll pick it up for the invoice when I do the final account. Did he say why he wanted a new lock? Had the vandals damaged that as well?'

'No, I got the impression it was to keep Anna out. He said she likes to mow the lawn but it's getting too much for her, so if she can't get in to the lawnmower, she can't do it. Anyway, I picked up a new padlock, so it's all secure now. The property has been improved with more cameras, and the new gate is finished. I've trimmed back the damaged plants, but I don't think they were sprayed with the weedkiller, they were just trampled. I'm hopeful they'll come back next year. They just need their repaired furniture back, and it'll all be good to go.'

'All of you have done a cracking job on this one. I know it's been hard work,' Steve said, 'but I'm sure the clients are well satisfied with it. And you've done it in excellent time.'

'Thanks, boss. It's been easier than I first thought it was going to be.'

Matt turned to take the tray of coffees from Paul, who said, 'She's fast asleep now. Out like a light once she sat on the sofa.'

All five of them took a cup, and stood and stared at the garden.

'I thought it would never look like this again,' Paul said, a slight crack in his voice. 'Steve, Matt, I need to speak to you in the kitchen, if you don't mind.'

Steve and Matt hid their surprise, and left the gardening team to finish their drink, then complete the final parts of the project.

They followed Paul into the house, and sat at the kitchen table.

'They'll be finished here today,' Steve began. 'And I understand in a couple more days your furniture will be returned to you. I'll not invoice you until then, and I'll put it all on one bill to make it easier for your insurance claim.'

Paul sipped at his drink. 'That's what I need to talk to you about. There'll be no insurance claim, I know who caused all this damage. I'm asking you to drop the investigation, Matt, and send me the bill for the work you've already done.'

Matt looked across the table thoughtfully, and picked up his cup.

'Anna?' He saw the light bulb moment in Steve's brain, and watched as Paul crumpled.

'Yes. It's not always apparent when you meet Anna for the first time, but she has been diagnosed with early onset Alzheimer's. I have lived with the knowledge for some time, and hadn't realised how much it had progressed. It started with the damn car accident, I suppose. We got into the car and I started the engine. I then returned to the house because she was panicking that she'd not picked up her handbag. I was just re-locking our door when I heard the bang. She'd slid over into the driver's seat, put it in reverse and barrelled down our drive. I got to her, pushed her over into the passenger seat, and took the blame.'

He sucked in air as if his lungs needed help to continue to breathe. 'Even then I didn't realise the deterioration. And I certainly didn't link the damage to the garden with her. She loved the garden. However, from her more lucid moments I'm getting a story that's almost of horror to her. It happened in the middle of the night. I was fast asleep and she got out of bed. I usually sense her moving, but had taken some painkillers for back pain. Not much fun getting old.' He smiled.

'From piecing it all together, it seems she wanted to water the lawn, but she did it with the weedkiller. Then she trampled on all the flowers and plants to avoid standing on the newly watered lawn, and soaking her carpet slippers. I keep the weed-killer right on the top shelf at the back, because we have the grandchildren over quite a lot, and I didn't want them touching it. I also didn't think Anna could reach it, but she did.'

'That trampoline?' Matt said gently.

'She decided it was ugly. The same with the furniture. She used the garden shears to slash the trampoline sides, and then started with the spray paint on the furniture. I only got the full story out of her in fits and starts last night, and I was waiting for her to have her morning nap before ringing you to tell you, but I think you guessed how she is, didn't you?'

Matt nodded. 'I did. But she didn't show there was a problem the first time I saw her. I wouldn't have guessed, not then...'

'I'm so sorry to hear this, Paul.' Steve spoke quietly. 'So this is why the shed has a new padlock. You're minimising danger to her, more than anything.'

'It's why I've had the new gate installed. There's been a tendency for her to wander off, which is a new development, so I'm hoping the freshness of the garden with its fencing, the lawn repaired and the furniture restored will create a welcoming environment for her. When you arrived, she was already at the gate, wasn't she? It's scary. Luckily I have family help, and even the grandkids are aware Nanny needs to be watched carefully. I honestly never thought about it being her, I just assumed vandals had done it. God forgive me, I even thought it was the feller across the road whose car she hit.' Paul stared into his coffee. 'It's a bleak future, but we'll cope. This behaviour is a new escalation, and a sudden one with no warning she was changing. A month ago she would have been horrified at the thought she would deteriorate into this sort of activity, but she is different. She's sleeping more, and I know one day I'll have to move her to live away to keep her safe, but that day isn't here yet, thank God.'

'There'll be no invoice from Forrester's,' Matt said. 'We've not actually done very much, to be honest, because we needed the garden work to finish before we could look at anything.'

'Last night she was almost the old Anna. She asked questions about the garden, said the new lawn looked lovely, and then asked if it needed watering. I said the lads would advise us on that, and she said she watered it last time with water out of the spray pump. I've got one of those fancy weedkiller canisters that you have to pump. She kept drifting in and out of lucidity, but eventually I got the full picture. She'd smartened up our furniture with a new coat of paint. I'd got three or four old rattle cans of spray paint from jobs over the years, and she used those to give it a new lease of life. We'd only had it since the beginning of the summer, that furniture. We talked for a couple of hours, and slowly it all fell into place. The security I had put in to prevent anybody else trashing our garden will keep Anna safe and at home, not wandering the streets and unable to remember where she lives. I know that point will come, but for now I can keep her safe.' He slumped into his chair. 'It's all a bloody nightmare.'

'I can't even begin to imagine,' Matt said. 'You have good medical help?'

'The best. I have an appointment for Anna tomorrow in view of this sudden escalation – maybe she needs her medication changing or something. I don't know. But there is a change within her so somebody needs to know about it. Thank you for listening and for understanding. I kind of feel I got you here under false pretences, but I honestly had no idea. After she'd done all the damage, she calmly came back to bed. I felt her get back under the covers and snuggle up to me. She was icy cold, but it never occurred to me it was because she'd been outside. I miss her so much, the real Anna.'

And he wiped the tears that suddenly were on his cheeks.

19

TUESDAY, 1 NOVEMBER

Carol listened to Matt and Steve telling the story of Paul and Anna Bancroft, then sighed. 'It's such a cruel illness,' she said. 'I've never experienced anyone with it, but it's such a protracted way to lose someone, and really you've actually lost them from the first moment there are any symptoms.'

'Well, the outcome is that we're simply cancelling the job. We did very little beyond visiting the house, and even that was on the gardening side of things, so it's down to Steve.'

Steve gave a slight nod. 'And our invoice to him, although substantial because of the fencing and the work that was initially booked in before the damage was discovered, will reflect a degree of sympathy in the charges.'

'I'll get the Forrester/Bancroft file closed and the names are already in WATSON. We'll leave them there, because it was an active investigation for a short time. I've reached 2019 in adding names, but still no sign of a Susan Hunter. I'm starting to think Dave met her well outside of the work environment, so her name wouldn't have cropped up in anything. And according to what you've told me, by 2019 she was already living in Australia.

I'm taking a lunch break today, going to nip over to the cemetery and take my friends a bunch of flowers. See if anybody else has done so. You took chrysanths, you said?'

'We did. Hopefully they'll still be okay. You remember where they are, your friends?'

She smiled. 'I've been two or three times since the funeral. I really did count both of them as friends. Intelligent men are hard to come by.'

'Hey!'

'Present company excepted, of course.' She grinned at both of them. 'So, I've been here a week. How am I doing?'

'Crap.'

'Garbage.'

'That's what I thought. As I said, intelligent men are hard to come by. You need me for anything else? Some of us have a database to build.'

Carol stood, gathered up her notebook and pen and looked at them both. In response, they waved dismissive hands, and she creased with laughter. 'Butterfly buns in five minutes. Make yourselves coffees, I'll do my own when I want one.'

As she closed the door gently, Matt looked at Steve. 'Intelligent men are hard to come by?'

'So she says. She could be right. We didn't spot the issue with Anna Bancroft, did we?'

'Maybe we would have if we'd ever known anybody with dementia or Alzheimer's, but I don't believe we've ever come across it before.' Matt sighed. 'It was pretty clear when she was standing by the gate this morning. She looked... dazed, I think is the word. And there was a touch of panic when he came out to find her. It's kind of rattled me. It's a relentless sort of illness, isn't it? No cure, can only get worse, and when the day comes when she doesn't know him, he'll give in.'

Steve walked by Matt's desk and through into the kitchen. 'I'll get the coffees. Never could resist a butterfly bun.'

* * *

Carol parked her car close by the graves, and sat for a few moments. Two good men. Gone far too early, still had such a lot of life to give. She wondered briefly how things would have panned out for Dave, had he still been around and with the return of Susan Hunter. Would they have rekindled what had clearly been a romance, albeit a secret one, or would he have moved on? She suspected the elusive Susan hadn't, but that was just a feeling. She wondered if the twinkle that was always in Dave's eyes would have still been twinkling for the woman who said they had been together, despite there being nothing to confirm or deny it.

She reached across and picked up the two bunches of large daisies that she knew would give off a splash of white in the darkness of the night, and opened the car door.

Knowing there were flowers already on the graves, she had brought along a couple of large jars she had used for pickling onions in that previous life when she'd prepared home-cooked food for the two of them. Now she bought her pickled onions from a shop, with no guilty feelings whatsoever.

She stood between the two graves.

'Hiya, you two. No scones today, but I've brought you some flowers.' She laid both bunches on Dave's grave, then walked across to put water in the two pickling jars.

The large daisies did indeed glow in the dimness of the grey afternoon light, and she smiled at the thought of how eerie they would look at midnight, with just the moon's glow to reflect off their petals, making them stand out.

'So, Dave Forrester,' she said. 'Tell me about Susan Hunter. Was it really a romantic liaison as she's claiming? Or was she somebody you failed to get arrested? Come on, pal, you've got us all concerned about this, and we can't find anything about her. And has she actually been to visit you and Johnny? She called asking where your graves are, said she wanted to bring flowers, but she's not been yet. You think she's perhaps saving to buy you a huge bunch of red roses? If there's any way you can communicate from the other side, now might be a good time to do it. I'm waiting...'

She began to place the flowers in the jars, and wished she'd brought an extra bunch to take home with her. They were truly pretty blooms. Once she had them standing in the jars, she wedged them in place on the two graves.

'I miss you two,' she said, continuing her conversation. 'And I'm working on all the cases you've ever had, putting everybody, clients and rogues, onto one database. But Susan Hunter isn't anywhere, so far. So come on, enlighten me.'

There was absolute silence. It did occur to her that it was for the best that there was silence; she would probably have died herself if there had been some form of response.

She placed a hand on Dave's headstone and levered herself upright, aware of twinges in her back and her knees as she did so. Getting older wasn't suiting her at all.

She blew a kiss to both headstones, and returned to her car, dashing away the odd tear that escaped her eyes.

* * *

Phil Newton was feeling frustrated. He had half hoped they would get some answers by bringing Aaron Peters and George Jackson in; confronting them with evidence of their lies should have resulted in their falling apart, crying for their mother and confessing to murder. It hadn't gone that way at all, and they had merely confessed to going to Gleadless, and then going home without even seeing Elise Langton, beyond her outline in the doorway of her home.

The answers they hoped to get had proved to be even more questions.

He had now returned to his desk, woken up his computer, and was rereading every report that had been uploaded by other team members and the forensics cohort. He checked the post-mortem results, wondering just what the implement had been that had caused the death of Elise. There were fragments of wood in the wound, so considerable force had been used for that to happen. It was attested that a baseball bat, with a rounded end, was not believed to be the weapon, but possibly a mallet, although this would only be confirmed if the actual murder weapon was found. The wooden fragments could be matched to it, with the indentation in Elise Langton's head checked for ratification.

He sighed. Surely Elise would have spotted a mallet in her assailant's hand? Then he remembered the lads saying the woman had worn a hoodie. What if it had been the sort that didn't have a zip, the type that went over the head and had a kangaroo pouch along the front? That would hide a mallet easily.

Elise would have had no idea what was to come, and she obviously had known the woman, because after the burglary she was on full alert. She wouldn't have allowed a stranger in, and definitely not at that time of night.

Phil reached for a piece of scrap paper and wrote *Elise's friends?* on it. He reckoned he could rule out neighbours – then ruled them straight back in because the lads said the woman had approached Elise's house in the same way that they had, in a direct line through the roadside tree area. This prevented having to pass any CCTV cameras pointing towards the little service road of ten houses. A neighbour would know this...

He looked around to see who was in, and called Ian and Kevin over. He explained his thoughts, and asked them to revisit the entire row of neighbours' houses, and make sure they spoke to every female over the age of eighteen. He wanted an accurate explanation of each resident's location for that evening at around half past nine and it would have to hold up to scrutiny. He was still smarting from not confirming the whereabouts of the burglarising duo fully. Every alibi would be double checked from now on.

Ian and Kevin left immediately, and Phil rang Rick.

'Hi, Rick. DC Newton here. You okay?'

'No,' was the short, sharp answer. Phil could sense the stress in the man's voice. 'Skye can't and won't accept her mummy isn't coming to see her any more, and she's just made it very clear she doesn't want Jenna instead.' He sighed. 'I know it will all take time, but at the moment it's like World War III here. Daniel has understood things have changed, and tries to make Skye understand, but it's not happening yet.'

'They're good kids, Rick. My boss took a proper shine to the little lass. Just have patience, it's only been a week.'

'You have something to tell me? An arrest?'

'No. We've had the two young lads in again just to go over what they were doing on the night of the murder, but they're in the clear for that. I just thought I'd give you a ring and ask about friends of your wife.'

Rick gave a short bark of laughter. 'She didn't really have friends. She liked her own company, and was never happier than when it was just her and the kids. She had acquaintances, other mums at school, but I don't think she would have even known where they live. They chatted while they waited for the kids to come out, but then she was back to her normal life. She was fairly close to Pippa, Jack's wife, but even that wasn't the sort of relationship where she would ring her just to have a chat. It was simply sisters-in-law, not friends who she would talk to about problems and worries.'

Again he sighed. 'It was the loneliness in my own life that was the real reason behind me seeing Jenna, but I'd give anything for that loneliness with Elise again.'

'Not working with Jenna then?' Phil asked, encouraging him to keep talking.

'It has to work now.' It was a short, pithy response. 'I can't bring up the kids on my own and manage the job I do. I work awkward hours, and it's only because I've been given bereavement leave that I'm coping at the moment. But I miss her, my Elise. I missed her as soon as she threw me out, but that lady wasn't for turning. She wouldn't listen to any apologies, any reasons, she just said I had to go, and we'd come to an arrangement about the children. So, really, in answer to your original question, DC Newton, I think the closest female person to her was Pippa Mitchell, and she'll probably not be able to tell you much more than I can, because simply none of us knew Elise all that well. Elise wouldn't allow it.'

20

TUESDAY, 1 NOVEMBER

Susan Hunter felt a surge of anger that seemed to start in her toes and work its way up her entire body, and it was all directed at the woman standing between the two headstones, obviously chatting to the occupants of the graves, even having a laugh with them.

She recognised her, although had no idea who she was, beyond her being the woman in the café at the antiques centre. Susan decided not to leave the safety of her car, but just to wait and see what happened – she could hardly go and make her first visit to Dave Forrester while another woman was placing flowers on his grave. She took a quick glance at her petrol gauge, saw there was almost half a tankful, and decided she would follow the woman and find out who she was. Maybe she was the reason Dave hadn't been particularly bothered when she had broken the news that she had to go to live in Australia. This woman seemed to care about him, it was a proper conversation she was having with two dead people.

* * *

Carol spotted the car with the woman in it as she walked back to get in her own car. And she knew. Susan Hunter. Even from the distance of a hundred yards or so, she knew.

She sat for a moment in her own car, wondering what to do. She had options. She could walk down to Susan and say hi, she could drive past and wave to show she knew who she was, or she could simply drive away and pretend she hadn't recognised her.

She went with that thought, and decided to simply drive away. She drove by Susan's car, a small white Peugeot, and continued down the long drive towards the cemetery exit, indicating to turn left as she passed through the cemetery gates.

She checked both ways, glanced in her rear-view mirror, and shivered as she saw the white Peugeot immediately behind her also indicating to turn left. She tried to read the number plate but couldn't see it. It was blocked by the rear end of her own car.

As she reached the Meadowhead roundabout she realised the little car had disappeared from her mirror, and she breathed a sigh of relief. Maybe she had been mistaken... but as she headed off up Bochum Parkway, she confirmed the Peugeot was still behind her, with three cars in between them.

She connected to the office, hoping Matt would be there.

'I think Susan Hunter is following me,' she said.

'Okay.' He paused for a moment. 'Come here, don't go home. It's probably better she doesn't know where you live, and there's absolutely no reason why you shouldn't just come here and put your car on the front. I'll go and stand outside as if I'm doing something important, and wait for your arrival. Where are you?'

'Just approaching the island at Norton. I'll be two minutes at the most.'

'I'll be here.'

They disconnected, and Matt grabbed his jacket and went outside, waiting for Carol's safe arrival. He saw her car with its left indicator flashing, and he waved at it. She pulled onto the parking area and stopped.

The Peugeot, still three cars behind Carol's car, slowed and indicated, then the indicator was cancelled and the little car sped up and carried on along White Lane.

'Thank you,' Carol said as they stood watching Susan Hunter disappear into the distance. 'I wasn't sure what to do. I didn't feel threatened, but I didn't want her to know where I worked either. I thought it would be handy if she didn't know me, but I guess we've blown that one, now.'

'I guess so,' Matt replied, smiling at her frustrated face. 'She followed you all the way from Hutcliffe cemetery?'

'She did. I recognised her when she was parked, while I was still chatting to Dave and Johnny. But I'll be honest, I only recognised her because we expected her to be there. It was a guess recognition thing. I realised I was correct when I drove past her, but then she was right behind me when I reached the cemetery gates. She's been within three cars of me all the way back to Gleadless. She's clearly decided not to follow me onto the parking area, but she'll be putting two and two together now, won't she? And I didn't get the number plate. Did you?'

Matt shook his head. 'No, it all happened too fast. I didn't manage to see any part of it.'

* * *

Susan stopped outside her home only three minutes later, and she sat for a short while pondering what the discovery meant for her. That damn woman clearly wasn't following her – with very few spaces and certainly no empty tables, she had chosen to go and sit at her table in the café, so that was pure coincidence.

But to be at the cemetery before her on the day she'd finally decided to go and visit the graves was damned annoying. And now it seemed she had a connection with the Forrester Agency. Could she be the invisible receptionist? She was obviously a friend of Dave's, as she had taken flowers to his grave.

She shook her head in frustration and got out of the car. Maybe the blasted woman had been the receptionist for some time, and maybe more than a receptionist to her Dave. Maybe that was why his emails had dried up towards the end.

She headed indoors, and went straight to the room she had decided would be her office. She sat down with a thud on the kitchen chair she was temporarily having to use until she found just the right antique wheeled chair along with some money to buy it, and leaned her head on her crossed arms.

Something wasn't right. Her plans had been to link up with Dave's family, to explain how close they had been, how much she had loved him, and her plans for becoming a part of the bigger Forrester family. Okay, they hadn't quite reached anything like that, but she had always known they would become a couple, she would say.

She remembered a conversation with Dave where she had said once Nicola had died she would return to be with him, and it also brought to mind the look of shock on his face. Maybe it had seemed a little blunt... but now the reason to rekindle the alliance with the business was urgent.

Nicola had taken longer to die than anyone could have foretold, and so it had meant being apart for five years, but surely the death of Dave Forrester didn't have to spoil her plans to be a part of his family? She needed access to that office as much as she needed to join that family, though of course, if it became necessary, she could forget about them once she had achieved her aim.

And this bloody woman, who'd already annoyed her by

having the last blueberry scone in the café, seemed now to be part of some conspiracy to keep her away from her targets.

She had liked Matt Forrester – had seen much of his dad in him – and as he spoke, she'd thought how that voice could have been coming out of Dave's mouth. The flatness of the Yorkshire dialect had been very evident in Matt, just as it had been in Dave, and she knew she would make a good substitute mother for him if she could only get to know him and Hermia better.

And she would certainly be a wonderful grandmother to little Harry. And then, maybe, one day, she wouldn't have financial worries any more. She would be able to buy things the moment she saw them, instead of having to come home, negotiate a loan, and then go back to see if the item was still there.

She lifted her head and looked at the bureau, a smile on her face. It had been worth getting a credit card, now all she had to do was find a way to clear the balance. And she had a way: become a valued member of the Forrester family, valued enough for her to get into that office and be trusted to be left on her own for a while.

* * *

It was around an hour later when Matt asked Carol to join him and Steve in his office. He poured them all a coffee, and Steve started the meeting by passing the folder of photographs that would be collected that afternoon by Tina Thornton as she finished work.

'Just have a quick flip through this, will you, Carol. Make sure there's no typos or anything.'

She grinned. 'You don't mean typos, you mean spelling mistakes. Of course I'll check it. What time do you need it for?'

'She's calling around half past four.'

'No problem.' She sipped at her drink and waited for the next issue to be raised by Matt, which she suspected would be the telling of her visit to the cemetery during her lunch break. Before she could begin, there was a tap at Matt's window. Carol rose to release the security lock. She didn't need to see identity proof for Karen Nelson.

Matt headed back to the kitchen to make a fourth coffee, and Karen sat between Steve and Carol.

She saw the report that Steve had produced, and leaned over it. 'Surveillance?' she asked.

'Yes. Bit boring. They had two hours of sex, and I had two hours of sitting in my car waiting for them to come out of the hotel. But I got the goods.'

He flicked over the page and showed her the photograph of the two people leaving the Travelodge, and she gasped. 'Is there one that shows her face a bit closer?'

Steve turned over to the next set of photographs, and Karen laughed.

'My God,' Karen said. 'Did you have to find out who she is? Or did the wife just want proof of infidelity?'

'The client just wanted proof, but we have a number plate for the woman's car, and if we'd needed it we were going to buy you a bouquet of roses and ask for a favour. You know her?'

'Oh, I definitely know her. She's obviously decided Anthony Dawson wasn't the man for her, so has moved on. This is Diana Marshall, wife of Liam Marshall of Marshall's transport, and mother of Niall Marshall, killer of Anthony Dawson. She's also the bit on the side of the late Anthony Dawson.'

Steve laughed. 'I remember it all now, but I'd never met her so didn't have any recognition. She gets about a bit then. Obviously doesn't rate Liam Marshall. Before I hand this report over to Tina, I'll add this information. She's bound to give us a five-star review then.'

'She was so in love with Dawson. It was quite pathetic, really, because on the night he was killed, he kicked her out, sent her back to her husband. Liam took her back, and I thought they seemed okay, standing by Niall and all that gumph.' Karen grinned as she took the coffee from Matt. 'So do I still qualify for my bouquet of flowers?'

'I would say so,' Carol jumped in quickly. 'We're lucky you called in.'

Karen held a thumb up towards Carol, and sipped at her drink. 'And I only called in for a coffee. I've only a spare five minutes anyway, so if you're having a meeting I'll be on my way as soon as I've drunk this.'

'There's no rush. We're having a chat about Susan Hunter. She's turned into a bit of a puzzle, although I'm not sure she's doing anything wrong. Just a bit strange.'

Matt continued to talk, telling the whole story, with Carol jumping in if he missed anything. The other two remained silent, listening intently.

Finally they all leaned back. 'You're right,' Steve said. 'It is a bit of a puzzle. So what do we do next?'

21

TUESDAY, 1 NOVEMBER

Phil Newton clattered down the stairs, just missing his boss by one minute. It didn't matter – he'd left her a note to say he was off to the George at Hathersage for a pint. In brackets he'd written shandy.

He didn't rush on the drive out to the Derbyshire village – nobody in their right mind would hurry through the Peak District, and he dropped down the long road from Surprise View into the heart of the village, and then into the pub car park. He sat for a moment just taking in the peace of the late afternoon, knowing it would be dark for his journey home. Summer was well and truly over, and autumn in the throes of becoming winter. The temperature was dropping, and as he got out of the car he zipped up his jacket. He didn't intend being in the pub long, just needed to double check the alibi of Rick Langton and Jenna Glaves before putting that little issue to rest. He'd taken a liking to Rick, although couldn't say he felt the same about Jenna. She seemed a little bit clingy; Rick was hers and she intended it staying that way. It must have been a godsend when the children arrived to stay with them on a permanent basis. Now she could really stake her claim.

Phil locked his car and walked across the car park and in through the front doors of the pub. Inside, the warmth was welcoming and he undid the jacket he'd just zipped up. He sat on a bar stool, and explained to the smiling man who came over to him that he didn't require a table, just a pint of shandy.

The bartender obliged, and placed the pint glass on a beer mat before turning to attend to another customer.

Phil watched him, waiting until he had finished serving, then held up a hand. The man returned to him, and he held out his warrant card.

'DC Phil Newton,' he said, 'just information gathering on a murder investigation. Would you have been on duty on the evening of Tuesday, 26 October? Last Tuesday?' He looked at the name on the man's badge. 'Vinnie?'

The bartender nodded. 'Vinnie Hancock. Somebody rang me and asked about a customer for that night, checking he was here with his girlfriend. He definitely was.'

'Thank you for your cooperation. I'm here purely to double check to put my mind at rest. If I show you pictures of the two people, Rick Langton and Jenna Glaves, can you just say yes or no to them? That's all I need.'

'Sure. No problem. Give me a minute to serve this chap and I'll be back.' He moved to the other end of the bar and Phil brought his pictures up on his phone, clicking on the screenshots he had taken of Rick and Jenna from their Facebook accounts.

He sipped at his drink while he waited, looking around. He'd never been inside the pub before, but had driven past it many times in his life. He'd have to bring Lauren out here for a meal, she'd really enjoy it. She needed some support and love at the moment, not having come to terms at all with losing her mother just a month earlier.

He watched as Vinnie finished what had proved to be a large, complex order, then waited until he returned to him.

'Sorry about that. The ladies all wanted convoluted drinks,' he said. 'Now, what can I do for you?'

'Is this the man who was here last Tuesday evening?' Phil held out his phone.

'Unless he's got a twin, that was definitely him.'

Phil swiped to the next picture and held his phone out once again. This time Vinnie took it off him, and looked closely at it. Then he lifted his head and spoke quietly. 'Unless she's cut all this long blonde hair off and dyed it red, this is definitely not who he brought to this pub last Tuesday.'

Phil wanted to punch the air. 'You're sure?'

'Absolutely sure. The woman who came with that feller looked nothing like this. This one looks quite skinny for a start.'

Phil's mind drifted to his last sight of Jenna as she had taken Skye out of the door. Definitely skinny. 'And the one he came here with wasn't skinny?'

Vinnie made a gesture with his hands, indicating his chest. 'Well-endowed,' he said. 'Not fat, but... comfortable. Short hair-cut, deep red. Pretty. They chatted all night, left ten-thirty-ish. She called him Ricky, though, not Rick. I noticed because it reminded me of *Eastenders* and Bianca always shouting Ricky.'

'Are all bartenders like you? Noticing every little detail?' Phil asked, grinning at the younger man.

'Pretty much. No point working behind a bar if you don't take an interest in the customers.'

'You get a break?'

Vinnie laughed. 'No. I finish at eleven, earlier if all our dining tables are clear.'

'And you were definitely still here when Rick Langton and his dining partner left around ten-thirty last week?'

'I was.'

'I'm going to need a statement from you. You work Wednesdays?'

'I do. I'm here for the two till eight shift tomorrow, but if you come about one o'clock, we can do it then. Does that help?'

Phil reached across and shook his hand. 'That's fine. I'll finish this off,' he waved his glass around, 'and leave you to it. See you tomorrow.'

He dropped down from the bar stool, and moved to a small table, then sat and stared at the shandy – half still remained in his glass – thinking. Nobody had actually interviewed the blonde-haired Jenna Glaves, they had taken Rick's word that he was there with his girlfriend at the George, and the George had confirmed he was. Nobody had realised that the phrase 'girl-friend' to Rick Langton could mean any female in the universe. Surely he must know they would eventually put two and two together? Phil was so relieved he'd decided to double check the alibi – he knew that without the fiasco at the boxing gym and the lies of the two boys, he wouldn't have rechecked this issue until they were at desperation point.

He finished his drink, waved a hand towards Vinnie, and left by the same door, heading towards his car. It flashed cheery lights as he remotely unlocked it, glowing brightly in the darkness of the night. There was only a tiny sliver of a moon, and it was quiet.

He slid into the driver's seat, and thought about ringing Karen to tell her things now seemed very different, but after checking the time he decided they would probably be eating. It could wait until he got home. On top of that, his Lauren needed him right now, to help her get through the days and nights of grief.

He drove to the edge of the car park and checked the road. He could see car lights in the far distance to his right, so he pulled out and turned left, climbing the hill out of Hathersage and heading back towards Sheffield. He needed his heater to warm up, he thought, that shandy had been pretty cold.

The car he'd spotted seemed to be getting closer and closer at a fast pace, its headlights on at full to compensate for the complete lack of street lighting on this well-used Derbyshire road. He was almost blinded by the full headlights, and dropped the angle of his interior mirror.

He put his foot down on the accelerator, thinking it might be better if he got round the ninety-degree bend at Surprise View before the car caught up to him, just in case the driver wasn't aware of the danger at that point. He knew he would feel a sense of relief once he was round that bend and the car behind him could overtake him in comparative safety on the wider road.

He was twenty-five metres from the safety of the bend, when another car came towards him on his side of the road. It too had its main beam on, and he pulled a hand in front of his eyes as he tried to see. Without realising what was happening, he swung to the right, as he had nowhere to go to his left. His car shot across the road, and the last sound that Phil Newton ever heard was the awful crunch of metal hitting the most famous dry-stone wall of Derbyshire, demolishing it and causing his car to tumble down the hillside just as many cars before had done over many years.

The car that had caused the problem, the one holding a young couple with their one-year-old daughter in a child seat, smashed into the bank of grass and trees and overturned, leaving only one of them alive.

The vehicle that had been speeding up to Phil on the drive

up the road, driven by an elderly lady who didn't like driving in the dark, was the one that managed to stop, and emergency services were called. Her husband in the passenger seat was struggling to breathe, and she prayed help would come quickly.

* * *

It took almost half an hour to reach Phil, but then the information was passed to the teams still at the top that there was no longer an emergency situation. There was no pulse to be found. The smashed car windows gave them access to him, and they could reach his wallet in the inside pocket of his jacket, where they also found his warrant card.

The road was closed at Fox House and also in the village of Hathersage. Everybody affected by the closures guessed it was another idiot taking the Surprise View bend too fast, but nobody guessed how bad it really was.

The driver and his girlfriend, from the Focus that had taken the bend on the wrong side of the road, were dead. Their child survived with minimal injuries.

The lady driving the car was shaken by the impact as she had collided with the car that had caused all the damage, but her husband died from a heart attack before the ambulance could get to them. Four people dead, two injured.

* * *

Karen received the news within ten minutes of Phil's warrant card having been found. Matt drove them over there in the Land Rover. She knew she wouldn't be safe to drive.

The roadblock officers they encountered at Fox House checked her own warrant card and ushered them through, expressing their condolences when she said the deceased constable was one of hers.

The scene was chaotic; blue flashing lights from emergency and police vehicles lit up the night sky. The elderly lady refused to leave her husband, remaining by his side on the road as the paramedics tried to restart a heart that would never beat again, before pronouncing time of death. She had blood running from her head, but said she would get treatment later, for now she had a husband to look after.

The child had been whisked away in the first ambulance to leave, and was on its way to the Children's Hospital, although Karen felt reassured by the fact that it was simply a precaution; the little girl seemed to have not been injured. Her grandparents, who had been on the phone with the child's mother at the moment of impact, would be meeting her at the hospital. That mobile phone had pealed out repeatedly until somebody answered it, and the news had to be conveyed to them in the worst way possible.

Karen had rung Ray, and he joined her and Matt within quarter of an hour, his face ashen. He pulled his boss into his arms and hugged her.

'I don't give a shit if this isn't allowed,' he whispered. 'I'm doing it.'

She rested her head on his shoulder, tears finally coming. 'It's allowed,' she said, 'it's allowed.'

22

TUESDAY, 1 NOVEMBER

Superintendent Brian Davies rang the bell of the semi-detached house, focusing on some pretty pink flowers growing by the door, clearly a winter-flowering variety as November was way beyond summer flowers, and waited patiently yet nervously. This was always the hardest part of a policeman's life, and one, as superintendent, he had to do this time. He couldn't fob this one off to the likes of Karen Nelson. If a serving police officer died, it had to be him.

A teenage boy opened the door, peering out.

'Oh,' he said. 'You're not Dad. Thought he'd forgotten his key again.' He turned his head and called for his mum.

Lauren Newton came down the hall and stood in front of him. 'I'm sorry, Superintendent Davis. If it's Phil you're after, he's not home yet. Shouldn't be long, though, he rang about an hour or so ago to tell me he was on his way.'

'Can I come in, Mrs Newton?'

And she knew.

* * *

Karen, Matt and Ray waited until the fire service people brought Phil up from the gorge below. His car was embedded in the trees upside down, and when the stretcher reached the top, Karen ran across the road to where he lay.

He was zipped into a body bag.

'Phil,' she said simply, touching his chest, then turned away, unable to hold back the anguish she felt. Matt pulled her to him and held her, letting her cry for as long as she needed to.

The accident investigation people reassured her she would get a copy of their report, but gave her the gist of what they had discovered even at this early stage. The road would probably be closed for at least another twelve hours, possibly longer, but from the skid marks, they could tell that the Focus had come around the bend at speed, and had cut the corner, ending up on the wrong side of the road just as the car now down in the gorge had reached that point. The vehicle behind DC Newton's car had been a little too close, but not dangerously so. The lady had tried to swerve, shown by the marks on the road surface, but the oncoming car hit her.

Vehicles were now arriving to move the damaged cars, in order to get a larger vehicle in position to winch up the one that was down in the gorge. Phil's body was taken away, and Ray and Karen agreed to meet up at Phil and Lauren's home. She had already spoken to a clearly upset Brian Davis, who said Lauren's sister had just joined her, so she wasn't on her own.

* * *

Lauren was nursing a cup of tea, having turned down a brandy. She looked up at her visitors, and stood.

'Karen...' she said, and burst into tears yet again. Her sister,

Maggie, took the cup from her and handed her the box of tissues.

'God, Lauren, I don't know what to say.' Karen seemed to crumple, and Matt led her to a chair.

'Can I make anybody a drink?' he said, looking around the room. Phil's fourteen-year-old twins were there, sitting quietly side by side on the sofa, and Maggie was hovering, unable to comfort anyone as she was obviously distraught herself. Phil had been loved.

'I've just made tea,' Maggie said. 'A potful. Can I offer anybody one?'

They all shook their heads, knowing this family wanted to be alone to grieve. They had done too many death notifications, knew the drill.

'Thank you for the offer,' Karen said, 'but we're not here to stay. I just needed to be with you for a few minutes, to let you know we're hurting as well. Phil was a close friend, not just a colleague, and I don't know how I'll manage without him.' She dabbed at her eyes and blew her nose. 'I'll be in work by seven, so you can contact me about anything.' She stood. 'Anything, Lauren.'

Karen moved to Matt's side, grateful for the comfort of this man she loved, and knowing he was hurting as well. Phil had been in his team when he had been a DI. She briefly wondered if DI Armitage had been informed by Brian Davis, guessing he would have. He certainly hadn't contacted her to see if she needed support. She dismissed him from her mind – he really wasn't worth any concern.

Lauren and Maggie escorted them to the door, and Karen gave both women a hug.

'The kids need you,' she whispered. 'They look so lost.'

Lauren nodded. 'I know. They haven't said anything, just

taking comfort from sitting on Dad's sofa, I think. That's the sofa he regularly falls asleep on – fell.' She corrected her words.

'I'll ring you tomorrow,' Karen said, and followed Matt to the car. As they drove off, Ray continued to sit in his car, his face a picture of misery.

* * *

It was almost midnight by the time Karen and Matt arrived home. Hermia and Steve were waiting for them.

'You're okay?' Hermia asked, hugging them both.

Matt gave a brief nod. 'Nightmare of a scene. There are four dead, a child in hospital and an elderly lady refusing to go get checked out because she's not leaving her dead husband. His heart gave out. We came away because it's not Karen's case, it's a Derbyshire one. We need them to complete their investigations and reach the truth, but I think it's all pretty clear what happened.'

He stood for a moment, lost. His friend and ex-colleague Phil was dead at forty; it didn't bear thinking about.

'Why was Phil out there?'

'He left a note on my desk telling me he was double-checking the alibi for Rick Langton and Jenna Glaves. It didn't sit well with him that we had taken the word of the gym owners but not checked for ourselves that what the two lads had said was the truth. And now, him doing his job to the best of his ability has resulted in his death. It's going to be a rough day tomorrow.' Karen ran her fingers through her hair. 'So bloody unfair.'

Steve put his arm around Hermia. 'Come on then wife-to-be, let's get home and leave these two to come round from this. We just wanted to be here for you both, make sure you were okay,' he explained.

'And thank you for that. Have you fed Oliver?'

'We have. He disappeared through the cat flap just before you arrived, so heaven knows where he is now.'

Matt smiled. 'He does seem to come and go at will these days. You suppose he's got a girlfriend?'

'It's more likely somebody else is feeding him as well as us. He's certainly a big cat these days,' Hermia said. 'Give us a shout if you need us.' She slipped on her jacket.

'Hang on a minute.' Matt went through to the lounge and returned carrying a laptop bag. 'When you've got a spare minute, Herms, can you have a quick look through this and see if you can find any reference to a Susan Hunter? It might even be in something Dad deleted, but I'm sure you're the person to ask.'

'Matt Forrester! There's around ten years of work on this laptop. It might take me longer than a minute.'

Steve took the bag from Matt. 'We paying her?'

Hermia's head lifted. 'You couldn't afford me. I'd best do it gratis.'

'You're a star, sis,' Matt said, and bent to kiss her cheek. 'And thanks for waiting for us. I feel a bit calmer now.'

'Who's Susan Hunter?' Hermia asked, after they'd left.

'She says she's an ex of your dad. We just need to check her out because we don't know her, and in the stuff back at the office she doesn't get any sort of mention. She says she's been in Australia for five years looking after her terminally ill daughter, and has just returned to Sheffield because her daughter has now died.'

'He never mentioned anyone called Susan to me, but I'll see what I can do. I'll ring in tomorrow and tell them I'm working from home.'

'Oh, good,' Steve replied. 'The university is paying you then? So we don't need to?'

'As if you'd pay me anyway.' She laughed. 'I'm just a skivvy for this company. Are you free on Saturday?'

'Could be.' He spoke cautiously. The last time he'd confessed to being free for a day, he'd ended up shopping in Sheffield city centre, not a pleasant thing to do in these current drug-infested times.

'Try to be. We need to go wedding venue shopping.'

'Well, that's a relief. For a minute I thought you were going to insist on "shopping" shopping, which isn't the same thing at all.'

* * *

Lauren Newton made the twins beans on toast because she knew they hadn't been fed. Both of them said they didn't want anything, but she pulled mother's rights and handed a plate to each. After ten minutes of chasing beans around the plate, they both emptied their dishes into the kitchen bin and headed upstairs. They needed alone time, and brother and sister shared a hug as they left each other on the landing to go to their own rooms.

Lauren and Maggie sat side by side in the lounge on Phil's sofa, neither one speaking initially. But then Maggie broke the silence.

'I'll stay over tonight.' She held up a hand as she saw Lauren's mouth open. 'No arguing, Lauren, I've already messaged to tell the family they'll have to sort themselves out until I come home. They've all sent their love, and told me to take as long as we need. And we'll do that. I'll know when you're ready to be alone, but I think you might have to identify Phil tomorrow, and I intend being with you all the way.'

'Oh, God, I haven't even thought of that. Will they expect me to do it? I thought probably Karen would do it, as she was his boss.'

'I'm pretty sure it has to be close family. I may be wrong but don't count on it.' She hesitated for a moment. 'This seems so unfair. Just as you were becoming settled financially and closer as a couple, this happens and takes Phil away from you. Did they say it had happened because of his job?'

'No, that superintendent didn't really say much, except how sorry he was, but he offered no real explanation for it. I suppose we'll find out more when the experts have checked the scene, but Phil was a police-trained driver...'

'Don't think about it, love, wait till we know more. You keeping the kids at home tomorrow?'

'I think so, just for one day. It gives me time to notify the school, make sure they're cared for. This is such a bloody mess, Mags, and I haven't a clue what I'm supposed to do about it, or how to handle what happens next.'

23

WEDNESDAY, 2 NOVEMBER

There had been a pall over the station when Karen arrived for work. She had deliberately got there early – just after half past six – but several of her team were already there, speaking in hushed voices, and showing nothing of the jokey side that usually started their days.

They all stood as she walked through the door of the briefing room, and she felt startled. They didn't normally stand as she entered. She would have put an immediate stop to this. But not today. Today she knew it wasn't for her, it was for Phil.

By seven, everybody had arrived; she stood facing them, with no idea how to get through the next few minutes without crying.

'Good morning, everybody,' she began, and there were several murmurings in response. 'I know you're all aware, but last night we lost Phil Newton to what appears to be a road traffic accident. Derbyshire police are in charge, and will let us have copies of all reports as soon as they have completed their work. I went out there to Surprise View as soon as I heard, and I also visited Lauren and their twins last night. Superintendent

Davis had already been to make the death notification, but I went on behalf of all of us.'

She stopped speaking for a moment, and tried to bring herself under control as images of the twins settled inside her brain.

'Does she need anything?' a voice asked from the back of the room.

'No, she's a very capable lady, and she has her sister with her, who came immediately after Superintendent Davis told her the news. I am expecting Lauren to be asked to go to Chesterfield today to identify Phil's remains, but I want to make sure we take her. Support her all the way. It's going to be a horrible time for all the family, and I want her to know we have her back. Jaime? Can you do it?'

A hand waved, indicating Jaime was listening and responding. 'I can, boss. I'll sort out with the morgue when they can accommodate her, and then I'll pop round to see her.' There was a definite catch in Jaime's voice.

* * *

Matt was deep in thought. He too had arrived for work early, not because he needed to, but because he wanted to. He wanted to think. They had left the cottage at the same time, with Karen turning right at the end of the drive, and him turning left to head over to Gleadless. It was a short journey and he arrived just before seven. He knew it wouldn't be long before Carol was in, because she would be able to see his car; she would want to know what was wrong.

He turned up the heating a little, and made himself a pot of coffee, before pulling out the file on Wesley Thornton. Steve had done a cracking job on the investigation, and had caught

Thornton almost with his pants down, so to speak. However, naming the woman in the case had put a slightly different slant on it, and he hadn't been surprised when Tina Thornton had asked if they had managed to uncover the identity of the woman she called the slag.

Their loyalty had been to their client, and Steve had quite rightly passed on the information obtained from Karen. She had merely thanked them, taken the collated file that was her copy, and paid her final bill.

But Matt felt uneasy. Steve had admitted she had been quite blasé about it all, and he had felt some concern about what she would do next, but he made a point of saying they couldn't babysit clients. They only needed to do what was required of them to fulfil the contract.

He stood by the window watching the world go by, although it was a little early for the world of Gleadless to be doing anything. He saw Carol's blue front door open, and a couple of seconds later she was locking it.

He went to release the security lock on the door to save her getting out her key, and smiled as she walked in.

'Something's wrong?' she asked.

'It is, and you're right, that's why I'm in early.' He handed her a cup of coffee and she followed him into his office.

'You've even made your coffee. What time did you come in?'

'Seven-ish. Karen had to be in early, and to be honest we haven't really slept.'

They both sat down and Matt told the story as he knew it. He faltered in places as it suddenly overcame him, and he knew there was no more Phil Newton. Carol waited for him to finish, sympathy evident on her face.

'My God, Matt, I'm so sorry. Is there anything I can do?'

He shook his head. 'I don't think so, Carol, thank you.

Karen's in a hell of a state about it, and it's out of her hands and in the hands of the Derbyshire Constabulary, but I know she feels as though that's wrong. He was her man. My man when I was there. Ray Ledger feels awful as well, and not just because they were close mates. Phil asked him if he wanted to go with him last night, just to have a pint together. It was only an alibi check, nothing big, but Ray had to say no. Mother-in-law's birthday, I think he said. Said it was more than his life was worth to miss that meal, so Phil went out to Hathersage on his own. We would have lost two of the team if Ray had gone with him.'

'And was the alibi confirmed?'

Matt bit his bottom lip. 'I have absolutely no idea. Karen didn't say Phil had rung her, which leads me to think it was proven to be correct, because if it wasn't I think he would have contacted her. Maybe.' He stood, suddenly infused with energy. 'I have to message Karen, ask her.'

Carol smiled at the sudden movement. 'Whoa, slow down, Matt. For one thing, I'm pretty sure Karen will have thought of that, and secondly, I thought you were persona non grata at Moss Way. Don't get her into bother with suggestions about her job.'

He laughed, then retook his seat. 'Okay, smart PA. I think she'll be calling in anyway at some point. I'll ask her then.'

'Good lad,' Carol said, and picked up her coffee. 'I'll go and get on, get WATSON finished, and start a run on it for Susan Hunter, Suzanne Hunter, Sue Hunter, Susie Hunter, and every other name I can think of. I wrote a long list last night of those that could have some connection to the name Susan Hunter, the only one we know her by. And in my lunch hour today I'm going for a drive around the Norton area.'

He looked at her. 'With a megaphone asking Susan Hunter to make herself known?'

'Of course not. I do know that she drives a small white Peugeot, and I've been on the internet looking at pictures. I think it's a Peugeot 107, so I thought I'd spend an hour just driving around Norton looking for it. It's the Peugeot with the big back window, know which one I mean?'

'I do. And you're right, it is that one. It was simply too far away to read the number plate, but it was near enough to see the back window. But here we go again, you working through your lunch break. You did that to go over to the cemetery, and that's not done.'

'I didn't need to tell you what I was doing,' she pointed out. 'I could have just gone out to meet some feller for lunch, and that would have been fine.'

'Meeting a feller for lunch?'

'No, of course not, but I could have let you think that and then there would have been no argument about it. Anyway, it's my decision what I do in my lunch break.'

He sipped at the coffee, which was now almost cold. 'Look, we need some sort of compromise here, because it strikes me you're exactly like Karen and Hermia, pig-headed and stubborn.'

'Yes,' Carol said, keeping her face straight. 'Not a lot you can do about it, though.'

He sighed. 'No, I don't suppose there is. Can I just ask that you keep me informed if you're going out and doing what I'm supposed to be doing, investigating?'

'Of course I'll tell you. Sometimes it might be when I get back, but if I need to do it outside of my lunch break, I'll definitely make a point of telling you. How does that sound?'

He thought it through. 'I don't know. I'm not actually sure what we've just reached agreement on, so I think I'll have to say it sounds okay. I'll talk it over with Steve when he gets here.'

'You do that,' she said, handing him her empty cup. 'And

thank you for the coffee, it was nice. I'm heading off to join forces with WATSON, but I reckon I only need another couple of hours for everything to be locked in. I've decided the best way to keep it updated is to have one set day a week when I upload names and cases, and I shall make that day every Friday. I'll do seven days' worth at a time.'

'Is there a reason behind it being a Friday?'

'Yes. I like Fridays.' She smiled at him, and left to go to her own office. WATSON awaited.

24

WEDNESDAY, 2 NOVEMBER

Hermia had been working intermittently on Dave's laptop for around three hours when she found the buried correspondence between him and Susan Hunter. He had loaded everything into a file named Escape, which in turn was loaded into a folder named AncientStuff. It wasn't hidden as such, and hadn't been deleted, forcing her to resurrect it, and to the casual observer it would simply have looked like personal emails, nothing work related.

The emails had started before Susan Hunter had left for Australia. She was clearly sorry to be leaving Dave Forrester, and Hermia smiled at the thought of her dad turning into a bit of a Romeo. The emails gave no clue as to how they had met – maybe it was simply Susan walking by the shop one day and stopping to chat with the man in the wheelchair, but however it had happened, she had become smitten!

As the time to leave for Australia approached, there was a hint of desperation in the Hunter emails, asking that Dave wait for her to return, requesting that he visit her if at all possible, and yet her father's responses were three or four days after he received each email. He was reticent, gave nothing anyway, explained the difficulty of a man in a wheelchair travelling for so many hours, and he knew he wouldn't be able to do it.

Susan was upset by that email and it showed in her response. She thought their relationship was strong, she expected a little more from him, he could still work from Australia – she had thrown everything at him, expecting him to capitulate. His killer email had requested that she not contact him again, and to make a new life for herself on the other side of the world. There had followed a flurry of emails that remained unanswered until eventually all contact stopped.

Hermia checked the ink levels on her printer, before instructing it to print the entire file. While she waited for the sheaf of papers to complete, she made herself a cheese and tomato sandwich, squirted salad cream on it and devoured it in a couple of minutes. It was only later, while drinking a glass of ice-cold milk, that she realised she had actually eaten tomatoes. Something she found boring, tasteless and better in a tin than the actual fruit. But she had opened the salad drawer, seen them in their little plastic box and knew she had to have one.

And to make matters even more incongruous, it wasn't even eleven o'clock, so she could hardly call it lunch. And she'd had her breakfast at around nine, so she couldn't pass it off as that meal either. This pregnancy seemed to be confusing her body clock and taste buds to a marked degree.

The printer gave a clunk and stopped, and she picked up the papers it had collated in the tray and took them to the coffee table, where she had laid out a couple of marker pens. She picked up the fluorescent pink one, and settled back on the sofa. A lap tray acted as a desk, and she began to reread all the emails.

Every time she spotted something significant or over the top, she highlighted it, alternating between fluorescent pink for the strange ones, and luminous yellow for the ones she considered to be more ominous. There were very few that didn't have a highlighted section. Her dad had been a kind and gentle man and had tried to let Susan Hunter down without it becoming nasty, but in the end he had been forced into just cutting her out of his life. And these emails showed a bullying aspect that he had clearly recognised and didn't want at any price.

Susan mentioned 'Family' in a couple of the emails – *I can't wait to become a big part of your family,* and *I hope your family will welcome me when I become a part of them* – and Hermia knew her dad had had a lucky escape from this woman. She was a stalker, wouldn't leave him alone, wouldn't take the hint to get lost, even though Hermia acknowledged he had never used such strong and hurtful words. And Susan obviously didn't want to give up, even when Dave had made it clear he was out of reach – she wanted to be part of his family.

More research would be needed by Matt to discover exactly who she was. Susan had used the excuse of wanting to visit Dave's grave to make contact with Matt. It had actually taken her a few days to make that visit, and then when she had, she'd been thwarted by Carol Flynn being there.

She knew, while she ate a Garibaldi biscuit, that this wasn't about her dad, it was about the rest of them. Susan Hunter wanted to be a part of the Forrester clan she had heard so much about.

* * *

Hermia waited for Matt to read through the emails before she would speak her conclusions. She knew he would eventually arrive at what she was seeing, especially when he'd worked through all the pink and yellow highlights, but she didn't want to influence him, she wanted him to arrive at the obvious all on his own. In the meantime, she munched on a scone that Carol had brought through for her. It was their first official meeting, and the two women had got on very well indeed.

Matt looked up from the paperwork. 'Is that your second scone?'

'Can't be. I wouldn't eat two.'

'Is it?'

'Yes.'

He nodded and dropped his head once more.

'I can't stop,' she said.

'Can't stop what?'

'Eating. I think I've had about four breakfasts today.'

'That's okay, you don't need to worry. From what I remember of Becky's pregnancy with Harry, she ate ravenously at the start, then about twelve weeks in she stopped because even the thought of it made her vomit. So you'll be okay in a couple of weeks.'

'I'll be like a balloon by then.'

'Mmmm,' he said, distracted by a yellow highlighted sentence. 'That's going to happen anyway.'

She finished the scone and pushed the plate to one side. 'You get scones and stuff every day then?'

'We do. Carol likes to bake, we like to receive them. It's a match made in heaven.'

'Steve's never said a word about this.'

'Perhaps Steve is a smart young man. You see, I told Karen, and now she questions me every day about how many I've had.'

'So now I can do the same with Steve...'

'But that will mean Steve will feel entitled to ask you how many breakfasts you've had, and so on.'

She thought about that for a few seconds. 'Yeah, you're right.

I'll wait till I stop eating, when I get to the sicky stage, before talking about his intake of scones.' She nodded as if agreeing with herself.

There was a period of quiet while she waited for him to reach the final page. Eventually he looked up at her.

'She's like a stalker.'

'Matt, she *is* a stalker. She probably thinks we're mega rich or something because we inherited Dad's business, this property, his money, but I'm not rich. Are you?'

He laughed. 'We've just taken Harry to Florida. We're definitely not rich now. I would say we're all comfortable, but comfortable isn't what she wants. She wants the whole feet under the table job, doesn't she?'

'She does, and she thought she'd got it with our dad until her daughter needed her in Australia. Pity she didn't stay there. So what do we do?'

'Cogitate.'

'Serious thinking then?'

'Definitely. I've never been stalked before. Have you?'

She nodded. 'Will Burgin at school. I told him to piss off, I wasn't interested, and the stalking stopped. He told somebody he didn't think I used language like that, and he was no longer interested. Don't think that tactic will work with this one, though, because it seems to me Dad tried that in a softly-softly way and she completely ignored it.'

'You never told me.'

'I didn't need my big brother rushing to my aid. Seems it was all too easy to put him off. It's a tactic I've used a couple of times since then.' She looked thoughtful, then grinned. 'Maybe I should have used it with Steve, then I wouldn't be eating for England right now.'

* * *

Once Hermia had left the office, Matt asked Carol if she could pop in for a chat. She guessed it was about Susan Hunter, and was still feeling irritated that they hadn't managed to get the registration of the woman's car. At least they could have found out an address with that information.

'Hermia's been through Dad's personal laptop and come up with the goods. There's a whole series of emails, mainly from Hunter to him. It's very obvious he's not interested, but she's persistent, I'll give her that. Herms printed them all out, then went through with a couple of highlighters. Take your time and see what you feel about these emails. However, the detecting side isn't part of your job description, so if you don't want to get involved, that's fine.'

He handed them to her and she glanced at the first page. 'Just for the record, boss, I am already involved in this as she followed me home. Secondly, I don't have a job description because I haven't created one yet. Do you mind if I take these home and study them?'

'Not at all, but we don't want you carrying on working after you leave here! You do enough for us.'

'It's fine. It'll stop me falling asleep like I normally do when I'm watching something boring on television. I'll tell you what I've picked up on tomorrow. That okay?'

'Absolutely fine.'

Carol tidied the papers and stood. 'Very pretty, your sister. I can see your dad in both of you, and your personalities match his. I'm almost at the end of uploading all the names into WATSON, should be finished by tomorrow, so we can run checks again for this woman, try different combinations, see what it throws up. You never know, we might just solve the whole mystery, us and WATSON, discover a little more about who she is and what she really wants.'

Matt grinned at her. Every day he reflected on how lucky they'd been that her stars had aligned with theirs at just the right moment, and she had joined the agency, making it a merry band of three.

He was most impressed by her enthusiasm. She didn't recognise negativity; her mantra seemed to be 'we can do this'. And he never doubted her for a minute. He wouldn't be one bit surprised if she did have an answer for them concerning Susan Hunter as soon as the listings for WATSON were complete.

She left his office carrying the printed copies, and he allowed his mind to reach to his dad. How had he felt about this Hunter woman? Was it an initial attraction that had started to fade when he realised she was becoming too intense? Or had he seen through her from the start and didn't know what to do about it? He had never been a ladies' man, quite the opposite, really. He seemed uncomfortable making small talk with members of the opposite sex, only comfortable with them when he knew them really well. He had been fine with Becky once he got to know her, but in a state of unease with other women.

So what had the situation been like with Susan Hunter? Or hadn't there been a situation? Was it just something in Susan's crazy mind? A need to belong to a family, albeit a readymade one? And did she just want a man with a significant amount of money behind him? A comfortable life at someone else's expense, and a considerable standing within the local community?

He swore to himself he would find out before being brutally candid with her and telling her, to use Hermia's fragrant language, to piss off.

25

WEDNESDAY, 2 NOVEMBER

It had been a quiet day until shortly after lunchtime. Then something approaching a tsunami erupted outside the office, with hands banging on the windows, and yells carrying across the car park, and probably across the tram tracks as well. Steve and Matt reached the front door at the same time, and Matt turned around to hold his hand up to Carol, who seemed about to leave her little office and join them.

'We've got it!' he called.

She nodded, and retook her seat, her hand clutching her mobile phone with 99 already keyed in, ready to add the final digit if it became necessary.

The two men stepped outside and the woman came towards them.

'Fucking idiots!' she yelled, and Steve grinned. He'd only been back in the office for mere seconds, and already things were proving interesting.

'Nice to meet you, Mrs Marshall. Slightly longer skirt this time.'

'I'll give you longer skirt,' she snarled and darted toward

Steve, brandishing a screwdriver. Matt stepped up behind her, and knocked it from her fingers.

'You either shut up, you moronic woman, or you get a punch to the jaw. Your choice,' he said.

She burst out crying.

'Well, that shut her up,' Steve said, bending down to pick up the screwdriver. 'Let's get her inside and find out what the hell she wants.'

They escorted her inside, one in front and one behind in case she had any more random weapons concealed about her person, but she was crying now, talking incoherently.

Steve put his hands on her shoulders and levered her down gently so that she was sitting on the chair opposite Matt. Matt pushed a box of tissues across to her, and waited until the tears had subsided a little.

'It seems we've managed to upset you, but I'm afraid you're going to have to explain how we did that. Niall's okay, is he?'

Niall was her only son who was now serving a lengthy prison sentence for murder. His reference to her son brought on a fresh bout of tears, but she did manage to gasp, 'He's okay.'

She blew her nose, then lifted her head.

'You told Tina fucking Thornton my name, and now she's told my husband what's been happening with me and Wes.'

Matt looked up to the still standing Steve before speaking. 'Steve, can you get Mrs Marshall a glass of water, please?'

'No problem,' Steve said.

'Now, maybe we should talk,' Matt said, a little more gently. 'Has Liam thrown you out? Again?'

She sniffled and reached for another tissue. 'Yes. No money, nothing.'

'You're definitely married?'

She sniffled again. 'We are. And I love him.' The last part came out as a wail.

'Then perhaps it might be a good idea not to sleep with other men.'

She didn't respond.

'So, for a start, you may be without money at this moment in time, but you are entitled, as his wife, to half of everything he has. Money, the haulage business, everything. Does that make you feel a bit better?'

She dabbed at her eyes, then turned as Steve handed her the glass of water. 'Thank you.' She smiled. Suddenly she had cheered up. 'It does make me feel better, but it doesn't solve my immediate problem. I had to catch a tram here, because I couldn't afford the taxi fare.'

'Look, I'm going to give you the name of a solicitor who will be able to help you.' He delved into his drawer and found one of Gloria Elland's cards. 'She's an excellent solicitor, will be able to steer you in the right direction. Is it definitely over between you and Liam?'

'Seems so. He's changed the locks, cancelled my cards, told me I can keep the Mini because he wouldn't be seen dead in it, but it needs petrol so I couldn't risk using that. I tried ringing Wes, but it goes straight to voicemail.'

'Give me five minutes,' Matt said, standing up. 'I'll see what I can organise for you.'

* * *

Steve looked at the woman sitting screwing a tissue into the tiniest ball imaginable, but he couldn't find much sympathy for her. Moving from one man's bed to another was never going to enamour her to her husband, and it seemed he,

Steve Rowlands, investigator extraordinaire, was the reason for her current predicament. She probably viewed him as the cause.

'So am I reading this correctly? Wes's wife approached your husband?'

'She did. The cow.'

'You can hardly blame her, Mrs Marshall. You did have an affair with her husband.'

'Oh, I'm not blaming her, I'm blaming you. Or this business, anyway. You've divulged my name, and there's laws about that now. I'm taking you to the fucking cleaners, I am.'

'Mrs Thornton was our client,' he explained gently, not wanting her to reach for the tissue box again. 'She employed us to find out who Wes was sleeping with, and we did. We just happened to know your name because of your affair with Anthony Dawson. We supplied her with everything she asked for. After that, it's completely out of our control what she does with the information.'

Matt re-entered his office and handed the shell-shocked woman a small piece of paper. 'Use your tram ticket to go back into the city centre, get off at the Cathedral stop and walk down the side of the Cathedral. You'll be in Paradise Square where Gloria Elland works. She'll stay until half past five, but if you're not there by then, she's going home.'

Diana Marshall stood, all thoughts of any compensation she could claim now flying out of the window. Meeting up with this solicitor could probably be a lot more lucrative.

She left the building and all three staff members breathed a sigh of relief. Carol had very little idea of what was going on, but had soon realised she was clearly the woman photographed in the file she had proofread for Steve. She had been on full alert for all the time Diana Marshall had been in Matt's office, and now she wanted to double lock the door and disconnect the entry system.

'How the hell did she know we'd done the surveillance work?' Steve muttered.

'My guess is that Tina Thornton told Liam Marshall that she'd employed us and he passed this on to Diana when he had a go at her.' He shrugged. 'My back's broad enough. I can take it. And he could be getting back at us for being partly responsible for sending his lad to prison. Payback time, I reckon. He's always kind of on the cusp of things, is that man. One day he'll find himself in the wrong prison cell at the wrong time.'

'He's a bad 'un,' Carol said, now standing behind them as they watched Diana Marshall running along White Lane, attempting to get to the tram stop before the next tram did. They guessed she would miss it by about fifteen seconds.

'Who's a bad 'un?' Steve asked.

'Liam Marshall.'

'You know him?'

'It's more that I know *of* him,' Carol said, 'rather than knowing him. Isn't afraid of bribing people to get what he wants. I came across him when I was working my previous job.'

Steve smiled. 'This would be the job we're not allowed to mention but we know who you worked for.'

'That's the job. And don't laugh at me, Steve Rowlands. You know how high he was in government, and I just prefer not to discuss it. In fact, the Official Secrets Act says I can't discuss it. But my previous job is how I know Liam Marshall should be locked up and the key thrown away. And that's all you'll get out of me, because I don't want you going down Charnock woods looking for my dead body. Okay?'

Steve knew she was half joking and half serious.

Matt turned around. 'Then we won't mention it again, I

promise. But if ever there comes a time when you do need to talk about anything from that time, we're here. And if there is anything further that should be mentioned about Liam Marshall, Karen might be your go-to gal.'

'I'll bear that in mind. Think Mrs Marshall caught that tram?'

'Hope so. When you just miss one, that fifteen-minute wait for the next one seems never-ending. Wonder if Liam Marshall has properly thought this through. I bet when he does, the marriage will miraculously be mended. He took her back after her fling with Anthony Dawson, and I thought then that he'd a lot more to lose than his wife. But I've put the idea of money into her mind now, so maybe it won't be quite as straightforward as Mr Marshall thinks.'

Snuggling down on the sofa with a new book downloaded onto her Kindle and a box of Quality Street that she'd bought and vowed to put away until Christmas, Tina Thornton smiled. She now had a king-size bed all to herself until she decided it was maybe time to share it, spare wardrobe space and the second chest of drawers back, and a remote control in her hands and not the calloused hands of Wes Thornton. As far as she could see, the only drawback was she had to pour her own gin and tonic. She sipped at her drink, pushed an orange cream into her mouth and opened her Kindle. Even that was compliant. It was over 80 per cent charged, and good to go. Really, she decided, revenge wasn't just a word in a dictionary, it was an actual thing.

And that Liam Marshall had been so polite, so welcoming. He hadn't seemed fazed at all by what she had to say, although she had been a bit puzzled by his comment around things having been put in place. She somehow thought he might know the definition of revenge as well.

She began to read. A few hours with J. D. Robb and a couple of gruesome murders, a pizza delivery, and then a *Silent Witness* rerun on television, what could be better? Calling in at the Forrester Agency had proved to be worth every penny, and visiting the Marshall haulage yard had been completely free of charge.

Her phone pinged and she saw the name of the text sender on her screen.

Liam Marshall.

Maybe that other side of the king-size bed wouldn't be empty for long, after all.

* * *

It was after five when Carol decided it was time to do her promised drive around the area. Her lunch break had somehow disappeared unnoticed in the excitement of adding the last of the information to WATSON, then double-checking everything had been done. She now felt satisfied that thoughts of files she had missed would no longer invade her dreams.

She threw her thick zip-up jacket on the back seat, a 'just in case' item she had grabbed at the last minute, and settled into the driver's seat. She selected Barry Manilow to accompany her, and she pulled away from her home. Gleadless and Norton are adjacent areas that virtually melded into one, and she turned left at the traffic lights and headed up Norton Avenue. The road changed its name within about a hundred yards to Bochum Parkway, and when she reached the first small traffic island, she went right, detouring off the main road. She knew she was now in Norton territory, and she leaned forward, peering along every road, into every parking area, every garage site, searching for a small white Peugeot.

After an hour of driving around, she pulled over and completed the filling in of the map she had taken with her. She had covered a large area, but it was now quite dark and she decided to head home. Even Barry Manilow was sounding a little fed up.

She had to pass the office to get back, and she automatically glanced at it to check everything looked okay. It didn't. There was a light on, yet she knew all three of them had left together at five o'clock. She tried to recall the conversation they'd had, and knew neither Matt nor Steve had mentioned returning to the office, so she quickly parked up outside her house and ran inside.

She rang Matt and breathlessly asked where he was.

'At home. Something wrong?'

'I saw a light in the office. And it's not Steve?'

'No, we arrived home at the same time. I'll drive over.'

'No, I'll go. Don't trail all the way back. I'll let you know what's wrong. Maybe we just left a light on...'

'And maybe we didn't. Don't go in, Carol.'

'I'll be fine. In fact, I'm looking at it now and I can't see a light. It was definitely there when I drove past. Like a torch, as if it was moving, now I come to think about it properly.'

'Wait ten minutes,' Matt said and then disconnected.

* * *

She didn't wait ten minutes. She didn't wait any minutes. She picked up the discarded jacket, and headed across the tram tracks, the mallet she used for bashing steak partially hanging out of her pocket.

She stood for a moment staring into Steve's office window, which was where she had seen the light, then moved across to Matt's. Could she have been mistaken? She tried the door but it was definitely locked, so she took out her key and inserted it. It worked fine, and immediately the alarm started its countdown, so she pushed her way in and keyed in the code.

She heard a sound behind her and froze for a split second, then slid her hand into the pocket, and began to withdraw the mallet. She didn't even get it halfway out before darkness descended and she crumpled to the floor.

She didn't hear the front door open and close, didn't see the assailant run away; she didn't hear Matt arrive on scene, and didn't wake up until the paramedics began to work on her.

26

THURSDAY, 3 NOVEMBER

Karen felt completely out of sorts and sleep deprived. Phil was never far from her thoughts, and now there was the attack on Carol. Suddenly it seemed that the cases she was investigating were all a little close to home. Okay, she wasn't investigating Phil's case, there didn't appear to be anything to investigate because the man who had come round that corner on the wrong side of the road was dead anyway, but it was Phil... the whole team was grieving, and quiet.

And now Carol. Matt had rung from the hospital to let her know where he was. He had reassured her Carol was out of danger, but all of these Gleadless cases suddenly felt as if they were intermingling, and she was sitting behind her desk waiting for news. Could the intruder in the Forrester office have anything to do with the killing of Elise Langton? She shook her head, having no idea where that thought had come from. There had been absolutely nothing that could have created a link in her mind, yet the thought persisted. There was no reason for anyone to break into the Forrester Agency, because the Forrester

Agency wasn't connected to the case. Or did someone think they were?

She stared at her phone, willing it to ring. When it did, she was mid-sip of her coffee.

'DS Nelson,' she said, mopping coffee from her desk surface.

'Switchboard here. I have a young man on who keeps mentioning DC Newton. Can I put him through to you?'

Karen threw the soggy, coffee-stained tissue towards her waste bin, where it landed on the floor. She shook her head, wondering how on earth she'd ever earned that place in the school netball team.

She heard the click as the call connected, and said her name.

'Oh, hi. My name is Vinnie Hancock, I'm the barman at the George in Hathersage. I was with one of your officers, a chap called Phil, on Tuesday evening. I helped him out with some information he needed, and he said he would send someone out to talk to me the following day, and to take a statement. But now I've found out that one of the fatalities in the smash at Surprise View was him. This must have happened within five minutes of his leaving me, he said he was going straight home.'

'Thank you for contacting us, Mr Hancock. I'm sorry we haven't sent anyone out to take your statement. Obviously, we knew nothing about it, as DC Newton did not have a chance to write his report.'

There was a brief moment of silence.

'Bloody shame. He was a nice man. We chatted for quite a while. The thing is I'm on holiday from Saturday onwards for a week, and I didn't want you sending someone then and me not being here.'

'Are you there this evening?'

'I am. Only until nine. It's been a week of strange shifts because we've got a couple of staff who are off ill.'

'And you'll be okay to take quarter of an hour off to complete a statement?'

'No problem. I'll not take a break till someone arrives.'

'It will be me, and hopefully we'll be there for six. I might just have to treat my partner to a meal. You have a spare table for two for around seven?'

'We do. Not many bookings tonight, which is why I can get away for nine.'

'Then I'll see you later, Mr Hancock.'

They disconnected and she sat and stared at the phone. It would have to be her who did this, she couldn't ask any of her team to drive past where Phil met his death, not yet. It was simply too raw with all of them. And it was only a statement, confirming Rick Langton and Jenna Glaves's alibi.

She picked up her mobile phone and sent a text to Matt, telling him she was treating him to a meal at the George that evening, and would he let her know if he couldn't make it, because she would need time to find another man.

His response was immediate.

Stop looking at other men. I'll be suited and booted for five. Xxx

She smiled. This man could always make her smile even when she was at a low ebb.

* * *

Matt had left home at the same time as Karen, going early into the office to look at CCTV before heading back to the hospital to bring Carol home once she was given the all-clear – the doctor had insisted she stay overnight, and Matt had agreed with them. Carol hadn't agreed, but Matt had been at his persuasive best, saying that she had nobody at home with her should she deteriorate, and that deterioration might well include being unable to use her phone.

He had been the first one to have eyes on her attacker, though it didn't help in any way. A ghoulish luminous mask covered the face, and black jogging bottoms combined with a black hoodie completely disguised whether they were male or female. Gloves completed the outfit, so he knew it would be a waste of police resources to fingerprint everything. Entry had been by a short ladder to the upper windows, where one had been smashed by a brick. Was this yet another opportunistic thief or was it someone who had targeted them specifically in order to remove something they didn't want the new regime of Forrester's to have? Steve had boarded the window up after Matt had left to follow the ambulance to the hospital, and after a quick phone call, Matt had organised having it repaired; he also considered that as it was obviously a weak point, it might be better to have bars on the outside of the window as well. He would make sure he was there to discuss it with the glazier.

When they first took over the premises, it had seemed a plus point that the premises weren't overlooked at the back by anything, and a row of hedgerow shrubs bordered the small paved back yard, but now he realised how easy it had been to effect an entry. And unlike when it had been his dad's home, it would have been in darkness.

He felt angry. They had concentrated on making the interior fully protected by CCTV, yet the state-of-the-art security systems had simply been inefficient. Yes, they had filmed the perpetrator, but to no avail. They couldn't even tell if the intruder was male or female. And they wouldn't have known about it until the following morning if Carol hadn't seen the light, a flashlight, she said.

The doctor had suggested that she was probably hit by that, in view of her quick recovery time, saying that if she'd been hit by anything heavier, she possibly wouldn't have been returning home at all.

* * *

He was at the hospital by eleven, collecting Carol from the ward. She needed no medication so they didn't have to wait around for the pharmacy to deliver her prescription to the ward, and by quarter past eleven he was helping her into his car.

'Thank you,' she said, flashing a quick smile at him. 'Now let's go and find the bugger who did this to me.'

'You're not employed on the investigation side,' he reminded her. 'You're our support staff. We'll find who did it. You take the rest of the week off.'

This time she didn't smile, she laughed. 'On your bike, Matt Forrester. It's my head she hit, not yours. And when I find her, it'll be her nose I aim for.'

'She?'

'I'm convinced it was a she. Wears Nina Ricci's L'Air du Temps. And what's more, she only meant to incapacitate me, not kill me. I think the blow would have been much worse if it had been a man, purely because of the extra strength a man has. I've had time to think this through during that long night,' she added apologetically. 'And it's somebody who wants something we've got, or she thinks we've got, but heaven only knows what that might be. I'm assuming you went through the flat with a fine-tooth comb when you were looking for the person who killed them, so is there something up there that you know about and nobody else does?'

'The only thing that was there was his journal. Yes, it was

hidden inside a hollowed-out fat volume of Shakespeare plays, but it's now actually at my home, not upstairs.'

'And is there anything in that journal that should maybe be on WATSON?'

'Never thought about that, because it's more about his thought processes, anything he needed to check on, that sort of thing. You want to wade through it just in case?'

Carol nodded. 'I do. As an outsider, I may just pick up on something that you would have taken for granted. And if there are any new names in it, I'll get them added even if we don't have a file for them. WATSON is our system, and doesn't need the same reasons as HOLMES for a case to be added.'

'So let's go back to this perfume.' He pulled up at the traffic lights and waited patiently for them to go to green. 'It's some talent when you can recognise a fragrance just like that.'

'No, it's not a talent. There are only two I would recognise anywhere, the Nina Ricci one and Dolce and Gabbana Light Blue, and that's because I wear them both. If she'd worn Chanel or Marc Jacobs, I wouldn't have recognised them at all, but I've found the ones I like and I stick to them. They become a sort of a signature for a woman, does a perfume. And L'Air du Temps is hers, just as much as it is mine. Your Karen favours Light Blue.'

Matt turned to look at her. 'She does! It's her weekday perfume. This is some skill you have.'

'It's not. Not all burglars and rogues wear Nina Ricci or Dolce and Gabbana. As I said, I only recognise these two because I wear them both.'

A car horn tooted behind them, and he set off, feeling guilty for being so immersed in the conversation he'd forgotten about the possibility that traffic lights do eventually change.

* * *

When they reached Gleadless, Carol was deep in thought. Matt pulled up outside her home, and jumped out so he could be there to help her out.

She smacked his hand. 'Away with you, Matt Forrester. This is the easiest car in the universe to get out of, and I'm not ill. I'm going to take a quick shower, and I'll be at work inside half an hour. I've a budgie to feed and some perfume to splash on.'

'You're not coming in to work.'

'I am.'

'It'll be noisy. We're having bars put on the back windows, all of them. They're drilling.'

'I have paracetamol. Matt, I'm coming to work. Now be a good lad and go get your dad's journal, and I'll see you in a bit.'

'I'm feeling bullied.'

'Good. Now let me go and work out how to wash my hair without causing pain on this lump site. And we'll probably hear Walter screeching as soon as I open the door. I let him have a fly every night, and I wasn't here to give him his freedom yesterday. I'm in deep trouble.'

He escorted her up to her front door, and then drove off to get Dave's journal. It had been some time since he had last looked through it, and he knew Carol would enjoy seeing the little side notes his father had made, especially the ones about his scone delivery arriving on time.

27

THURSDAY, 3 NOVEMBER

Matt handed Carol the small journal. 'It's tiny writing.'

'It's a tiny book.' She stood. 'Come here, big man.'

He moved towards her, and she held her wrist towards his face. 'That's L'Air du Temps. I'm surer than ever now that this was the perfume she wore, and that it was definitely a woman.'

'She has good taste,' he said.

'Well, let's hope this little book gives us a clue to who she is.'

'Although it's not that easy to judge on CCTV, I'd say whoever hit you was about the same height as you. And it was the torch that was used, so they didn't come prepared to hurt anybody. You must have given her a hell of a shock walking through the front door. This has shown us the weak spots in our security, and I've booked a meeting with the company who installed everything for next week. We have to do some major upgrades, I fear.'

'I did wonder if there was enough on the back of the property. There's a lot at the front, but the rear is vulnerable.'

'Not for much longer. There'll be bars on every window except the two big front ones, so she could end up wishing she'd hung around. Because she'll not get in again. I have no idea if she's taken anything, and she wasn't here that long according to the CCTV. About three minutes, I reckon.'

'She didn't get into your office. It would have been nothing short of a miracle if she had, with that keycode. I hate it that we now have to double up our security. It's not about the cost, it's about the inconvenience and the bars on the windows.'

'You know, if she was here to get anything from the computers, even if she physically removed them, we wouldn't lose the work. Everything that I do is backed up on a separate hard drive that I was no longer using at home, and it's all saved to the cloud anyway. Whoever set these three laptops up linked them all together.'

'That would be Hermia. I asked her to sort us out, so she did, and with one arm in a sling. Hermia and computers were made for each other, not so much me. Steve is okay with them, but Herms runs rings around us.'

Carol gave a slight nod. 'I'm going to clear the external hard drive of everything, still leave it connected and visible on my desk, then if anybody else wants info from here hopefully they'll grab that and go. They'll get nothing but they'll think they've got everything. That's until they plug it into their own machine. You think it was info she was after?'

'No idea. She walloped you and went. I think you got away light, it could have been so much worse. But watch my lips. Under no circumstances can this ever happen again. I don't care if the bloody place is on fire, you don't attempt to come inside. You risked your life. God, you're just like Herms. I told her not to go into her flat on her own. Then she shows a prospective buyer around, and he threw her over the third-floor balcony.'

Carol looked down at the floor. 'Sorry,' she said. 'I thought I would be okay because I knew you would be on your way. Is Steve going to shout at me as well?'

'Probably. It's only because you could have been killed, and I think we'd miss you. Who'd update WATSON for us?'

'You're all heart, boss, all heart. How many men are there working on the windows?'

'Two, I think.'

'Then go and see if they want a hot drink. I'll switch on the kettle.'

* * *

Carol had been forcibly evicted from the office and despatched to her own home, with instructions not to cross the tram tracks again that evening. Matt explained where he was going – his partner had invited him out on a date with the lure of a meal, but if Carol needed him...

She said she wouldn't, and he watched as she entered through her blue door before locking the office and getting into his own car. He was home for half past four, and could hear Karen singing in the shower. It was pretty tuneless, but it made him smile. He'd had a rubbish few days, and this woman could make him feel so much better without even trying.

He fed Oliver, who miaowed his gratitude, then headed upstairs.

Karen was dressed in smart black trousers with a white blouse that was almost sheer but not quite. He whistled.

'Too much?' she asked, turning a worried face towards the mirror.

'Not enough,' he said, and bent to kiss the back of her neck.

'Don't do that,' she reprimanded. 'I have to have my work head on for this first part of the evening. I need to take a statement, then we can forget about it and enjoy the meal. I've never been to the George, so I'm looking forward to it.'

He kissed her again, and headed for the bathroom. 'I'll grab a quick shower and maybe we can sit down for half an hour and just relax. We've had a bloody awful few days, and we probably need a little time out, a chat about inconsequential rubbish, maybe even a cup of tea.'

Karen took the hint and went downstairs to make a pot of tea. It had become an evening ritual between them to always make it in the teapot – they had stopped making them straight in the mug – as it felt more civilised to do it that way.

She was putting the tea bags in the pot when she heard the front door open and Hermia shout, 'S'me.'

'Hello, Smee. You lost your pirate ship?'

Hermia looked puzzled.

'Never mind,' Karen laughed. 'Just my warped sense of humour. You need something?'

'Bacon. I swear to God this child is going to come out looking like a fat little piglet. I could eat it for every meal. Steve's starting to notice we're having it a lot, so I've made him a shepherd's pie which he loves, but it's not floating my boat, so I'm having bacon. Except I've only one rasher left.'

Karen opened the fridge and removed a full pack. 'Enjoy,' she said.

'Thanks, you're a pal. I'll replace it tomorrow. You having anything nice?'

Karen shrugged. 'No idea. We're going to the George at Hathersage for a meal. Actually, I'm going because I need to take a statement, but I booked us a table for after I've finished. I could hazard a guess your brother will go for steak, but I'll wait until I see the menu.'

'You're taking a statement?'

'Yes. It was Phil's last job. He went to double check an alibi after he felt he ballsed up with the boxing gym one, but he didn't get the statement because the barman was working. Said he would organise it for the day after, and of course he...' She halted, unable to finish her sentence.

'So you're going to finish off what he started,' Hermia said gently. 'He'd appreciate that.'

Karen nodded. 'I know. I didn't want to give it to anybody else, I felt I had to do it. I'm going to miss Phil so much. He was on a par with Ray Ledger – I could trust them implicitly, and get everything he tackled done quickly. Which, of course, is why Phil was out at Hathersage that night, not because I asked him, but because he wanted to tidy up what he considered were loose ends.'

'I'll leave you to get ready. But I'll be thinking about you both; it'll be as bad for Matt as it is for you. I know how much he misses his team.' She kissed Karen's cheek, and walked back to her own home next door.

Karen didn't move, suddenly overwhelmed by grief. They would all miss Phil in so many ways – his awful coffees and his expert teas, his patience when teaching something new, particularly to new recruits, his skills on the computer – what would they all do without him? This wasn't only about the way she was feeling, it was the whole team.

She was still dabbing at her eyes when Matt walked into the kitchen. He enfolded her into his arms.

He didn't speak; he didn't have to, he knew exactly what was wrong.

* * *

The drive out to Hathersage was in darkness. It had been a grey day, and it was as if the daylight had given up on itself, welcoming the night's blackness with a sense of relief. They rounded the Surprise View bend, noting that work had already started on repairs to the dry-stone wall.

Matt reached across and grasped her hand.

'Okay?'

She nodded. 'As much as I'll ever be.'

He put on his indicators and pulled into a layby, which was used almost exclusively for stargazing. Being far away from the bright lights of any cities and towns, the area was noted for being a mecca for astronomy aficionados.

Matt and Karen looked at the skies that had witnessed such horrors at that spot earlier in the week.

The stars were limited – the cloud base was patchy, providing intermittent flashes of light, but Matt knew it would settle Karen's thoughts before their arrival in the village at the bottom of the hill.

They sat for five minutes, each lost in their own thoughts, then Matt squeezed her hand again. 'Ready?'

'I am. Let's go and drink a toast to our friend.'

'With non-alcoholic wine? He'd laugh at us. Probably make us a coffee to finish off the meal.'

'I wish,' she said quietly, as Matt slipped the car into drive and headed downhill.

The car park was almost empty, and Karen felt grateful. It meant Vinnie would be able to give his statement quickly, then they could have their meal and get back home.

Vinnie came towards them as they approached, and Karen quickly held up her warrant card and slipped it back in her bag.

'That's the quietest spot,' he said, pointing to a small table in a corner. 'I put a reserved sign on it for us. I'll be with you in one minute.'

Matt and Karen walked across, and Karen took out the statement form. She wanted this to be a quick job; this man was working. She guessed it had been a much busier night when Phil had come in, leading him to decide to take the statement the day after. Tying up loose ends.

Vinnie joined them, glancing back at the bar and the one female staff member standing there as he did so.

'This is only her third night, so I just need to keep an eye out for any problems, but apart from that I'm free for a bit. She can cope,' he said.

Karen smiled at him. 'Good to meet you, Vinnie, and thank you for contacting the station. Please remember we received nothing from DC Newton, so everything you can remember of what you told him is new to us.'

'Well, I need to start by saying I liked him. He was polite, didn't rush me, and the only problem was it was a busy night. He had a shandy, so drink was nothing to do with what happened later – on his part, anyway. And I am so sorry it happened. It's a bad spot for accidents, and it really threw me when I found out who had died.'

'You have a lot?'

'A lot of bumps and bangs, not so many fatalities. But there were three cars involved in this one. Am I right? That usually ends up with at least one death, and emergency vehicles blocking the road out of the village. When you live here, you learn to accept that.'

28

THURSDAY, 3 NOVEMBER

'Thank you, Vinnie.' Karen picked up her pen and wrote his name at the top of the statement form. He told her his address in Hathersage, and she smiled. 'That's up by the church with Little John's grave in the graveyard, isn't it?'

'It is. You know it?'

'I would say the grave is my most visited place in Derbyshire. I was always fascinated by the size of it, and whether it truly is Little John or not – and let's face it, Robin Hood isn't around any more to confirm or deny it – I preferred to believe it was the truth. That's why I knew the name of the road where you live.'

'I still live with Mum and Dad, sort of. They had a little dwelling built for me in the back garden, so I live there, but that was because it's almost impossible to get a place in Derbyshire, and Hathersage never has property coming on the market. I get the best of all worlds, a property that is mine, cost me nothing, Mum cleans it for me, and Dad keeps my freezer stocked. He's the chef in the family, so Mum lets him do it.'

'Happy life,' Matt commented. 'I used to visit here for the open-air swimming baths, but as you get older, things like that die away and you forget how brilliant they were. So you were born here?'

'I was. So was Mum. Our house goes back in our family for four generations, I believe. But I bet that's true of most of the inhabitants of Hathersage. Very close-knit community.'

'So,' Karen said, her pen poised to write Vinnie's words down. 'I'll take your statement in rough, then transfer it to the official form. If you'll then sign it, that should be fine, and you'll never hear from us again unless we come back for a meal. That okay?'

'That's fine, but...'

'But?'

Vinnie shrugged. 'But nothing, really. It's just it isn't as straightforward as you're thinking. And I'm only saying that because it was obvious Phil was a bit surprised by what I had to say, so you may see me again. Possibly in a court room?'

'Then I'm going to record this as well as write it down.' She felt slightly puzzled by his words. She fished in her bag for her small recorder, hoped the batteries were good, and switched it on.

After confirming the date and location, and the name of the interviewee, she turned to Vinnie.

'We know DC Newton was here to confirm an alibi that the George Hotel had already confirmed. Did DC Newton show you images of your customers, Rick Langton and Jenna Glaves?'

'Rick Langton, yes, Jenna Glaves, no. Jenna Glaves hasn't been a customer here.'

'Can you expand?'

'I can. The booking was made over the phone, and the party of two arrived on time. I confirmed from the pictures shown to me by DC Newton that the man was Rick Langton, but the woman's face he showed me was definitely not the woman Rick brought here that evening. We had no name for her, it was booked in Mr Langton's name.'

'You're absolutely sure it wasn't Jenna Glaves? Long blonde hair, very slim.'

'The lady who came here with Mr Langton had red hair, styled very short, curvy but not overweight. Buxom, I'd say, and she made sure Mr Langton had an unobstructed view. Extremely low-cut top she had on. I didn't catch her name, although they chatted all the time they were here. I got the impression it wasn't a new relationship, more like a long-term one. In this trade, you learn to tell the difference.'

Karen was writing everything down, and was glad she'd put the recorder on the table. 'And what time did they leave?'

'Around half past ten, give or take five minutes. And that's all I can tell you. I'd never seen them here before, don't know what car they came in, but I can tell you she had seabass and he had steak. And he slipped a tenner into my hand before he left.'

Karen sat for a moment, looking at her notes. Vinnie had been, thankfully, quite observant, and she knew that what he had told them had been coaxed out of him already by Phil. 'Thank you, Vinnie. I'll get this written up in a coherent way, because it's highly likely this could end up in court, so we'll get it perfect at this point.' She glanced at her phone. 'We've forty-five minutes until our meal is booked, so I'll complete this and ask you to do a read-through of it before signing it, then we can enjoy the rest of our evening. Thank you so much for this, it's opened up a whole new line of investigation.'

'You're welcome. Now can I get you a drink while you're waiting for your table?'

Matt accompanied Vinnie to the bar, and Karen began to write.

* * *

With the signed statement safely tucked away in her bag, Karen sat across from Matt at their table for two.

'This opens up the whole thing with Elise Langton, doesn't it? We have signed statements from everyone – her brother, her neighbours either side, her sister-in-law confirming her brother's statement, you name it, we've got a statement. Even one from Rick Langton saying he was at the George, with a note on it of verification from here that he was here, accompanied by a female.'

'So why don't you have one from Jenna Glaves?'

'I suspect because Rick Langton's statement encompassed both of them. He was clearly in a blue funk about the discovery of this other woman, and every time he spoke of being at the George, he said it was with Jenna. But he never said anything when Jenna was there. In fact, I've only seen Jenna once, and she couldn't wait to get away from me. Like a scared little mouse, she was. I thought nothing of it other than her life must have changed a lot, because she suddenly had two children to bring up on a full-time basis, instead of the couple of times a week it had been before Elise was killed. It's strange, but when I did see her, she took his daughter out, keen to get Skye and her away from me. She'll get such a shock tomorrow when I bring both her and Rick in for a little heart-to-heart, so to speak.'

She sipped at the watermelon cooler she had ordered, both of them aware that alcohol was out of the question. Matt had opted to drive, and Karen refrained during the week. Matt had asked for water.

'You know, don't you?' Matt said.

'But as you very well know, ex-DI Forrester, knowing and proving are two different things. It will happen, I'll get the proof and Elise will get justice. But one step at a time, one statement at a time, and the CPS will say we're okay to charge. One more day and I'll have this locked up.' She looked up and smiled as Vinnie appeared bearing two plates.

'This slow-cooked lamb shank is superb, DS Nelson. I told our chefs you were a special customer, so treat it with reverence.'

'I will,' she promised, staring at the huge plate of food in front of her, and suddenly aware of how ravenous she felt.

'And you, Mr Forrester, have an equally superb sage and chorizo-stuffed pork fillet, which, I might add, is a particular favourite of mine. Is there anything else I can get either of you?'

They both shook their heads, said no, they were fine, and Vinnie left them to enjoy the meal.

They ate without speaking for several minutes, until Karen leaned back and asked if they could afford to employ a chef full time, one they could steal from the George.

'Not yet,' he said. 'Give me a couple of years. This,' he stabbed at his pork fillet, 'is truly amazing.'

Matt held up his glass of water, and she followed with her watermelon soft drink.

'To Phil, may he rest in peace.'

They clinked glasses and Karen responded with a further, 'Rest in peace.'

* * *

An hour later, after a final word with Vinnie regarding his planned holiday and the date of his return should they need to contact him again, they left the George.

'I have a food baby the size of a six-month foetus,' Karen said as she eased herself into the passenger seat. 'I am almost a happy woman right now. You know, Phil has done this. Even if he had managed to get the statement from Vinnie, we would have found it in his car after the accident, but he organised with Vinnie that he would get the statement the following day, and thereby causing Vinnie to contact me. This is Phil's work, and he handled it perfectly.'

'He did. You want to stop in that layby and walk up to the bend to say goodbye properly?'

'No, it's just too damn dangerous for oncoming cars. If they see us there, they might just swerve and end up in all sorts of trouble. I'll wait until the funeral for my goodbyes, and my thanks.'

Matt noticeably slowed as they reached the bad bend, and Karen blew a kiss across the landscape of the Surprise View.

* * *

Thursday evening closed with an impromptu call on Carol. Matt simply wanted to check she was okay, and as they were passing through Gleadless on their way to Ridgeway anyway...

She invited them in, and Matt wasn't the least bit surprised to see she was going through the printouts of the emails between his father and Susan Hunter.

They refused her offer of drinks, having finished their meal off with coffees, but agreed to sit down for a few minutes, instead of just rushing off.

'I rarely have visitors now,' she explained. 'My job meant I wasn't encouraged to have close friends, and when my husband died, his circle of friends seemed to fade away as well. Don't get me wrong, I'm a person who enjoys her own company, but I do like it when someone does call, even if it's at bedtime.'

'You're not fooling me,' Matt said. 'You're not even preparing for bed. You're reading the emails.'

'I don't like her,' she said, waving one of the pages in the air, 'this woman. And neither did your dad. I'm getting a strong impression he was relieved when she went off to Australia because communication then dried up between them.'

'That's what Hermia said. I reckon wherever Dad is watching over us now, he'll be mighty relieved we haven't been taken in by her. What I don't understand is what it is she's after. What does she think we have that she could possibly claim?'

'Do you think it was her who attacked me?' Carol looked at both of them.

Matt spoke first. 'I don't know. Do you want to pursue it with Karen? I know you said you didn't want to take it further, because you're okay, but as a police officer I would always advise that you push for justice.'

She grinned. '*Ex*-police officer.'

'But Karen isn't ex anything, and she's here with us right now. Karen, talk to her.' He turned to his partner.

'I wouldn't dare. If you decide to report it, Carol, obviously we'll take it on, but I do get what you mean. My advice to you is wait until the day you do find out who she is, and punch her in the nose with a good right hook. You'll get so much more satisfaction than it going to court and her getting a slap on the wrist. But don't quote me on this. I'm sure I'm not allowed to give out this sort of advice, and I'll deny I ever said it if it ever goes to court.'

29

FRIDAY, 4 NOVEMBER

Ray Ledger arrived at the home shared by Rick Langton and Jenna Glaves at just after seven. Having two police cars parked on the road outside the Langton home had caused several curtains to move, people watching was happening, and speculating amongst their immediate families about what the couple had done.

They also saw the speedy arrival of Jack Mitchell, Elise Langton's brother, who left the street two minutes later with both children strapped into the back of his car.

Within a minute of this, Rick Langton was placed in the back of Ray's car, with Jenna Glaves helped into the rear seat of the second, a hand firmly pushing down on her head to help her get in. She seemed reluctant to go.

Ray booked both of them into the custody suite on their arrival at Moss Way, handed them a bottle of water each without mentioning they had tea and coffee for custodial visitors, and left them to await duty solicitors. That had been the first thing they had demanded on arrival at the booking-in desk. He doubted the solicitors would be there much before ten, so he simply left them in the interview rooms to either become increasingly bored, or terminally angry.

'Booked in, boss,' he said, 'and very happy to do it. Thanks for the late-night call. I slept better for knowing what was happening, and the part Phil played in it.'

Karen gave a slight nod of her head, acknowledging his words. 'Phil actually solved it for us, unless this smart-arse woman comes up with some other spectacular alibi. Rick was definitely at the George, but not with Jenna. So where was Jenna? She's obviously trying to hold on to a man who actually is pretty damn worthless. He supposedly wanted Elise back in his life, but was at the George with some other woman, name unknown as yet, while Jenna was at home alone. I'll bet anything he thought he'd got away with it, because now he really needs Jenna to have his kids. I'm not sure it will have occurred to him that she is a suspect. He'll be more concerned about his lie coming out about his companion that night.'

'I'm going to enjoy this interview whether it's talking to him or to her. You decided which one yet?'

Karen pursed her lips as if still undecided. 'I think it has to be her. I'd probably lose my temper with Mr Smartarse Langton, who thinks he can get away with everything short of murder, when actually it's his girlfriend who's scored the goal there.'

Her desk phone rang and she reached across to pick up the receiver. 'DS Nelson.'

'Hi, DS Nelson. It's Jack Mitchell. Elise's brother.'

'Yes, Jack. What can I do for you?'

'The first thing is to tell me the father of these two kids didn't have anything to do with the death of my sister.'

'You know I can't discuss anything, but Rick was where he said he was at the time of Elise's death. Does that help you?'

She heard the exhale of relief. 'Thank you. There is something else, though. The kids are rather upset at having to get up and come over here at this time in the morning, to say nothing of my headteacher, who's now having to take my class. Skye is busy ironing a load of tea towels as usual but Daniel is noticeably upset. He's lost his mum, and now fears he's lost Jenna as well. No – let me correct myself there. It's not so much the thought he might have lost Jenna, it's more he's lost mother number two. It could have been anybody, but she's the mother figure he desperately needs. But that's a little irrelevant, and I know I'm waffling, but do you think you could pop by at some point and talk to him?'

She felt surprised. The kids hardly knew her, and she herself wasn't that good at interacting with anybody under the age of eighteen, yet she found herself agreeing.

'I'm not needed here until about ten-ish, so I'll nip over now. Is it urgent?'

'I don't know.' She could almost imagine the shrug. 'It could be, I suppose, and...' He hesitated. 'Look, forget it, I'm possibly dragging you over here for nothing at all.'

'Let me be the judge of that, Jack. I'll be there in about fifteen minutes.'

* * *

Ray had volunteered to drive and she had been happy to let him. They pulled up outside Jack Mitchell's smart semi-detached home on Quarry Vale Road, and Karen gave a small wave as she saw Skye standing in the bay window, presumably waiting for them as she was jumping up and down in excitement.

Jack opened the front door and escorted them through to the kitchen where Daniel was sitting at the table. Skye had been removed by Pippa Mitchell, and a sort of peace descended.

'She's an absolute bundle of electricity, that child,' Jack said with a smile that caused his eyes to crinkle at the edges. He clearly loved the little girl. 'Daniel, you need any more milk?'

'No, thanks, Uncle Jack.' He pushed his glass to one side, and looked carefully at Karen and Ray. 'You're not taking me away, like you took Dad away?'

'Of course not, Daniel,' she reassured the child. 'We've called round for a little chat with your Uncle Jack. And we never take little ones away anyway.'

He seemed reassured, and Karen nodded to Jack to indicate he should lead them into whatever he wanted them to hear. She quietly placed her recorder on the table.

'Daniel, remember what we were talking about earlier?'

Daniel frowned. 'Was I naughty to say it?'

'Of course not,' Jack reassured his nephew. 'You should know by now you can say anything to me and it won't be naughty. So, tell Karen what you told me about Jenna.'

The pause seemed to go on forever, and then suddenly, after a quick glance at Jack, Daniel spoke. 'She hurt Mummy.'

'You saw her hurt Mummy?' Karen led the child gently.

He shook his head. 'I was still awake because Skye was being a pain, and wanting to iron me. I kept telling her we had to go to sleep and Mummy would be mad if she knew Skye was trying to iron me and make me like Flat Stanley.'

Just for a second, Karen was puzzled, but Jack explained. 'I gave them my old copy from my childhood of a book called *Flat Stanley*. They love it. It's quite funny, you should read it some-time. Apparently on that night, Skye wanted Daniel to be like Flat Stanley and able to slide under doors without opening them. Okay, Daniel, carry on. Just tell Karen what you told me.'

Daniel nodded. 'I went to my bedroom door to push her out and back to her own room. Then someone came to the door. I stopped moving because I didn't want Mummy to know I was still awake. Then I heard Jenna say a naughty word. And she asked where my dad was. They were shouting at each other, then there was a big crash, like something had fallen over, then I heard the front door slam and it all went quiet again. I pushed Skye into her own room because I knew it was a naughty word that Jenna had said and she shouldn't have said it while Skye was near. I went to bed and fell asleep.'

Karen looked at Jack and wanted the pair of them to huddle in each other's arms and cry. This child was their only witness to the murder of his mother. And he had no idea of the gravity of what he was saying, he was more concerned that his little sister didn't hear naughty words.

'Ray, stay with Daniel a moment, will you? I need a quick word with Jack.' She switched off the recorder and stood. Jack led her through to the conservatory and they sat facing each other.

Karen spoke before Jack had the chance. 'You were damn right to ring me,' she said. 'However, I am going to try my hardest to make sure this child doesn't have to repeat any of this in a court of law. If we can't get a confession out of her, then he may well be needed. He won't be seen, he will be protected, and he won't see anything because he will be in a separate room.'

He nodded. 'I think I knew it could come to that when I rang you, and I'll be honest, I was tempted not to do it. He's only a child, not old enough for the evil side of this bloody world, but he'll still have his dad. And us.'

'Thank you for doing this, Jack. I know it must have been hard. The urge to protect a child comes naturally to you as a father and a teacher, and I have much respect for you making the right decision. And I promise I'll try to keep him away from having to repeat any of this ever again. Hopefully Jenna will do the right thing.'

'Well, she's not managed that so far, has she? In fact, she couldn't have got anything more wrong. Elise and I were very close. Mum was always ill, and we really only had each other. Now she's taken that away from me.'

'I do, of course, have to ask you and your wife not to discuss this with anyone. It should be in the public domain by tomorrow, but even that's not a given, so keep it to yourself until you see a front-page story telling the news.'

'We will. We don't want anything jeopardising what she has coming to her, the evil bitch. What Daniel said this morning came as a shock, as you can imagine, because as far as we were concerned, Jenna was at the George with Rick. So who was Rick there with?'

Karen laughed. 'You want a job with the police? I honestly don't know but I should do in about two or three hours, if he suddenly discovers a way of telling the truth.'

She stood, and headed back to the kitchen to find Ray teaching Daniel how to draw fireworks. 'He's supposed to be going to a communal bonfire tomorrow,' he said. 'When I taught my kids how to draw them, they obliged by painting them on the walls all the way up the stairs. Just thought I'd better warn you.'

Jack grinned. 'We'll have a small one in the back garden, I think. Too much happening at the moment, it needs to be a bit quieter than a communal bonfire. Think it's time this government cancelled bonfire night once and for all, it's a nightmare. We've had bangs every night for the best part of the last two weeks, and it's bound to continue for a good week after the fifth of November.'

'And every copper and fireman and NHS employee would agree with you. Come on, Van Gogh, let's head back to the station. We have work to do. Thank you so much, Daniel, for talking to me.' She reached into her purse and removed the only cash she had on her. 'Here's a twenty-pound note. Get Uncle Jack to take you to buy some fireworks, pretty ones that Skye will like, not bangers that frighten cats and dogs. And me.'

* * *

Ray started the car. 'Lovely kid. Think you can keep him out of court?'

'If that cow of a woman confesses, I'll do my best. He won't be needed then, but we can, if necessary, let the judge have hearing of this recorded interview with Daniel, so that he can determine how long he's going to send her away for. I know she'll get life, but he can add or subtract with that. Let's try and make sure he adds.'

30

FRIDAY, 4 NOVEMBER

Karen was staring at Jenna Glaves, watching the way she couldn't keep her hands still, couldn't control a slight up and down jiggle in her legs, couldn't stop the constant back and forth of her head as if she was looking for something.

Jenna's duty solicitor was someone Karen hadn't seen before, but she had been notified he was called Ethan Gardner. They clearly had little to say to each other; Gardner was reading through some notes he had made, and Jenna was concentrating on how she was moving every bit of her body.

The woman was unhappy.

'We ready?' Karen asked Ray and he nodded.

They entered interview room A, carrying coffees, and both held a file. Karen's contained crime scene photographs, but she knew the main part of her interrogation would be around the deliberate lie told by Rick Langton that Jenna Glaves was with him on the night Elise was murdered.

Ray logged every person in for the benefit of the recording, then Karen began her questioning.

'Jenna, you have been cautioned. Did you understand the caution?'

'Of course I did. I'm not thick, you know.'

'Good. Then please don't pretend you don't understand any of the questions I'm about to ask you.'

Jenna shuffled on her chair.

'So, I want to take you back ten days or so, to the evening of Tuesday, 25 October 2022. Can you tell me what you did on that evening, please?'

'No.'

'Why not? Is there a reason?'

'I can't remember.'

'It's not much more than a week ago. Allow me to remind you about things that happened the day after. You received two children to look after, Daniel and Skye Langton, the children of your partner Rick Langton, who is currently in the interview room next door to you. The children were brought to you because their mother had been quite brutally murdered. Does that refresh your memory?'

She shrugged. 'Yeah. You could have just said the day Elise died.'

'Elise didn't simply die, did she? As I said, she was brutally murdered. Okay, tell me your movements between eight and ten o'clock that evening.'

She shrugged. 'I was home.'

'Doing what?'

'Watching TV.'

'Jenna, this is like pulling teeth. What did you watch on TV?'

Again she shrugged. 'Can't remember.'

'Where was Rick? Was he home with you? Maybe he knows what you watched on television.'

'He might do.' Her thumbs were circling each other at warp speed.

'DC Ledger, can you pop next door and ask Mr Langton what they watched on television on the night his wife died?'

'She's not his fucking wife!' Jenna's response was loud.

'When did they divorce?'

'It was going through.' The response this time was mumbled.

'Then in future we'll refer to Elise Langton as Rick Langton's wife. In this country, you're married until the Decree Absolute is in your possession. That hadn't happened, I understand.'

'He was going to marry me,' she said, her tone acerbic.

'Not in this lifetime,' Karen replied, 'according to him, anyway.'

Jenna pushed her chair away from the table and stood up. 'Can she speak to me like this?'

Ethan Gardner spoke for the first time. 'Sit down and shut up, Jenna. And yes, she can speak to you like this. I'll let you know when and if she crosses a line.'

Jenna retook her seat and resumed twirling her thumbs. Her right leg was beginning to have an almost violent tremble and Ray asked her if she would like a drink.

She smiled gratefully and asked if she could please have a cup of tea. He stood. 'DC Ledger leaving the room to get a drink for Miss Glaves.'

Ray stopped outside the door and smiled to himself. He normally addressed all females brought in for questioning by the title of Ms, but he had deliberately used the title Miss. She hadn't been pleased. It served to emphasise her single status, and she had clearly considered herself married to the philandering Rick Langton.

He got her a tea from the machine and carried it back inside the interview room, logging himself back in as he did so.

'Thank you,' she said, and almost smiled at him.

'You're welcome, Miss Glaves,' he said, and watched the smile disappear, possibly for ever. His boss was certainly winding her up.

Karen resumed her questioning.

'Okay, Jenna, let's go back to that night. We do know for definite that Rick wasn't with you until around eleven on Tuesday evening, 25 October. We have indisputable proof of that. He was at the George Hotel at Hathersage, having steak for his meal.'

Again she stood up, and again Gardner told her to sit down. Gardner was beginning to see the jealousy erupting out of her, and he knew he was powerless to stop her signing away a long stretch of her life. She seemed to have completely disregarded his advice to use no comment whenever things got a bit rough, she was answering everything.

'Who was he there with? What's her name? It wasn't bloody Elise. So who else has he got?'

'How do you know it wasn't bloody Elise?' Karen asked quietly.

There was utter silence for a moment as the woman who had stated she wasn't thick suddenly realised just how thick she had proved herself to be. Then she remembered Gardner's instruction.

'No comment.'

'We don't have the information yet as to who Rick was at the George with, but I imagine my officers have already discovered her name. They're speaking with him now. He's going to be charged with perverting the course of justice by deliberately making a false statement and giving you an alibi when you don't have one, but he will be released shortly. I can tell you she was curvy and buxom, with short red hair – this is from a description given by the bartender at the George.'

Jenna's eyes widened and filled with tears. 'Toyah Plant. My best mate. I asked her to be my bridesmaid. I'll fucking kill her.'

'Like you killed Elise Langton?' Karen deliberately lowered her voice.

Jenna screamed and banged her fists onto the table. And continued to scream then dropped the volume to sobs. 'I thought he was with her. I thought he was spending the evening with her. With Elise. I took a mallet with me, to frighten them, but she was on her own and she came for me, tried to take the mallet, so I hit her.'

Jenna was now blubbering wildly, wiping her nose and her eyes on her cardigan sleeve.

Despite Gardner's words advising her to shut the fuck up, it was obvious even to him that she had just confirmed she had murdered Elise Langton. This was his first duty solicitor job, and he hoped the rest of them he'd have in his life wouldn't be as difficult as this.

Ray passed a box of tissues across to the sobbing woman, who now seemed to have shrunk in front of their eyes. Every word she had uttered had been recorded and she accepted in her own mind that nothing she could say from here on out would take away what she'd said about the mallet that Elise had tried to take from her – 'so I hit her.' That phrase would reverberate around the courtroom.

She had lost everything.

Karen hadn't even opened the file with the crime scene photographs. She simply tucked it under her arm, and rose to leave. 'DC Ledger, take Miss Glaves to be charged with the murder of Elise Langton. DS Karen Nelson leaving the interview at...' she glanced at her watch, '11.23 p.m.'

* * *

Rick Langton was outside interview room B, with Ian Jameson.

'Everything okay?' Karen asked.

'It is. He's going to be charged because of the deliberate false statement, but then he'll be going home.'

She turned to Rick. 'Your children are with Jack and Pippa Mitchell. I spoke to them this morning, and I have to tell you that your son gave us valuable information about who murdered your wife. He was still awake when Jenna called at Elise's home, expecting to find you there. They had a shouting match, Elise tried to take the mallet from Jenna and Jenna hit her. Hard. Daniel heard it all, but even now I don't think he realises the significance of what happened. I'm hoping he won't have to attend court, but we'll cross that bridge if we ever get to it. Oh, and Jenna now knows just who you were with at the George that night, she recognised my description of her. Her best friend? Really?' She turned to Ian. 'Take him and charge him, DC Jameson.'

She headed back up to the briefing room, where everybody seemed to be waiting with bated breath. She held up a thumb, and there was a spontaneous round of applause.

'She confessed on tape,' she told them. 'Just don't let her anywhere near Rick Langton because I think she'll kill him as well. The woman he took to the George was her best mate.'

'Ouch,' someone at the back said clearly, and the round of applause happened again.

'Okay. Has anything come in? I'm going to get this interview written up and on the case file, and then hopefully I can finish around four. We've put a lot of foot hours in on this one, a lot of doorstep interviewing, so no overtime tonight, get home to your families. I've got a meat and potato pie to make for my particular family.'

Karen moved into her own office, and looked around at what everyone was doing. It was mainly smiling. This was how good it felt to get a result, and Phil Newton had played such an important part in it.

She pulled her keyboard towards her and began to type up the report of the interview. Everything felt peaceful, and she knew that sooner or later she would have to come up with a replacement for Phil. But not yet. Maybe in a month or two. Or a year or two.

She looked up to see Ray's face at her door window. She waved him in. 'Everything go okay?'

He nodded. 'She seemed to deflate. Gardner didn't speak at all, so whether she'll want him for her defence counsel I've no idea. She said nothing when she was charged, and she was escorted down to the cells. She's in front of the magistrates in the morning, and they'll remand her from there, so we've only got her overnight. Strange one this, wasn't it? There was nothing for quite a few days of some intense policing, and then bam! It all gets cleared up.'

'It feels good that we've tied it up, but it's exhausting. You fancy nipping round to Starbucks and getting us a latte? I'll pay.' She delved into her bag and took out her purse. 'Oh...'

He laughed at her. 'You gave all your money to the kids for some fireworks. I'll get them. You want a bun as well?'

'I daren't. I had this huge lamb shank last night, and I'll be honest, I've not wanted anything since. And I've to make a meat and potato pie for tonight, and eat it! I'll be on a diet all next week. So thanks for the offer, but a latte is enough. I'm hoping it will give me some energy, today has drained me. It's all very well knowing she's guilty, but until we're over the finishing line and actually charging her, everyone's on tenterhooks.'

'I'll be back in fifteen minutes or so. Don't fall asleep while you're waiting.'

'Fat chance. I've to finish the report of the interview, get the statement from Vinnie at the George logged onto the system, all sorts of niggling little bits to do. I said I was going home at four, but that might not actually happen.'

31

SATURDAY, 5 NOVEMBER

Carol sat at the breakfast bar, eating a slice of toast and studying her map of Norton. Having woken at the ridiculous hour of six, she decided it would be a good idea to have a coffee and head off out for a drive, trusting that if Hunter had parked her car overnight, it would potentially still be parked at such an early hour.

When she first handed in her CV to Matt Forrester, she had anticipated a more than satisfactory ending to her working life, being polite to visitors to the practice, keeping files in order, generally watching over the two men who had welcomed her so warmly. Instead, she had so far had one working day in hospital, done a major piece of work with WATSON, and now was – in her own small way – adding her own investigative work to the list. It was proving to be nothing like she had imagined it would be, and she was loving it. Even the lump on her head was slowly diminishing. And that was why she was heading out on a Saturday morning, not officially working, but sort of.

She folded her map, slipped her plate and cup into the dishwasher, and picked up her coat and bag. Time for action.

She drove once again up Norton Avenue and along Bochum Parkway, but this time veered left instead of right at the traffic island. She followed the long straight road to the next island and turned to her right, into the older part of Norton. She loved this area, it had a different vibe to the part she had already checked, and when they had been looking for a house around here, they had seen a perfect one that they immediately offered on, only to find an offer had been accepted the day before. Their next perfect house had been the one at Gleadless, possibly bought because of its blue front door.

She drove, her eyes peeled for a small white Peugeot. And within ten minutes, she saw it.

It was parked outside a bungalow, on the driveway. She had driven up the small cul-de-sac, around the turning circle at the end and back down, and it was on the return journey she saw it. In her two days of searching, this was the only white one she had seen, and her fingers tingled. She picked up her phone and took a picture, scribbled the address on her notepad, and drove quickly away before anybody came to ask questions.

She continued to drive around until she had covered the rest of her earlier designated area, then headed back towards Gleadless. She parked her car on her own drive, then instead of going inside, she crossed the main road to go to the office.

Matt and Steve's cars were parked on the front, and once inside, she pressed her intercom to say good morning to both of them.

As if by magic, they appeared at her office door.

'You okay?' Matt asked.

'Should you be at work?' Steve asked. 'You do know we don't work Saturdays?'

'Away with you. Go and find criminals. I've been at work for the past hour, Saturday or not, and yes, I'm fine. Hardly hurt at all when I washed my hair this morning, so even the lump's going down.'

'You've been at work for the past hour?' Matt said, suddenly recalling her words.

'I have. I figured if Hunter parked her car last night, it would still be parked up early this morning, so I was out and about early, singing along to Billy Joel. There are worse things to do.'

'I thought you were taking it easy.' Matt frowned.

'I did. You can't go above forty in any part of Norton, and most of it is a twenty zone. Couldn't take it much easier. I found one white Peugeot, right model.' She took out her phone, scrolled to pictures and handed it to Matt. 'Think we can persuade some friendly police person to track who owns this?'

Matt stared at the picture. 'Give me quarter of an hour.'

* * *

Ray answered his mobile phone with a small sigh that was part regret and part pleasure. It was good to see Matt Forrester's name on his screen once again.

'Boss? Everything okay?'

'It's fine, Ray. And you? And maybe you didn't get the memo, but I'm no longer your boss. Shall we make it Matt from now on?'

'Yes, boss. Been a funny old week, but a result yesterday made it feel better. What can I do for you?'

'A car registration. We have the address where it's parked, just really want to know we have the right owner.' He read out the number plate from the small picture on Carol's phone, and Ray said he would ring him as soon as he had the information.

* * *

As they sat around Matt's desk discussing ongoing cases, large ongoing ones and smaller more immediate ones, Steve was trying to check Carol out surreptitiously. She looked okay, but the blow had been serious enough to necessitate an overnight stay in hospital...

'Steve, I am absolutely fine.' She spoke without looking at him, knowing exactly what he was thinking. 'Even the headache has gone now. I had a brilliant night's sleep, and I am not taking time off work, Saturday or not. This case has become personal. Besides, I haven't had the pleasure of punching my attacker in the nose yet.'

Matt and Carol grinned at each other, and Matt tried to hide the laughter as he spoke. 'That might have been suggested as a form of retaliation because she didn't want to formally report the attack to Karen.'

'What? That allowed then?'

'Only if you do it without witnesses. And don't get blood on your clothes; they can tell anything with DNA these days.'

'Seems a lot easier being a landscape gardener.'

'Not as much fun, though,' Matt said and then returned to the task at hand. 'Okay, we have to make it a priority to find out who broke in here, but more importantly, why.'

Steve shrugged. 'There's nothing here worth taking. We don't carry cash on the premises, every bit of information in this place is also in the cloud so even if they take it, we've still got it. It doesn't make sense. Even if they just want to access our files, it's not a two-minute job. I am right, aren't I?'

Carol nodded. 'You are. You do have expensive top-of-the-range equipment with these computers, plus expensive state-of-the-art security—'

'Except it was easily breached with a ladder and a well-disguised burglar.' There was a touch of anger in Matt's tone.

'But everything's now sorted with the vulnerable windows. And the whole system will be connected directly to Moss Way within the next week. We're paying mega bucks for that, but we need safety as a priority. It seems as soon as we start investigating anything, somebody tries to muscle in. Won't happen again. Carol, this is no longer a drop-in centre, everything is by appointment only and there are only five key holders: the three of us, plus Herms and Karen. Only Steve and I know the key code to your office, and basically you hold everything that goes off in here in the palm of your hand. I have no idea what else we can do except buy a Kalashnikov or something similar on a just-in-case basis.'

Carol laughed. 'That sounds like an excellent idea, and in other circumstances I might have thought it was a joke. Seems it's not.'

'It's all for your protection, Carol.' Matt sounded serious. 'If anything happens to you, we've blown it because we don't know how anything works.'

'Gee, thanks,' Carol responded. 'I feel so needed.'

All three of them burst out laughing, and in the midst of it, Matt's phone rang.

'Boss?'

'Yes, Ray. It's Matt.'

'Sorry, boss, I forgot. That car belongs to a Susan Hunter. Is that all you need?'

'Thanks, Ray. You're a star. I owe you one.'

'A pint with froth on?'

He laughed. 'Any time, pal.'

The other two had heard both sides of the conversation, and Carol punched the air. 'Yes! Well worth getting up early. So now what do we do?'

'We cogitate.'

* * *

Becky Davis was finally able to enjoy a little bit of peace. Florence was fed and asleep in her crib in the corner of the lounge, Harry was upstairs on his computer, and Brian was in his office doing whatever it was Brian did in his office. The lounge was reasonably tidy given a new baby now lived there, and Becky had no intention of doing anything other than putting up her feet and relaxing for half an hour with a book. A book about murder, and she wanted nothing about babies to be in that book. She scrolled through the library on her Kindle to see what delights she had downloaded after recommendations from book group members on Facebook, and realised she had two L.J. Ross books to catch up. Problem solved. She completed the download of *Bamburgh* and rested her head on the cushion. By page five, she was asleep, utterly exhausted after baby Florence's restless night.

She dreamt. Easy dreams of going on holiday with Brian and the two children, easy dreams of a life without stress, without controlling arguments that usually revolved around Matt Forrester.

She didn't hear Brian come in, walk over to the baby, and walk out again, closing the door – none of which was loud enough to wake her up.

But was just loud enough to wake Florence.

She didn't cry, just snuffled quietly, expecting – even at this young age – that someone would arrive to pick her up.

Harry came in looking for his headphone charger, and still Becky slept on. He found the charger, and glanced at his baby sister as he passed by. Her blue eyes fixed on him, and Harry fell in love. He reached towards her, and she curled her hand around his forefinger. He was entranced. Brian had actively discouraged him from touching her, quoting germs as a reason for the non-contact, but Harry was revelling in this tiny human clinging on to his finger, germs or no germs.

Until the door opened again, this time with a bang, and Brian roared.

'Get away from that child. I've warned you about passing germs on to her.'

Harry gently removed his finger from the tiny hand, and without saying anything walked past Brian, intending to head back upstairs. Brian raised his hand and hit him with considerable force on the back of the head, knocking Harry into the door jamb.

'Get upstairs, young man. I'll deal with you later.'

Harry rubbed his forehead, feeling a lump already starting to form. When he took his hand away, there was blood on it. He wouldn't give in to tears, not in front of Dickhead, but once his dad saw his head, he knew there would be problems.

Harry reached his room and sat on his bed. He didn't move for half an hour, then pulled a holdall out of his wardrobe. He packed what he thought he might need, then filled his school backpack with a sleeping bag and two blankets. He switched off his phone, thankful it was fully charged, stuffed his charger cable into the bag along with it and closed the zipper. This life wasn't what he wanted, and it was a life he didn't need to have. He would just have to work on his dad, convince him everything would be much better if he could live with him and Karen.

He popped into the bathroom before leaving, where he dabbed at his forehead while trying not to make a sound, cleaning away the now dried-up blood. It looked pretty bad to him.

He stood at the top of the stairs, his heavyweight coat on, his Wednesday hat on his head, scarf around his neck, his backpack in place, and his holdall grasped in his hand. He had almost seventy pounds in money, and that he slipped into his pocket.

He listened and could hear Dickhead and his mother in the kitchen. He would have liked to have seen baby Florence before he left but he couldn't risk being discovered. He crept down the stairs, opened the front door and slipped outside. Closing the door created a soft click, and he picked up the holdall, and moved as fast as he could.

Dickhead had won. He had what he wanted now, his mother and his baby sister. And Harry felt free, exhilarated as he raced around the corner and out of sight of anybody looking out of the bay window of his home. His ex-home.

Harry knew he was on his own for the foreseeable future; he couldn't take the risk of his dad seeing what Dickhead had done to him, but Harry knew a place he could go.

He would keep moving, keep one step in front, or behind, any searchers that he guessed would be out looking for him.

Then, once the lump had gone, he could go to his dad.

32

SATURDAY, 5 NOVEMBER

By mutual agreement, Matt, Steve and Carol decided to forget Susan Hunter until Monday morning and by eleven the office was locked up and as secure as it could be without yet being connected directly to the police.

Matt hoped he could put it on a back burner until Monday, but the truth of the matter was that inside he was raging – he wanted to know what this woman was playing at, why she was targeting the Forrester Agency, and what the story was about her friendship with his father, because he couldn't see much of a friendship in any of the emails. Dave had avoided her as much as he could, eventually blocking any communications.

He followed Steve's car home, and they parked up side by side.

'Carol's proving to be a bit of a gem, isn't she?'

'Certainly is,' Matt agreed. 'We're going to have to start paying her.'

Steve grinned. 'Might be a good idea. Harry coming over later?'

'Yep. Having a bit of a bonfire in the back, watch a few fireworks, eat chestnuts. You coming across?'

'Would Hermia miss it? Yeah, we'll be there. Six-ish?'

'That's fine. Ask Herms if she can make some bonfire toffee. She's ace at that.'

The two men headed for their own homes, and Matt tracked Karen down to the bedroom where she was fast asleep. He leaned across and gently kissed her. She stirred, opening her eyes. Then she sat up and looked around, as if lost.

'I came up for a shower,' she said. 'I only rested my head for a minute.'

'Then get your shower now, and I'll go make us a sandwich for lunch. Don't forget Harry's coming over and we're having a bonfire later.'

'I put a slow cooker full of hash on early this morning. Well prepared. That'll feed all of us and keep us warm. What time is Harry arriving, or do you have to go get him?'

'I said I'd pick him up at three. That okay? He can help build the bonfire then.'

'That's fine. He's staying overnight?'

'He is. I spoke to him yesterday and he was really looking forward to it. Must admit, it was always a high spot of my childhood, was bonfire night. Is Herms making a Guy Fawkes?'

'Yes. I saw her earlier, before I fell asleep, and she asked for some of your old joggers, and an old T-shirt.'

He paused. 'You told her to get lost, didn't you?'

'Not at all, I gave her those old black ones that are covered in paint, and that old Metallica T-shirt.'

She watched the colour fade from his face.

'That's okay, isn't it, sweetheart?'

* * *

Matt ran around the corner to Steve and Hermia's place and barged through their back door.

'Where's my clothes?' he gasped.

'In your wardrobe? Chest of drawers?' Steve suggested, while Hermia stared at her brother.

'What do you mean?'

'My painting joggers and my Metallica T-shirt! Karen's given them to you for Guy Fawkes, she said.'

Hermia took hold of his hand and took him through to the lounge. 'Come and meet this year's Mr Fawkes.'

The Guy was lounging on the sofa, dressed in an old pair of jeans stuffed with newspaper, and a huge yellow jumper. Matt slumped onto a chair. His head dropped into his hands and he groaned.

'She's just having me on, isn't she? It was the Metallica T-shirt. She knows how important it is, how much I cherish it. Is it murder or manslaughter if I go back home and kill her?'

'Murder, I think,' Hermia said, 'so not worth it. For what it's worth, I think it's hilarious and I wish I'd been there when she first told you.'

He trudged back home, and found Karen wrapped in a towel, heading into the bedroom to get changed.

'You lied.'

'True story. I did.'

'Why?'

'I wanted to see how much panic would show on a grown man's face at the thought of losing a much-loved T-shirt.' She dropped the towel. 'Now come here and let me make it up to you, show you it doesn't really matter because I love you so much.'

Matt stared at her. 'You want to give Hermia anything else, if this is what I get when you do?'

'You didn't recognise the big yellow jumper then?'

She pulled him into an incredibly, unbelievably beautiful long kiss. By the time she'd finished making him feel better, he'd forgotten all about the big yellow jumper.

* * *

Matt looked at his watch and stood. 'I'm nipping over to get Harry. Be about twenty minutes. Anything you need from the shops while I'm out and about?'

'We've about half a bottle of Henderson's Relish. Think it's enough?'

He pursed his lips. 'Maybe. But there'll be some at Herm's house if we run out.'

'Then we have everything we need.'

He leaned over her and kissed her. 'And so do we.'

* * *

Matt was a careful driver; always had been, always would be. He reached the Davis home in eleven minutes, and knocked on the door.

Brian opened it, saying, 'Becky's feeding Florence. I'll go and get Harry.'

Matt leaned against the porch and waited for the mad scramble as his son tumbled down the stairs, eager to be with his dad. He heard several doors slam, and then Davis running down the stairs.

'He's not here. Where the fuck is he?'

Matt pushed past him and went up to Harry's room, taking the stairs two at a time. He opened the door and quietly said his name.

'You in here, Harry? You're not in any trouble, I'm here for you. For the bonfire.' There was no response, so he walked across to check his wardrobe. The familiar blue and white of his football shirts, all three of them, were noticeable by their absence.

Davis appeared in the doorway.

'Where does he keep his Wednesday gear?' Matt asked him. 'His scarves and hats?'

'Top drawer, I believe.'

Matt pulled it open and there was very little in it, and certainly nothing in blue and white.

'He's gone. What the fuck's happened here that would make him take off?' He pushed Davis up against the wall. 'You'd better start praying that nothing's happened to my lad, Davis.'

'I'll have you arrested for aggressive behaviour towards a senior officer, Forrester.'

Matt looked him up and down in disgust. 'That's not aggressive yet, believe me. But if my son isn't with me in the next hour, you'd better start praying, because I just know it's you that's caused him to run.'

He ran back down the stairs and into the lounge, where Becky was breastfeeding Florence. She quickly covered herself with a small cloth, but Matt just looked at her. 'Seen it all before, Becky. Harry's gone. Now think where he will have gone to. Any friends who'd give him a bed for the night?'

'He doesn't really have friends.'

Matt could see tears in her eyes, a woman who had no idea what was going on, having only just found out that one of her children had disappeared.

'When did you last see him?'

She looked blank. 'Lunchtime? I think so, anyway. I just

assumed he was upstairs on his computer. We don't see that much of him.'

'Becky, for fuck's sake, he's your son. Your firstborn. And you don't see that much of him?'

There was no sign of Brian Davis, so Matt went through the whole house checking every room, then into the back garden where he checked the summer house and the tool shed. But Harry was nowhere, and Matt had to admit temporary defeat.

'Karen, we have a problem.' He explained the situation over the phone, and Karen said she would be with him in ten minutes, along with Steve.

He tried Harry's phone number for a third time, but knew his son had switched it off as it went directly to voicemail. While he waited, he began to walk the surrounding streets, calling out his son's name, speaking to people, asking them to check their outbuildings.

Steve pulled up alongside him and they headed back to the Davis house to get Matt's car, then all three of them split up and began to drive round the area, asking everyone they came across if they'd seen a young lad, probably wearing a Sheffield Wednesday scarf and hat.

When they next regrouped outside the Davis home, Brian and Becky came out to them.

'Anything?' Brian asked.

Matt shook his head. 'Has something happened to make him do this? Has there been an argument, an altercation?'

'No, not really. I told him to stop holding Florence's hand, but that's all.'

'You didn't touch him?'

'How dare you?'

'I'll repeat it, and for my child I'll dare anything. Davis, did you touch him?'

'He fell into the door jamb. Got a bit of a lump on his forehead.'

Matt pulled back his arm and smashed his fist straight into Davis's face. There was a splatter of blood, and Karen turned away.

'DS Nelson, arrest this thug.' Davis couldn't have said it any louder.

'Whatever for?' she said. 'He's not done anything.'

'He just hit me.'

'Well, I didn't see it. Did you, Steve?'

Steve shook his head. 'No, but I saw Superintendent Davis walk into the door jamb of his front door. That's not a crime, is it?'

'Okay, this is getting us nowhere,' Karen said. 'We need officers out looking. I'm going to Moss Way, see who I can pull in, although we're going to be stretched because it's bonfire night. Get out of my sight, Davis, or I'll arrest you for aggravated assault of a child. It may still happen when we find Harry and find out what went off here today.'

She turned her back on her superior officer and walked back to her car.

'I'll ring you as soon as I know how many feet on streets I can muster, Matt. If you and Steve can continue to cover the area, it will be a start.'

She could see the pain on Matt's face, so she walked over to him and kissed him. 'We'll find him,' she said quietly, then disappeared at high speed.

Becky was standing in the doorway, tears rolling down her cheeks. She looked at her husband.

'Brian, you have blood all over your face. I suggest you go and have a wash.' She reached up to his face, intentionally coating her hand with his blood, then transferred it to the door jamb. 'I'll wash the paintwork down where you walked into it, and then when we get back inside, I want to know exactly what you've done to make my son leave home. He's an eleven-year-old out there all alone, and if anything happens to him...'

Davis said nothing, simply walked inside his home, and up the stairs.

'I'm sorry, Matt,' Becky said. 'Please go and find him. Bring him home.'

'I'm sorry too, Becky, but know this, and know it well. When I find our son, he will visit you at weekends only, and only if I consider it safe that he is here. The rest of the time, he will live with Karen and me, Steve and Hermia. It's what he wants, and I think it's time we all listened to him. One thing that is definite is that I won't allow him to live with Dickhead Davis.'

He left her standing on the doorstep, the cries of her new baby reaching her, but still she didn't move. She knew if she attempted to walk at that moment in time, she would fall in a blubbering heap at the foot of her stairs. She leaned against the blood-smeared door jamb, and let her head drop, sobbing until she thought her heart would crack open with the agony of the moment. It was over. Her marriage was done. She wanted this man out of her home and her life.

33

SATURDAY, 5 NOVEMBER

They arrived in droves. Everyone Karen contacted left their bonfire preparations, their families, their own lives, to help find the missing child.

She held a briefing within half an hour of making the first call, and ten minutes after that, the room emptied as everyone ran for either squad cars or their own vehicles. A missing child was always responded to with immediacy, but this missing child was one of their own close-knit police family, and all resources would be made available.

'Where's Davis?' Ray asked, before heading out.

'Don't even ask,' Karen snarled. 'I couldn't tell everybody this, but it seems to me that he's the reason behind our lad running away. We have to get him back before nightfall, Ray, it's so bloody cold at night, and he's only eleven. According to his mother he doesn't have friends as such, presumably because Dickhead doesn't encourage it, so I think he's left without any sort of plan, just a need to escape. We've left Hermia at home in case he turns up there, but he's taken a sleeping bag and warm clothes, so I guess he's planning on sleeping out. He's running scared, and it's breaking my heart.'

Ray hugged her. 'We'll find him. I'm going in my car, frees up a squad car. I'll keep you informed, boss. Stay strong.'

She watched him leave the room, then grabbed her bag and headed towards her Kia.

* * *

The streets were alive with police officers and squad cars, loud hailers notifying communities of why there was all the activity in their area, and requesting that they check their outbuildings.

By five o'clock, the daylight was fading to a gloomy greyness, with the temperature dropping rapidly, although there was no loss of hope in finding Harry before the end of the evening.

Small bonfires, where the children of the family were very young, were already starting to appear, with the odd rocket or two shooting up into the heavens. It brought Daniel and Skye Langton into Karen's mind, and she hoped they could enjoy the evening Uncle Jack had organised for them. She tried to put Rick Langton out of her mind, feeling overwhelming anger towards him for not having told the truth in the first place. If he had, Phil would be out and about, joining in this search for Harry.

The ranks were swelled, and depleted, throughout the course of the night. Night shift workers were despatched as they arrived on duty, and the wearier day shift workers went home for a few hours of rest, planning on re-joining the search the next day if Harry wasn't found overnight.

It was a stressful first day of searching, and Matt, Karen and Steve arrived home after midnight, supposedly to get some rest before starting again.

Hermia looked grey. The worry had taken its toll, and Steve sent her straight home to bed, saying he would follow her ten minutes later. That didn't happen.

Matt made a pot of coffee, and they sat around a large ordnance survey map which covered the kitchen table, tracing potential routes Harry could have taken.

Steve rubbed his forehead in frustration. 'He could even have left the area, got on a train and be anywhere in the country.'

Matt shook his head. 'He's not that worldly wise. I feel he's here.' He stabbed his finger onto the map. 'I don't think he's ever been on a train, it's not something we've done. Even the odd away match we've reached by car, so I don't think that would even occur to him. So, on here we need to search for anywhere that would offer him some sort of shelter.' He groaned. 'When we were refurbing this place – and finishing refurbing Steve's house – we taught him a lot about building dens. Remember?'

Steve nodded. 'He got pretty good at it, kept taking our best bits of wood, tying it all together with string and duct tape. On the plus side, if it gets him safely through the cold of tonight, I'll take that. We called him Bear Grylls, didn't we?'

Matt nodded. 'And that's what he's doing, I know it is. He needed time to plan, and he'll have gone to ground somewhere and barricaded himself under some kind of cover. Maybe if he's still not been found by morning, the helicopter will be able to spot something. But I know he's in this area, and at some point he's going to contact me. He's not daft. His phone's off now because he's angry at his mum and Dickhead, but he also knows he needs to conserve his battery. He can't plug a charger into a stone wall or a tree trunk. So...'

Matt moved his finger back to the red cross that indicated the Davis home.

Steve also leaned forward. 'And he would know to stop before it got dark so he could see what he was doing. I reckon he has to be in a couple of miles' radius of Becky's house.'

Karen handed Matt a pencil. 'Work out the two-mile radius and let's see what sort of terrain we're dealing with. Then let's try and think like an eleven-year-old who is so unhappy he's had to leave home. Why hasn't he come here?'

Matt dropped his head. 'I said he could come and live with us in a couple of years, but I felt he needed his mum right now. I'm such a bloody idiot. Did I miss a sign?'

Karen reached across and squeezed his hand. 'You missed nothing, Matt. We had to trust that Becky would choose wisely in picking a stepdad for our boy, even knowing what we knew about Davis. And Becky is a good mum. I think I can probably forecast what will happen next in her life, new baby or no new baby. But no matter what happens in the Davis household, we give Harry the power to choose where he wants to live, and if he chooses here, we work around the obvious problems, like our jobs.'

'There are four of us,' Steve said. 'We will work it out. Let's just get him away from that thug. You think he hit Harry?'

Matt nodded. 'I do. It's going to be talked through when Harry gets home, and I'll find out if there's been any other physical abuse. If there has, a busted nose is the least of Davis's worries.' He gestured to the map. 'So, this is the two-mile area. It takes in Charnock woods, heading towards Ford and further on into Eckington. He knows these places, and it would make sense for him to go there. However, there's also Shire Brook Valley, which holds a myriad of hiding places.' Just for a second, a smile flashed across Matt's face. 'I lost my virginity in a tent in the Shire Brook Valley.'

Karen grinned. 'Me too.' She traced her finger along the line drawn by Matt. 'Would he have walked this far?'

'Yes, don't forget we searched in the opposite direction at the beginning, before we had dozens of coppers arrive to help us, so he initially could have had a good start on us. And Birley Spa Wood is dense enough to give him lots of cover, plus water from the Shire Brook itself. Remember how he researched Bear Grylls after we laughingly said he was in training to take over from him? It's the fact that I know he's capable that's keeping me going. The thing that is flattening me is that he's only eleven, and he's too trusting.'

Karen's phone rang and she grabbed at it.

'DS Nelson.'

She listened for a minute, and looked at Matt, shaking her head. Matt slumped, resting his head in his hands.

'Thanks,' Karen said. 'And tell everybody I'll be in the briefing room for six, to sort out where we go next. We've been promised an early start with the helicopter tomorrow, weather permitting. Please thank everybody for their help.'

She disconnected. 'They're heading either home or back to Moss Way, until dawn. They can see nothing tonight, especially now all the bonfires have burnt out. It's very smoky out there, as we know, so they've had to stop until they can see again – they'd probably miss him anyway in the dark. Much as I wanted to scream at them to keep looking, I have to accept the facts. There's not even a bright moon to see anything by.' She stood. 'Okay, I'm setting my alarm for five, so let's grab a few hours of sleep, and let's trust our boy that he's hunkered down somewhere safe, he's snug in that amazing sleeping bag of his, and hopefully sheltered from the rain that's promised for about three o'clock. I know Harry, he'll have sorted it.'

Steve said goodnight and went home. Matt and Karen,

despite being convinced they wouldn't sleep, were asleep in five minutes, their arms around each other, taking comfort and solace from their love for each other and for Harry.

* * *

The cockerel call alarm on Karen's phone pierced the early-morning air, and she yelled at it to shut up. Then she remembered. Matt was already sitting on the edge of the bed, shaking his head and trying to inject some sort of life into his body that had walked so much the day before. He knew it would be on repeat until he found his son.

'Is it raining?' he asked.

Karen peered through the curtains. 'Not at the moment. Ground looks dry, so hopefully it hasn't rained on Harry either. I'll go and put the percolator on while you shower, then I'll have mine. Okay?'

He nodded, misery written onto his face. 'Where is he, Karen?'

'We'll find him today. We have a full twelve hours or so as opposed to only a couple of workable hours yesterday. Come on, be strong, and let's get out there and organise the people we do have.'

As Karen reached the bottom of the stairs, the doorbell rang. She let Steve in, and he followed her to the kitchen.

'Hermia's staying put, but she's been out and checked all our sheds and summer houses already, just in case he's arrived since the last of the five inspections she did yesterday. That boy is in for a proper telling-off from Aunty Herms, I'm telling you. After she's covered him in sloppy kisses, I might add.'

'I know exactly how she feels.' Karen switched on the coffee machine and placed three cups at the side of it. 'I could shake him, I feel so angry, but it's what love is about, isn't it? When we were in Florida, I saw what a special lad he was: kind, considerate, funny. But I'm not laughing now. Pour the coffees out, will you, Steve, when it's finished dripping and gurgling. And stick some bread in the toaster; it may be all we get to eat today.'

Wearily, she climbed the stairs and reached the top the same time as Matt left the bathroom, towelling his hair. 'It's all yours. Steve here?'

'Yep, cooking breakfast.'

'I don't think—'

'Matt, it's toast. We have to have some sort of fuel inside us, and this is probably all we'll get today, so a couple of slices will help. And coffee is on.'

She walked into the bathroom, slid the door lock across, sat on the edge of the toilet seat, cried, and prayed.

34

SUNDAY, 6 NOVEMBER

Radio Sheffield launched an appeal at 7 a.m., and by 7.30 there had been several reported sightings, none of which proved to be viable. Volunteers had assembled in Jaunty Park, and Karen had despatched Kevin Potter and Jaime Hanover, who was suffering with a sprained ankle, to organise and direct activities.

By eight, the helicopter was buzzing around like a giant dragonfly high on heroin, and everyone was eyeing the dark clouds with trepidation. Most of the volunteers had arrived with rainwear – they were the smart ones who had checked the weather forecast before leaving home.

Karen had remained with her team, but Matt and Steve walked their pre-planned route, heading towards Hackenthorpe and Beighton, and dropping down into the beautiful Shire Brook Valley. They walked the paths leading down to the pond, veering off every few yards to check dense thickets of old branches, overpopulated areas of trees, and anything that could conceivably hide a small child. Every few minutes, Matt checked his phone in case he had missed a call, but there was nothing.

They reached the pond and sat down to ease their aching legs for a few minutes.

A pair of swans paddled over to inspect them and to check if they had brought food, and Matt had to smile as he heard Steve apologising to them, explaining they were there to find a missing child and hadn't thought to bring some bread.

The pond was a place of peace, and the two men sat quietly, simply taking it all in.

'Who was it then?' Steve asked.

'Amy Warrington,' Matt replied, knowing the question about his lost virginity would come sooner or later.

Steve gave a quick nod. 'Nice lass.'

'She moved from Sheffield about two weeks after that, and I met Becky.'

'You didn't mention it at the time.'

'I know. I knew you'd take the piss, and probably spread it around half the school.'

'As if. Come on, let's crack on and find this lad of ours.'

They stood and completed the full circuit of the pond before continuing deeper into the valley. The helicopter passed over twice, but still Matt's phone remained silent.

* * *

Harry shivered and snuggled further down into his sleeping bag. He remembered his dad laughing at him when he had chosen it, saying it would keep him warm on his next visit to the Arctic, but his dad obviously didn't know how cold it could get in Eckington woods in November.

He pulled his hat further down, wincing as it touched the lump on his forehead. He couldn't go home to his dad until the lump disappeared, he knew that. If his dad found out what had happened, he would go for Dickhead and get himself in big trouble. He couldn't go home until he could explain it away by saying he had hit it on something innocuous, like a low-hanging branch.

Sleep had only been sporadic. He had chosen a well-hidden place behind rocks that in happier times he had clambered over, but the bangs of fireworks had gone on until after midnight, and it had definitely been colder than he imagined it would be. In the early hours, he had dragged bundles of dead branches and fashioned a shelter of sorts, but had returned to his sleeping bag as soon as he could, eager to warm himself.

On his journey over here, he had called into a shop and bought crisps, biscuits, sausage rolls and a large bottle of Coke. He'd stashed the bottle upright between two of the rocks, and put the food into his now empty backpack. He had to ration the food. He knew he was stuck here until the lump disappeared, so the food had to last him. He couldn't risk venturing out for more, his picture would shortly be plastered everywhere.

He knew enough about phones that they could track where you were, almost pinpoint the exact spot, so he had to leave it switched off. Phil Newton had once explained the intricacies of mobile phones and their value to detectives.

He felt tears prick his eyes as he thought about Phil. He'd always liked him. He ignored the little voice inside his head that was saying his dad had enough on his plate following the death of his friend, without his son going missing.

And Harry now had another issue – he needed a wee.

* * *

Matt and Steve had passed other searchers on their way back to the entry point of the valley, and they exited on to the Hackenthorpe estate, where they sank gratefully into Matt's car.

'Helicopter seems to have disappeared,' Steve said.

'It's a limited time thing, borrowing that,' Matt explained. 'It's a good tool to have when you're searching for a moving object, say a car or a burglar legging it from the crime scene, but I reckon Harry has morphed into Bear Grylls and decided to go to ground until all the fuss has died down. The helicopter is a bit high to spot something that isn't moving, and if Harry has built a hide of some sort, it'll blend into the winter background for sure.'

Steve turned to face Matt. 'He'll come home, you know. And he'll come home to you. He'll not want anything more to do with Dickhead, which in some ways is a good thing, but at the moment he's licking his wounds and trying to be a big brave man like his dad. I'm trying hard to trust his skills, knowing him as I do, but I'd feel a lot happier if he was five years older.'

'Me too. My brain keeps saying *but he's only eleven.*' Matt sighed. 'So where next? Let's try and think like an eleven-year-old kid.'

'He'll have gone somewhere he knows well. Where do you take him when you're not playing at being a detective?'

Matt waved a hand. 'Here. We also do Charnock woods, the Ford area, and Eckington woods. Let's go to Jaunty Park, find out where they need to send people. Apparently Jaime and Kevin are supervising that.'

He switched on the engine and headed out of the valley and up to the top of one of Sheffield's famous seven hills, before dropping down slightly to reach Jaunty Park.

Jaime spotted the two of them and limped over.

'Hi, boss. So sorry this has happened. We've got volunteers out all over the place, but no reports of any sightings yet.'

'Thanks, Jaime. Have you got anybody in Eckington woods, or around the Ford area? They're spots Harry knows well.'

Jaime opened her file and showed him the map. 'We're fully covered in Charnock woods as you can imagine, because it's the closest point and easiest for the less able to navigate, but Ford and Eckington are a bit further afield. There's around six volunteers at each one but our own personnel are also there. No responses so far.'

'Then we'll go down there, and join that group at Eckington, before it gets too dark to see. Have you seen Karen?'

'Yes, she's been all over the place. Her voice is a bit rusty, she says she's been yelling Harry's name for hours.'

'Thanks, Jaime. And are you okay? You're limping...'

'Yes, boss. Jumped out of the way of a firework on Friday night and my ankle gave way. It's better than it was, but I'm on standing still duty today because of it.'

'Anything you're doing is gratefully acknowledged. And it's not boss any more, it's Matt.' He knew his words were simply going over the top of her head. She heard them, and ignored them. Just as Ray Ledger did. Just as Phil Newton had.

He left her advising a group of three teenagers, who had just turned up wanting to know if they could help, and he and Steve headed back to the car.

'Eckington woods it is, then. Would have been a bit of a walk for Harry, but he's done it before. Let's go see if he's done it again.'

* * *

It was starting to drizzle as they parked the car, and Matt felt his heart lurch. Not only would his son be cold, scared and miserable, but he could now add wet to the list. He hoped with all his lurching heart that Harry had built himself a shelter just as he and Steve had taught him over the years.

Pine fronds will stop light rain. He tried to project the thoughts to his son, knowing there was no way of doing that.

At the entrance to the woods, they spoke to the constable on duty who had spent all day directing volunteers on which way to go to search. He recognised Matt immediately and also called him boss. Matt gave up. Would they never stop thinking of him like that?

They were shown the map hastily cobbled together and photocopied by Karen before she let anybody loose in the woods.

'Can you remember where you took him before?' Steve was inspecting the details on the map closely.

'He liked to be near the river. Liked to be muddied up to his chin, if he could manage it, but the river really was what he loved. Having said that, it's too damp and muddy to sleep by the river, and the cover isn't dense enough, so I think we can discount that and go for further away from the water. He just loves woods, so I can't really say where we should start to look. And he's going to squirrel himself away properly now, because he'll think he's in trouble.'

Matt paused to brush away a tear.

'Steve, he'll be freezing. This will be his second night under the stars, and that's no good for a little lad. I've been thanking God all day that I paid for an expensive sleeping bag, because he was going camping just after Christmas with the Scouts, and I didn't want him to be cold. What if I hadn't been able to afford the best one in Go Outdoors? We don't know what else he's got with him, but I hope he brought other warm stuff as well.'

* * *

Harry could hear voices not too far away, women he thought, and gathered up everything that wasn't already pushed between the two big rocks. As quietly as he could, he stuffed everything into the gap, then followed, pulling the large branches behind him to hide the opening. He pummelled his sleeping bag into a chair shape, and sat, holding the branches up so that nothing could be seen externally. He hoped.

The voices drew closer, and he could hear them intermittently calling his name. He remained absolutely still and silent. The voices eventually became quieter and the people passed by, but still he remained immobile. It was only when he could no longer hear them calling his name that he dared to move.

He lowered the branches to the floor cautiously, knowing they would become his bed for the second night running, yet he still didn't move from his place of safety. He couldn't let his dad see his head.

Gradually the darkness deepened and only then did he move from between the rocks. He put the two blankets on top of the branches that had helped cushion the hardness of the packed earth underneath, then pulled out the sleeping bag. He was shivering with cold and fear, but fear of his father going to prison for hammering Dickhead overrode all other sensations. He made himself as warm as he could, wrapping his scarf around his nose and mouth, bringing the two ends together at the front, before zipping his coat all the way up to his throat, then he yanked his hat down to cover his ears, wincing as it passed over the forehead bump. His hood then went up around his hat and he completely zipped up his coat.

Harry immediately felt warmer. He took some biscuits out of his bag, had a drink from the bottle and finished off with a packet of crisps. He stuffed everything away in his backpack, closed up both bags in case he needed to move quickly, and snuggled down in his sleeping bag.

The night sounds in the woods were strange to his ears: snuffling sounds, the creaking of trees in the wind that was increasing in strength, and the gentle pitter patter of the rain that seemed to get just a little bit heavier with every passing minute. He wriggled his body, which was encased like an Egyptian mummy, until the rock almost hung over him, and he felt a little more sheltered. Eventually his eyes closed with exhaustion, and he slept.

35

SUNDAY, 6 NOVEMBER

Carol, at her own suggestion, had spent the day in the office, another base covered in case Harry would consider it to be a safe place. She had tidied, she had made frequent trips out to the couple of sheds in the back of the property, and she had attempted to read her book.

She tried not to let her mind travel to the possibility of abduction – the criminal community hadn't liked Dave Forrester, and they most certainly didn't like Matt. Could this be somebody taking revenge? Matt had told her what they knew and therefore it didn't point to abduction, it pointed to a runaway scared little boy who couldn't take the home situation any longer, but there was still that small niggle at the back of her mind.

What if somebody had recognised the signs? A small lad with a backpack and a holdall, trudging along a road, possibly showing signs of being upset. *Need some help, young man? Let me take you to this café and get you a hot drink.* She didn't even want to think about that scenario.

During that long day, she spent some time on the computer,

trawling through the internet searching for anything on Susan Hunter. There was nothing. The woman was a complete mystery. Carol remained in the office until just after eight, not wanting to go home just in case. She checked her own summer house, but it was exactly as it was at eight in the morning – Harry hadn't been there.

She sat with her legs curled under her, reflecting on how much had changed in her life over the previous couple of weeks. Given a choice, she would no longer want to work for the supposedly great and good of the country, she would stay doing exactly what she was doing now, organising the men whom she considered to be her boys.

She went to bed, having made the decision to go out early and see if Susan went to a place of work, or indeed anywhere else. Her boys had enough on their plate, and yet she felt the woman was an ever-present threat to the business, or even to one of them. She had no doubt that her attacker had been Susan, and she was determined to find out why she'd been in the Forrester offices and what she was looking for.

* * *

Matt and Karen were back home by eight, exhausted and frightened. It seemed unbelievable that there had still been no sightings of Harry, and the conclusion was that he had simply ignored the places he knew and loved, and had found somewhere he knew his dad wouldn't look for him.

Matt, Karen, Steve and Hermia spent the evening in Matt's kitchen, the map once again spread out while they nibbled unenthusiastically on pizza. They were out of ideas, exhausted, demoralised.

* * *

Harry was getting wetter in the persistent drizzle, and he wanted to cry. He needed proper shelter.

He packed everything into his bags, having the common sense to make sure his remaining food didn't get wet by wrapping it tightly in the carrier bag he had received it in, and then peered out from behind the rocks. He was pretty sure nobody would be out looking in the dark, and, with his torch at the ready, he left the comfort of the shelter that had kept him hidden all day. He didn't know Eckington woods as well as he did his home area of Charnock woods, so he took his time, heading always downhill. Finally he arrived in the small town of Eckington, and he huddled into a shop doorway. The church clock said it was just after quarter past eight, and he hesitated, wondering what to do. He didn't know the little town very well, only the shops at the bottom of the hill where he was currently sheltering, but he did know there was a housing estate not too far away. With sheds in gardens.

The roads were quiet, and he kept to the shadows as much as he could; in particular he didn't want to spot any police cars, who could still be out and about looking for him.

He reached the housing estate, and turned off the main road with a feeling of relief.

Now to find a shed that was open.

He tried to get into two back gardens, but security lights came on, so he moved away. Then he saw a car approaching and froze. He dropped behind a hedge as the car slowed and stopped two houses further up the road than he was.

A man and woman emerged from the front door of the house, both wheeling large suitcases. That was the point when he realised it was a taxi.

The driver got out and stashed their cases into his boot, the woman got into the back seat, and the man went back to lock the front door before returning to the waiting car. As the man took his place by the driver, he heard the man say, 'Thank God we're flying from Birmingham and not Manchester on this bloody awful night,' and then the taxi drove away.

The house was now in complete darkness. Harry made himself wait ten minutes behind the bush that was hiding him. Then he moved. His legs ached from being bent, and he jumped up and down a couple of times to loosen his muscles. He was aware he might just have to run.

Cautiously he walked down the path that ran down the side of the recently vacated house, and round to the back garden. Only one security light came on, and he knew that was a lucky break because it didn't light up the back of the house, only the side access. The shed was small and situated right at the bottom of the garden hidden by plastic leaves on a tall trellis, and he guessed it held the lawnmower and garden tools, but none of that mattered. It had a roof, that was the most important thing. He just had to hope that the lock wasn't some clever thing that required a degree in science to unlock it.

It was a padlock, and just made to look as if it was locked. He smiled for a moment. His mum's shed had been like that until burglars had arrived one night and stolen their Flymo. But he wasn't here to steal anything, or to damage anything. He just wanted to get out of the rain and find somewhere to sleep. He removed the padlock, and opened the door. It creaked, but only for a couple of seconds.

The shed was pretty full, but he knew he could make enough space for his makeshift bed. What was a plus was that it had electric power. There was a kettle on the side, and several bottles of water, a canister marked tea, and powdered milk. He folded down the handle of the lawnmower, then carried it outside, stashing it down the side of the shed.

There was even a rug on the floor, and a fold-up chair hanging on the wall. Harry presumed the husband liked to escape to his little shed; it was certainly comfortable and reasonably tidy. There was only one window, but it did have an old blind, which Harry lowered. The window didn't worry him – it looked out onto a very tall privet hedge.

It took him ten minutes to sort out his new home, and then he crawled into his sleeping bag. Stomach cramps were an indication that he would need toilet facilities before much longer, but he fell asleep quickly.

The rain continued all night, but Harry didn't get any wetter thanks to a holiday flight from Birmingham.

Brian Davis had moved into a hotel. His night was spent in comfort, but he spent it cursing the kid who had brought the wrath of Becky down on his head. She had made it very clear she never wanted him to darken her door or any other part of *her* property again, and had even stuffed his clothes into his suitcase. *Her* property was emphasised several times during the conversation, so he gave in, wondering what it would take to talk her round.

But did he really want to talk her round? She had taken the side of bloody Forrester after he'd hit him, and as for Karen Nelson – she'd never proceed beyond DS, he'd see to that.

At just after two, he suddenly sat up. What was keeping him in Sheffield? He apparently had no family now, no home as Becky owned the house they currently lived in... he'd apply for a transfer to the Met. She'd no doubt want a divorce, so it would be a completely fresh start for him. He'd have eighteen years or so of paying out for Florence, who he already knew would never be allowed anywhere near him thanks to the lump on Harry's forehead, but he could cope with that.

He finally dropped off to sleep, dreaming of being welcomed with open arms in London.

Not once during that long night did he give a thought to the whereabouts of the boy he had brought up as his son for at least three years.

* * *

Becky Davis felt alone. The police had been in and out of her home all day, the Family Liaison Officer had been reassuring, but still her boy hadn't been found. Matt had been quiet, but she guessed he would be until she could tell him the news that Brian was out of their lives.

She cradled Florence in her arms and stared out of the large bay window at the dark night sky. No stars tonight, drizzling with the incessant rain that had been there most of the day. She ached for Harry. Was he afraid? Was he dry? She hated the thought that he might be uncomfortably soaked through. Where was he?

Her breasts were starting to feel full and she knew Florence would be awake soon, hungry for her mother's milk. But now, as she slept soundly in her arms, it was supposed to be a peaceful time, one she would normally enjoy and appreciate. But without Harry upstairs playing on his PlayStation, nipping up and down the stairs for food to keep him going, there was no peace.

She had checked his room at the same time the FLO had. Harry had emptied his money box, but she had no idea how much had been in it. He came back every week with £10 from his dad for what he said his dad called 'incidentals but not fags or drugs', but he rarely spent it and when it reached £100 he'd put it in the bank. He had taken no food that she could see, but the two blankets he always had at the bottom of his bed, just in case it turned cold during the night, were missing. Plus, of course, he had the sleeping bag. She had complained to Matt about spending so much on it, but now she thanked God he had done so.

He had, of course, taken his Sheffield Wednesday shirts, hats and scarves. All of them. That was all her son had to sustain him.

Florence waved an arm, and then began to snuffle, turning her head, seeking a nipple.

Becky moved away from the window, sank down onto the sofa, and began to feed her tiny one while crying inwardly and outwardly for her bigger one.

36

MONDAY, 7 NOVEMBER

Monday brought sunshine. The rain had passed over the country during the night, bringing with it optimism that Harry would be found.

Carol woke feeling as if she hadn't really slept. It was still only five o'clock, and she knew she wouldn't be able to drop off to sleep again because her thoughts immediately flew to Harry. She showered, dried her hair in a haphazard fashion because it was still quite painful to touch the sore spot with a brush, and went downstairs. She fed Walter then fed herself with a toasted bagel; she made her first coffee of the morning, but also filled her flask. She was going to confront Susan Hunter today if it killed her. As it could quite easily have done at their last meeting.

She smiled as she sat at the kitchen table. She had no proof whatsoever that it was Susan who had been in the Forrester offices that night, but she knew. She knew.

What she didn't know was why Susan felt she had anything to do with the Forresters. It was clear from the exchange of emails that Dave didn't see her as a romantic presence in his life.

In fact, what she felt about the emails, having studied them care-fully, was that Dave was simply being polite, until in the end he had to be fairly brutal and cease all communications with her.

Susan must have seen that, so why was she now trying to play the 'Dave and I' card? It didn't make sense. So what was it she really needed from the Forrester Agency? Something inside the office, clearly, but Carol had no idea what the daft woman thought could possibly be in there for her.

Carol swapped her handbag for a tote and placed her flask inside it. She also packed her iPad, and a packet of digestives in case she got peckish. Surveillance was new to her, quite exciting, really.

It was just after six when she considered herself ready. She debated sending a text to Matt, but the previous evening he'd said don't open the office until we've found Harry, so she decided she wasn't officially at work. He would only say don't do it anyway. But this was personal, this was a lump on her head, this was being followed by a small white Peugeot, this was infringing on her personal space and life, and the woman wasn't going to get away with it.

She went out into the early-morning sunshine and shivered, and so quickly returned to her front door, went back inside and changed her coat for a padded one. She warmed the car up before setting off, deciding that the sun was out just to fool everybody. It was bloody freezing.

With the heating on full and warming the interior of the car nicely, she headed back to the road where she had found the Peugeot.

She parked about ten yards away, feeling like a spy. Her own car was hidden by a large Leylandii hedge, which she normally disliked intensely, but today she applauded the foresight of its owner.

The clock in the car said it was 7.20, which meant it was 6.20 because she hadn't got around to putting it back by an hour a month earlier; she figured she could sit back and enjoy being warm for a bit before Susan surfaced. If indeed she was going to surface at all.

* * *

When she saw Susan's front door open, Carol's clock said 8.22. Susan walked across to her car and got into the driving seat. Before she could drive off, Carol opened and closed her car door as quietly as she could and walked up to the Peugeot. To her immense joy and surprise, in view of the cold conditions, Susan lowered her window to adjust her side mirror.

Carol placed her hand firmly on Susan's arm, and watched as the woman's head swivelled. She got the distinct fragrance of L'Air du Temps as it wafted out of the car.

She reached in and removed the car keys.

'We use the same perfume, Susan,' she said.

'What?'

'You heard. It's the perfume you had on the other night in the offices of Matt Forrester, the night you hit me over the head with a torch.'

'No...'

Carol could hear fear in Susan's voice, and she put her left hand on the back of Susan's head.

'Okay, here's what's going to happen. You're going to tell me what it is you want from us, because you sure as hell have never been a girlfriend of Dave Forrester. That's bunkum. There was something you tried to get from him, but it sure as hell wasn't love. So what was it?'

'You're talking rubbish.'

Carol tightened her grip on the back of Susan's head. 'You have two minutes to tell me, and if I don't hear the truth in that time, I shall smash your face into your steering wheel. It's a bit like an eye for an eye type of punishment, really, but in my case it's a head for a face. I didn't report you to the police because I needed to know what you're up to, but at any time I can do this as I'm sure you know of the Forrester connection with the police. Now start talking.'

'Fuck off.'

Carol pushed Susan's face to within an inch of the steering wheel and held it there.

'Wrong answer, Hunter. I said start talking, and we'll begin with what it is you want from the offices that made you break in, with some difficulty, I might add. We'll talk compensation for the damage after. And if I push your head again, brace yourself because I won't stop.'

The sob that escaped Susan's lips came as a surprise. Carol waited, not relinquishing her hold on the back of Susan's neck one bit.

'I said talk.'

'What can I say?' Susan wailed, the sob now turning to torrential tears. 'He's dead, and I don't know if he dropped me in it.'

'Who's dead?' Carol increased the pressure of her hand.

'Bloody Anthony Dawson.'

Carol's brain did a somersault. She let go of Susan and opened the driver side door. 'I'll hold on to your car keys until I know you're telling the truth. Shall we go inside?'

Susan climbed out, still crying, and fishing around in her coat pockets for a tissue.

'Then will you leave me alone?'

'It's more a case of you leaving us alone. You've haunted the place, and me, for a couple of weeks now, and I can tell you my bosses are a heartbeat away from taking it to the police because they don't know what you want. So start talking, before this whole thing escalates.'

She followed Susan to her front door, used the woman's keys to get them inside the house and then they headed through to her kitchen. They sat at the table, and Carol said, 'Well?'

Susan took a deep breath. 'Anthony Dawson and I are brother and sister. Five years ago, he told me about a business opportunity that would guarantee a 100 per cent return, for an initial outlay of ten thousand pounds. I fell for it. He said it was importing fabrics like silk, high-cost goods, and I would see my initial money double in three months. I managed to scrape it up, and sat back and waited. He told me he'd been to see Dave Forrester, who was also investing, and I believed him because Dave and I had been acquaintances who I tried to keep in touch with, but that faded away once I left for Australia. It was the fact that honest Dave was investing that convinced me it was kosher.'

Carol waited, realising that maybe Dave and Susan had been close, until Dave called a halt to the relationship because Australia was a little too far away.

Susan paused for a moment. 'I received nothing, and Anthony wasn't taking any calls from me. In the meantime, my daughter in Australia died – all that part was true. I desperately need that money; I returned from Australia with nothing, and I thought I could perhaps find something in Dave's files that would direct me. When you came in after the place was closed, I panicked and whacked you with my torch so I could get away. I really am sorry, but I don't know how else to find anything out.'

'So the visit to Dave's grave was just that? Just a desire to visit it?'

'It was. I did at one time think we might get together, but he wasn't interested. And now Anthony's dead, I don't know what to do.'

'You could have tried explaining this to Matt Forrester; that might have been a smart idea.'

'You still don't understand. I can't afford anything, especially not to employ Matt Forrester.'

'So you came to steal the Dawson file? That's what all this has been about?'

Susan nodded.

'Then I can help, because the Dawson file contains nothing more than a surveillance report showing he was screwing around with another man's wife. He never had dealings with Dave Forrester until just before he was killed, and he was killed by the son of the woman he was seeing on the side. He clearly used the name of a totally honest man to convince you to part with your money. Some brother he was, Susan.'

Carol watched as the woman before her deflated.

'So here's what happens now, Susan. You write all this down, send it in an email to me at work,' she fished a business card out of her pocket, 'and all this will go away. You will not come near the offices again or we will slap you with a bill for repairs, and know this for definite, Susan, your brother not only lied to you about Dave Forrester. The fabrics he imported were more than likely drugs. If you pursue it, it may just show what exactly was going on and as an investor, you will be liable for any consequences that may arise from any illegal activities.'

Carol stood up.

'I'll leave you now, but if I hear of you again, I'll be back. Understood?' She placed Susan's car keys on the table and walked out.

* * *

Fifteen minutes later, Carol was sitting at her own kitchen table pouring a coffee from the flask she had taken with her. It felt good that she could report she had sorted the Susan Hunter mystery, but she decided she might have to sanitise her actions when she told the full story. Matt and Steve seemed to think she was kind, gentle Carol. Best leave them to their illusions.

She finished her drink, then ran across the tram tracks to the office. She checked the entire building, then the back of the property, hoping against hope that she would find a young boy hiding from the world.

It was distressing to think Harry was still somewhere out there, scared, vulnerable, missing his parents but now probably too frightened to just simply return home.

And deep down, she knew her actions that morning with Susan Hunter had been born out of her angst and worries over Harry Forrester; she wasn't aggressive by nature, although it could surface when it was needed, but as she sipped her coffee, she wondered if she would have actually tightened her grip even more on the back of Susan's head and smashed it straight into the steering wheel, leaving a mix of gore and blood all over the interior of the little Peugeot.

Her life as a PA to a leading member of the government hadn't just been about keeping his diary and sending emails on his behalf, the security aspect of the job had given her qualifications that Matt and Steve had seen on her CV, and she knew that when she confessed the entire truth about her activities on this cold Monday morning, they would believe every word.

She finished her coffee, rubbed the lump on the back of her head that was now healing and itching, and knew it had been worth it.

37

MONDAY, 7 NOVEMBER

Harry solved the problem of the pains in his stomach by attaching himself to other people. He left his hut and walked to the front of the house and back onto the road. Two women and three children were walking down; he waited until they had gone by before tagging on to the little group. When he reached the community centre, he nipped inside and found the toilets, which he could vaguely remember from a previous visit with his dad.

Ten minutes later and with his pains now gone, he felt so much better, but was aware that it was a school day and he would stand out so early in the morning. Feeling exposed and nervous, he used the same trick for walking back up to his shed, but this time staying quite close to a man out walking a couple of dogs.

He slipped back into his shed with a feeling of relief, and climbed back into his sleeping bag. He slept for a couple of hours, now free from pain, and when he woke, he had lunch. A sausage roll and a packet of crisps helped the craving for food, and thanks to the shed's amenities, he now could make a hot drink which would also satisfy the emptiness in his stomach.

He wished he dared to use his phone, even if it was just to keep boredom at bay, but he knew the second it went on he would find himself surrounded by police, all there to rescue him. Not going to happen.

There was a broken piece of mirror in the shed, and he had looked at the bump carefully. It was now spectacular shades of purple and yellow, with dark blue at the centre, and a very pronounced bump. He couldn't go home yet; his dad would probably consider murder a suitable option. But he would like to speak to him...

The day seemed to stretch for ever. He set up the folding chair, dragged one of the blankets across his knees, and made himself a hot tea. He didn't like the powdered milk, but it was better than nothing.

He realised he felt quite poorly, but guessed the cold had a lot to do with it, plus getting wet through the previous day. It had even felt damp throughout the night in the sleeping bag, but he guessed his own body warmth was drying that out.

He used some of the bottled water to rinse out the cup he had used, and folded the chair, before hanging it back on the wall. He remade his bed with the blanket underneath him and crawled back into it. He'd found a book about gardening still inside its brown Amazon envelope, probably to keep it clean, and supposed that the man who owned the property kept the book in the shed for such times as this, sitting with a cup of tea. Harry started to read it. He found it a bit uninteresting, but it was better than nothing. The section about trees was pretty cool.

Slowly the boredom drove him to sleep, and the night darkened once again.

* * *

Matt felt as if he was going out of his mind. The son he thought he knew so well was in none of the places they had explored together and where he would have expected him to be, but surely he couldn't be too far? He was on foot. Bus drivers had been asked to look out for him, train stations had been checked for CCTV sightings, but nothing was helping.

Volunteers and officers had been out all over the south-east of the city for the second full day running, and yet there had been nothing. Karen was in an exhausted sleep by his side, yet tired as he was, Matt's eyes wouldn't close. His mind was constantly re-visiting every place he and Harry had checked out since his son had been able to walk any sort of distance, but in his heart he knew they had covered all of them.

And it seemed that he was partly to blame. Having discussed cases, where they had talked of criminals who had used their phones while committing crimes, passing on his knowledge of forensics, he'd given Harry the knowledge that to stay hidden, his phone had to remain off.

Matt knew Becky was falling apart. He had seen it in her eyes when he had called round to check on her – that was the point when she told him Brian had moved out and wouldn't be returning under any circumstances.

His mind also thought about Carol's information regarding Susan Hunter, and what had transpired on that front. It seemed she had completely ignored him and sorted the situation – possibly the only thing that had put a smile on his face that day.

Slowly and inexorably, Matt's eyes did close and he drifted into surface sleep.

* * *

Harry came awake to a noise, a dog barking, and he pulled his sleeping bag as far up his body as possible. He was cold, he was hot, he was freezing, he was shivering, and he felt ill. He wanted his mum. She always knew what to give him when he was poorly. Then he was too hot and dithering, so he pushed the bag down to his waist, only to pull it back up two minutes later. He didn't know how to stop the shivers, and his leg was actually banging against the metal leg of the work bench. He could do nothing to stop it, and the grown-up Harry who had bravely walked away from a man he despised gave in to the child Harry, and began to cry. He needed help.

He pulled his bag towards him and took out his phone. The gardening book in its Amazon packaging where it was stored to keep it clean was by his side, ready for him to read out the address.

He switched on the phone, pressed Dad and waited all of three seconds.

'Harry?'

'Dad, I'm so cold and I think I might be a bit poorly.'

ACKNOWLEDGMENTS

My starter thanks have to go to the entire team at Boldwood, particularly my editor, Emily Yau, my copy editor, Cecily Blench, and my proofreader, Candida Bradford. Their insightful comments have seen this book to its conclusion, yet ready for the next in the series.

And now I have to thank certain people for lending me their real names – Carol Flynn, Susan Hunter, Karen Nelson, Oliver, my late cat, and Walter, my daughter's budgie. Stars, all of you.

Two author friends in particular are my absolute rocks: Valerie Keogh and Judith Baker, I can't thank you enough for your support.

The same goes for my team of beta readers, and my team of ARC readers, you're all magnificent, and make sure your reviews are in on time!

Lastly, I have to thank my family, who are truly wonderful in their support of me. You all know who you are.

And finally, my readers. Without you, none of this would be worthwhile, and I promise to try to write a bit faster!

Anita xxx

ABOUT THE AUTHOR

Anita Waller is the author of many bestselling psychological thrillers and the Kat and Mouse crime series. She lives in Sheffield, which continues to be the setting of many of her thrillers, and was first published by Bloodhound at the age of sixty-nine.

Sign up to Anita Waller's mailing list for news, competitions and updates on future books.

Visit Anita's website: https://anitawaller.co.uk/

Follow Anita on social media here:

facebook.com/anita.m.waller

twitter.com/anitamayw

instagram.com/anitawallerauthor

ALSO BY ANITA WALLER

One Hot Summer

The Family at No. 12

The Couple Across The Street

The Forrester Detective Agency Mysteries

Fatal Secrets

Fatal Lies

THE

Murder

LIST

THE MURDER LIST IS A NEWSLETTER DEDICATED TO SPINE-CHILLING FICTION AND GRIPPING PAGE-TURNERS!

SIGN UP TO MAKE SURE YOU'RE ON OUR HIT LIST FOR EXCLUSIVE DEALS, AUTHOR CONTENT, AND COMPETITIONS.

SIGN UP TO OUR NEWSLETTER

BIT.LY/THEMURDERLISTNEWS

Boldwood

Boldwood Books is an award-winning fiction publishing company seeking out the best stories from around the world.

Find out more at www.boldwoodbooks.com

Join our reader community for brilliant books, competitions and offers!

Follow us
@BoldwoodBooks
@TheBoldBookClub

Sign up to our weekly deals newsletter

https://bit.ly/BoldwoodBNewsletter

Printed in Great Britain
by Amazon

30060097R00155